ALSO BY RACHEL COHN

Gingerbread
The Steps

RACHEL COHN

SIMON & SCHUSTER BOOKS FOR YOUNG READERS
New York   London   Toronto   Sydney   Singapore

SIMON & SCHUSTER BOOKS FOR YOUNG READERS
An imprint of Simon & Schuster Children's Publishing Division
1230 Avenue of the Americas, New York, New York 10020

SIMON & SCHUSTER BOOKS FOR YOUNG READERS
is a trademark of Simon & Schuster.

Book design by Ann Sullivan
The text for this book is set in Garamond 3.

Manufactured in the United States of America
2 4 6 8 10 9 7 5 3 1
Library of Congress Cataloging-in-Publication Data
Cohn, Rachel.
Pop princess / Rachel Cohn.
p. cm.
Summary: Yearning to escape the small Massachusetts town where
her family retreated after her sister's death, Wonder Blake gets her
chance when her sister's manager offers Wonder a record contract on
her sixteenth birthday.
ISBN 0-689-85205-3
[1. Singers—Fiction. 2. Music trade—Fiction.
3. Popular music—Fiction. 4. Family problems—Fiction.
5. Interpersonal relations—Fiction.
6. Massachusetts—Fiction.] I. Title.
PZ7.C6665 Po 2004
[Fic]—dc21   2003000171

FIRST
EDITION

For skgj,
Boston's original pop princess

Part One

Shades of Blonde
Brunette

One

My life as a pop princess began at the Dairy Queen.

I could tell you that at the time, I was your average fifteen-year-old girl with slacker grades, dysfunctional family, bad hair days, and a love for singing out loud to every pop song on the radio. But that was the Wonder Blake who appeared doomed to live out her junior year as a social oddity at her new high school on Cape Cod.

The other Wonder Blake, the one who slaved away at the DQ every afternoon, she sang aloud to every song on the radio in order to drown out customers' voices so her mind could focus on her real ambition: escape. Sing-aloud Wonder dreamed of escape from Cape Cod, escape from high school, escape to Somewhere, Anywhere (okay, preferably New York or L.A., though London or Paris would probably do, as would any dark steamy Latin American beach metropolis like in the *telenovelas* on the Spanish language channel). She also longed for escape from parents whose marriage was on nuclear meltdown, escape from the sorrow that had overwhelmed our household since my sister's death. In whatever glam city happened to be Somewhere, Anywhere, the other Wonder Blake would go and reinvent herself, become a sophisticated emancipated teen

with a hot bod and ridiculous confidence. She could be like some Presidential Fitness teen ambassador; she'd have a kick-ass designer wardrobe and a smile that could light the world on fire. That chick would know how to make new friends like *that* and she would have guys lining up to date her, instead of the regular ole Wonder Blake, who you could tell guys thought was kinda not bad-looking but why's she always by herself staring out into space, and anyway isn't she the girl who used to be on TV, what's her deal, how'd she get stranded here?

The regular ole Wonder Blake had two years of high school left to go, two more years trapped in sleepy Devonport, Massachusetts. Escape for now would have to come from singing aloud at her job at the Dairy Queen, passing the time in her own reverie.

And so it happened that I was discovered by Gerald Tiggs, the powerful talent manager, at a chance meeting at said DQ. Tig (as he was known) walked into the DQ at the end of my shift late one Saturday evening. I was mopping the floor, using the mop as a pretend microphone as I strutted across the wet floor, a Discman on my ears as I sang "Smells Like Teen Spirit" out loud—very loudly. My rendition of Kurt Cobain was closer to down-home gospel than to grunge wail. I had no idea a customer was lurking until Katie, my one friend in my family's new hometown and also my DQ coworker, practically knocked me over, sprung the headphones from my ears, and shouted, "Wonder! The guy's trying to talk to you!"

I looked up. Labor Day had passed, taking the Dairy Queen's late night customers with it. Yet here was one standing before me at 10 P.M., clutching a chocolate-dipped soft-serve cone, his teeth flashing so bright in the flickering strobe lighting I thought I saw my reflection in them. He said, "Don't I know you? You look familiar."

Of course I recognized him. Who could forget those killer-shark eyes and the fine Italian tailored suits he wore even during 99 percent humidity? I told him, "Think a little harder."

He did, and then he knew. The killer eyes turned sad when he made the connection. "You're Lucky's kid sister."

"That's me." My big sister had been dead almost two years, yet it seemed I would always be known as "Lucky's kid sister." I wouldn't have minded having my name legally changed to "Lucky's Kid Sister" if it had meant I could have even one more day with her.

"I didn't know you sang too." He paused, as if he was seeing me for the first time, even though I must have met him several times before, with Lucky. His eyes looked me up and down, slowly, as if he was appraising me, not in a scamming way, but more like I was a piece of fruit. "You were a B-Kid also, right?"

I nodded, embarrassed. That was my old life, when we still lived in Cambridge, when my parents still liked each other. Back then, my sister and I trekked

every Saturday to a television studio in Boston to tape *Beantown Kidz,* or *B-Kidz* as it became known, a kids' variety show that developed a cult following through-out New England. In the time since the show's can-cellation, several B-Kidz had emerged to become major film, television, and music stars. My sister Lucky had been slated to become one of those B-Kidz alums.

"Do you have a demo tape?" Musicians and singers struggle for years to hear a major talent scout ask them that question. I got it over a mop and pail with no desire for it whatsoever.

"Oh sure," I said. "I made one while I was singing in the shower this morning. Let me just have my people FedEx it over to you." Katie, who had been watching the whole scene, busted out laughing. Everyone in the small town on Cape Cod where my family had recently moved knew that our house was one in chaos—and on a downward monetary slide.

Tig raised his eyebrow at me, then he laughed too. "Wanna make one?" he said.

"What, do you have a karaoke machine handy?" I asked. Ours was a small town made up of rich people's summer homes and working-class people's regular homes. Lights, camera, action was not what you would expect to find in Devonport, Mass.

Tig said, "No, but I've got a little recording studio setup in my summer house on the beach, and I've got a soon-to-be ex-wife back in Manhattan that my lawyer has advised me to avoid for the next couple weeks by just laying low, so what better way to hide out than by discovering a new pop sensation during the off-season? C'mon, it'd be fun; help an old guy have some fun in this beautiful boring town."

The conversation would have ended there, with the "You must be crazy" I was about to offer Tig, had my mother not arrived at exactly that moment to pick me up at the end of my shift. "Tig!" she cried out, which was funny—my mom, the ex-law librarian, frumpy dresser with the bad perm, getting down with the hep nicknames. "How long has it been? What are you doing in this godforsaken town? Do you summer here?"

When my mom is nervous, she babbles. When she is intimidated and nervous, she babbles moronically.

"Ah, Marie," Tig said. His shoulders appeared to slump and the sheen cast off his glossy teeth smile dimmed, like maybe now he was remembering the other side of dealing with Lucky's family. "Long time." He gestured toward me. "I was just thinking your other daughter here should make a demo tape. Looks to me like she's got the same qualities Luck—" He stopped himself from saying her name. I was used to that by now. People around me acted like they couldn't use the words "lucky," "death," "die," or "accident" in a sentence for fear I would fall apart in hysterics on the spot.

"Wonder would love to!" my mom blurted out.

"Anna!" I corrected her. "My name now is Anna!"

"It so is not," murmured Katie, who thought her name was boring but that "Wonder" was exotic and interesting. Since we'd moved to the Cape, I had been waging an unsuccessful campaign to be called by my middle name, Anna, a perfect name in my opinion: "a" followed by "n," then the "n" and "a" in reverse. Nice. Normal. Girl next door.

My parents had been told they would not be able to conceive children. They had been married seven years when my sister Lucky arrived to prove that medical wisdom wrong. Two years later, their second unexpected wonder arrived, Wonder Anna Blake, me. By the time my little brother arrived less than eighteen months later, my parents no longer believed in miracles. They named him Charles.

Tig asked, "Which is it? Wonder or Anna?" He answered his own question before I could respond. "It's Wonder—of course it's Wonder. That's the name to sell records."

My mother nodded knowingly at Tig. I could see her large chest rising and falling rapidly. She hadn't been this excited since Lucky was on the brink of signing a major record deal.

"Our Wonder has a lovely voice," Mom said. "She used to be an *incredible* dancer." Mom stopped herself, and I knew what she might have liked to add: Wonder had been an *incredible* dancer back when we lived in Cambridge, until . . . you know . . . and since then

Wonder has let her body go to hell and she's stopped caring about her God-given talents. Wonder was a B-Kid too, you know! Tig, can you save her?

Tig looked at me like I was a puppet whose strings my mother would pull and I would dance on command. Not. I couldn't imagine how Mom could possibly embarrass me more. I did not want to find out. I whined, "Ma, I thought you were going to wait outside for me after my shift." Please, I thought, please don't let anyone from Devonport High walk in right now and witness this scene. It was bad enough that Katie was seeing it.

Tig scribbled a phone number on a napkin. He started to hand it to me, then appeared to think better of it and handed the napkin to Mom instead. "Let's talk," he said. "I'll be in town through the end of September." He walked outside, and we heard the beep of his Mercedes' car alarm turning off.

My mother's eyes were bright and her cheeks flushed. Since Lucky's death, the day didn't pass that Mom's complexion didn't appear gray and her eyes dead. Seeing Mom liven up, I knew it would be hard not to let her persuade me to take Tig up on his offer. On the plus side, perhaps I could score a few days out of school over it.

Mom patted the top of my head, then reached behind me to loosen my hair from the DQ hair net. My light brown hair fell around my shoulders. Mom touched the bottom of my chin gently. As she gazed

into my eyes I knew she was looking through me, trying to see Lucky.

She said, "I knew you could be a star, too. Like, you know . . ."

"I'm not Lucky," I whispered to her.

"Tig thinks you could be," she whispered back. "He would know."

Two

In my list of ambitions, tripping into a pop princess career did not register. That had been Lucky's deal, not mine. When I wasn't plotting fantasy escape from Devonport and I was dealing in reality land, my ranking of ambitions went like this: (1) save enough money to get my own car (please a Jetta, please), which would allow for (2) a better-paying job at a mall in the larger Cape town of Hyannis, which in turn would lead to (3) a major cash stash that would finance a post-high-school yearlong trek to like Norway or Madagascar or Tasmania or some place way far Far FAR from Massachusetts, an ultimate adventure from which I would emerge (4) totally in love with some hot foreign guy and then maybe one day, I would (5) have a career as, like, a veterinarian or a travel book writer or a professional chocolate taster. Easy.

First I had to survive high school. Two years down, two to go.

My freshman year, the year Lucky died, had flown by in a haze of C-minus grades from teachers who felt sorry for me, and crying jags in the bathroom between class periods. I had no real friends; I didn't think I knew *how* to make good friends. Lucky had been my

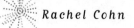

best friend, and our friends had been other B-Kidz or girls from our dance classes. Those friends had either graduated or were in private school. Money was getting tight in our family, so I went to public school. I wouldn't be making friends through performing either: *Beantown Kidz* had just been canceled, and I stopped going to dance class, the one area where I actually excelled. Performing was out that year, anyway. It hurt too much without Lucky. I'd only been a B-Kid because I wanted to do whatever my big sister did. As for the grades, the parentals let the issue slide that year. I'd never been a star student like Lucky, and nobody expected me to start now.

On Labor Day before sophomore year Dad sat me down for The Talk, the "You're such a smart girl, if you'd only *apply* yourself" speech. I responded that while I didn't aspire to be some airhead twit, I really didn't care if anybody thought I was smart and a good student so would it be okay if I just dropped out of school and got a job? The big fat answer was NO.

My GPA improved to a staggering C-plus average that year, which didn't impress my parents at all, but what really sent them over the top was the new gang of girls who let me hang with them, more because I had been a B-Kid than because they actually liked me. With these girls, I was caught smoking in the bathroom; with them, I got busted for skipping school and hanging out in Harvard Square cafes, flirting with college guys and pretending we were college girls highly in need of invites to their keg parties.

Mom said, We're moving; I won't tolerate this behavior. To Mom, it didn't matter if I explained it was one cigarette—my first—and I didn't even like it, didn't matter when I said I was just skipping school because it was all one big bore, I never actually went to one of those keg parties. Mom said, My therapist is worried that you're a follower, you just go where the wind blows. You need direction. Lucky had motivation and drive—don't you want that for yourself?

Dad said, We're broke. We can't afford to live in Cambridge anymore. We're moving to a quiet, safe place where my children will have nothing better to do than study.

Bye-bye big city, hello small town with the sea breeze and fresh-cut grass and white lace curtains at every house. Yawn. Whatever.

No one said what we all knew: No move could bring Lucky back, and no change of scenery was going to make us forget our loss.

We'd been living in Devonport, Cape Cod, for three months now and the most exciting thing that had happened was Gerald Tiggs coming into the Dairy Queen.

I had been planning to remind Mom that a music career was not an ambition of mine, when the morning after our encounter with Tig, I walked into the kitchen and found her telling Dad and Charles about it.

"Wonder could have a record deal within a month, with Tig!"

Dad's face had not adopted the newfound glow on Mom's. He sat at the kitchen table, not looking up from his newspaper, his fork absently moving around pieces of scrambled eggs he likely would not finish. In the two years since Lucky died, he'd lost a lot of weight, and now stood tall and skinny as a rail, his hair completely gray. I think Mom ate for him: Her wardrobe had graduated from black career suits to poly-stretch pants from Target.

Dad said, "Unless those grades go up, Wonder can forget about it. The agreement with Lucky was a 3.5 or higher GPA if she wanted to pursue the music career. Wonder clocked in at, what, 2.5 last year? As it is, unless there's a marked grade improvement at this new school, she can kiss the Dairy Queen job good-bye."

That comment really pissed me off. I could feel my disinterest in Tig's offer turning into *Just try and tell me I can't make a demo, Dad.*

Our dog, Cash, was wagging his tail at Dad's feet, waiting for the leftovers Cash knew Dad would be discreetly discarding. The condition of us getting a dog had been that Dad got to name it. He named the dog after his favorite "pop" star. Cash was my man in black, the most gorgeous black Lab/poodle mutt mix you ever saw.

Charles said, "Stupid fucking record people. Don't do it, Wonder." To Charles, "record deal" equaled "death." On that terrible day, Lucky and I had been walking down our street in Cambridge and Lucky was giddy: She and her two best friends, Kayla and Trina, were close to signing a major label record deal for their girl group, Trinity. Mom and Charles were across the street waiting on the porch for us to return with the groceries she'd sent us out to buy for a celebration dinner. Mom waved, Lucky waved back. Lucky was all *Trinity this, record deal that,* and in her excitement, she stepped out into the street without looking. A car ran a red light and hit her. Drunk driver.

Two years later, our family was just starting to get on with our lives, but we were all going through the motions, as if we expected that at any moment our lives could again change in a random instant: irrevocably, horribly. The two years of litigation with the family of the driver of the car that killed Lucky had ended with the driver in jail, but that brought us no satisfaction. Lucky was still gone, and my parents' love for each other seemed to have gone along with her. The expense of the court costs had drained their finances until they finally gave up the lawsuit, sold our house in Cambridge, and moved us to Cape Cod for a fresh start. The custody battle over their marriage ended in a dead heat, with the two backing off into separate corners: Dad took permanent custody of the living room, with his computer; Mom took the bedroom, with her TV; and the kitchen was the open arena reserved for occasional sparring.

"No cursing at breakfast," Dad mumbled after Charles's use of the F-word. Charles kicked at his skateboard under the table. Cash growled at Charles.

"But it's okay at dinner?" I asked.

Dad looked up at me. He almost smiled. "Only on alternating Tuesdays in leap years," he said.

Just then we heard a crash in the living room. Cash barked and ran to the door, tail wagging. We ventured into the living room to find that a small piece of the ceiling had cracked and fallen, knocking over an antique lamp and spreading debris over the shabby, worn-out wooden floors. Our home was on prime oceanfront property, but the house, built by Dad's grandfather, was falling apart everywhere, and we had no money to fix it.

Since Dad, a college dean, had been placed on "sabbatical" by the university in Boston, and the only job Mom had been able to get in town was as a cashier at the grocery store, my parents had barely enough money to pay for our move from Cambridge to this ancient rickety house my father had inherited. Dad was supposedly going to use the profit from the sale of the Cambridge house to support our family while he used the peace and quiet of the Cape house to write a great novel that would make us rich beyond our wildest dreams. I think Cash was the only family member who believed Dad could do it. Cash sat at Dad's feet every day while Dad stared at the blank computer screen, usually playing solitaire or surfing the Net when he thought we weren't looking.

"Please let me call Tig, Wonder," Mom said in my ear. "Please."

"Sure," I muttered. I was glad I hadn't blown my summer savings from the Dairy Queen on a new stereo for my room. Looking at the plaster falling from the ceiling, I knew I would have to use that money for school clothes.

Three

I went upstairs to my room for Sunday sanctuary. It was still weird to go inside my bedroom and not see two beds. Lucky and I had shared a room in the house where we'd grown up in Cambridge, and we'd shared a room in this house on the Cape when we spent summers here. Now that we lived permanently at the Cape, I had moved into the guest bedroom. Lucky's and my old room was locked and nobody ever asked Mom for the key. My new room had a great view, though. I could wake up in the morning and lie in bed, watching the blue ocean rolling right outside the window, the ocean's rocking motions making me feel as if my bed were moving to its rhythm. The roar of the ocean and the waves breaking below the window helped drown out the silence that had existed in our family home since Lucky had gone. Sometimes it felt like we had become a family of ghosts.

There was a knock on my door and I snapped, "I said I'd do it!" thinking Mom was at the door wanting to talk about Tig again, but instead Katie and her twin brother, Henry, aka Science Project, walked in. Henry and Katie lived next door. I'd been hanging out with them every summer since we were babies.

Katie flopped on my bed. "Guess what! Mom told us

at church this morning. Only the second week of school and school's going to be canceled this week! They found asbestos somewhere so the whole school has to shut down to get it cleaned up so we don't all like die during homeroom."

I did a gospel *Messiah* jig around my room, singing, "Hallelujah! Hallelujah!"

My initial week at Devonport High had been beyond painful. A summer becoming a permanent townie? Who does she think she is?

The kids my age in town were forever separated by whether they were townies or summers. Townies lived in Devonport year-round, and had families that could not afford vacation homes. Townies had jobs working at the fish stands that the summers frequented, and the townies' parents often had side jobs looking out for the summers' houses during the winter. Summers, the group I had been part of before, were only in attendance on the Cape in July and August, refugees from the heat and humidity in New York, Washington, and Boston. They drove expensive cars, went to fancy private schools, and did not spend their school vacations slaving for minimum wage. Our family had been a summer one, but we were never rich, just lucky to have inherited a house on awesome oceanfront property. I no longer belonged to either group. I was glad to have spent the past summer buried inside the Dairy Queen with a uniform visor half-covering my face.

"I'm so excited you live here year-round now!"

Katie chirped. She threw what I referred to as her Popularity Kit—beauty and celeb mags, makeup samples, and hair accessories—onto my bed: her idea of Sunday entertainment. If there could be an award for Girl Most Determined to Be Popular Despite Her Acne and Braces and Kmart Clothes Collection, Katie had it nailed. She should have been popular just based on how nice she was. I'd spent a whole summer at the DQ watching her give free vanilla dips to college students so broke they paid for their Value Meals with rolls of dimes, helping old people to the bathroom, giving little kids a reassuring rub on the back before she had to clean up the peanut butter sauce they'd just spewed all over the condiment table. I could barely manage minimum-wage-level pleasant.

Katie tossed me a soap opera magazine. "Check out the cover—I brought this one special for you." The my-reason-for-living gorgeous face of Will Nieves, the hottest actor on daytime television, stared back at me, all black eyes and chiseled cheekbones, cinnamon skin and tousled black hair. Will Nieves, star of *South Coast,* the one soap I never missed, the reason I took the five-to-ten rather than the three-to-eight shift two nights a week at the DQ, since our family VCR was on the blitz and no way could I miss my daily dose of Will. I smacked my lips onto Will's picture.

Henry said, "You seriously think that guy's hot?"

"Shah!" I said back.

Henry made a *blech* face. In the last year, he had

grown very tall, but way gawky. His thin, dark blond hair had turned golden from the summer's rays, and his usually pale skin was pink and healthy. He almost looked cute, except for his pants always looking like they would fall right down off of his skinny white ass. Henry/Science Project looked like both his name and his nickname: he had that *aw shucks* thing going with a pleasant puppy dog face, but he also had perpetually wrinkled brows and intense stares because his head was always computing computing computing. He had this habit of coming into my room with Katie for no reason; like today, he'd seen Katie carry the Popularity Kit to my house and there was no way he planned to do girly stuff with us, yet here he was in my room.

"You two are not honestly going to spend the day slobbering over pictures of that guy and putting on makeup, are you?" Henry asked.

"You bet we are," Katie said.

"Katie, I thought you said you would help me build the new computer for Dad's birthday today."

"No, Science Project, that's *your* project, not mine!" Katie said. "Wonder and I want to do something fun!" She wrinkled her eyebrows, then asked me, "Hey, did you ever call that Tig guy?"

I shrugged, and Katie let the subject drop. She said, "I know! Let's prank-call Doug Chase!"

That idea interested me. I told Henry, "Charles is gonna go hang out with his pseudocool skater dudes if you wanna go hang with him." I did not need Science Project's geek karma infiltrating my room if I was going to prank-call my crush. Will Nieves may have been the man I intended to marry, but Doug Chase was the fer-real guy I was seriously lusting over.

Henry squinted up at the sun beaming into my bedroom through the window. "Gimme pseudocool skater dudes over Doug Chase any day," he mumbled, then got up from the window seat and left my room.

I had been drooling over Doug Chase all summer, though really I had been crushing on him since the summer after fourth grade when he caught me in a game of Marco Polo at the community pool. He had crystal blue eyes, tattoos covering both his upper arms, and he was practically a rock star in Devonport— everyone had heard his band play at the Fourth of July Devonport town festival. Even though he was like one of the most popular seniors at Devonport High, even though I had about as much of a shot with Doug as I did with the prime minister of Canada, I couldn't help fantasizing about him. I had gone from a size eight to a size ten over the past summer from eating pizza where he worked every day, just so I could scam on him while cheese was probably oozing down my blouse, for all that he noticed me. I loved to watch the slither of the serpent tattoo on Doug's left bicep while he flipped the pizza dough in circles. I had lost a summer of lunchtimes watching that dough twirl and fantasizing that Doug and I were on a blanket on the beach at midnight, with moonlight streaming down onto us as I ran my fingers along the serpent—an extreme sensual touch that would have Doug's lips finding mine in no time.

Now that we lived in dullsville Devonport, dreaming about kissing Doug was my only entertainment besides dreaming about kissing Will Nieves from *South Coast*.

I was just shy of my sixteenth birthday, and I still hadn't kissed—I mean *really* kissed—a guy. I didn't count the awkward and random encounter in the B-Kidz dressing room when I was twelve with Freddy Porter, a fellow B-Kid who went on to become a member in a monster popular boy band.

The Blake family had moved to the Cape to start our lives over. My resolution was that I would have a boyfriend as part of my new life by the ocean, and that boyfriend would be Doug Chase.

Lucky always said I knew how to dream big.

Four

Tig's summer home was less than a mile from ours.
Mom stepped out of our beat-up Volvo on Monday
morning and admired the new shingles on the two-
story house with the spotless windows. "Wouldn't it be
nice to have a house like this?" she asked.

"You mean not falling apart?" I said.

Tig came outside to greet us. The wind flapped his
white suit against his dark skin. The guy was the
smartest dresser I have ever seen. He had a round face
that would have appeared youthfully innocent and kind
were it not for those shark gray eyes framed by short
spiked black braids. He said, "Thanks for dropping her
off, Marie. Great seeing you. We'll call you later when
she's ready to come home." He flashed the killer smile
and put his arm around my shoulders before Mom had
a chance to protest. She had definitely expected to stay
with me, not drop me off.

Tig's house was decorated with frilly, flowery pat-
terns, New England quilts on the walls, and awful lace
curtains, and it smelled like carpet cleaner. I guess Tig
could see the look of confusion on my face because he
said, "The soon-to-be ex decorated the house. Sucks,
doesn't it?"

I tried again, but this time was worse. I saw my sister's face on the other side of the microphone, holding the headset to her ear with one hand. Her blond curls hung down her shoulders, and her cheeks were rosy and happy with the joy she found in singing. She was such a pretty girl, especially when she sang.

Tig announced, "I see your feet tapping and your hips rocking, Wonder. I know you have more in you."

One more time I started,

I've known you so long.

Tig shook his head, frowning. I'd blown it. Now he knew me for the fraud I was, a pretender to my dead sister's throne.

Before I could apologize to Tig for wasting his time, I heard the music to a familiar, and favorite, song coming through the headset. Tig nodded to me and without thinking I just started singing. The song was "Like a Prayer."

Tig must have remembered that Lucky hated Madonna songs. Lucky's face and voice effectively blocked, I started to wail the song. As I got more into it, I felt my body relax and my voice strengthen. There was an extraterrestrial cool quality coming from my voice that I hadn't known existed.

"You're showing off now, Wonder," Tig said into my headset, but I kept singing anyway, and I saw him smiling—and smiling big, like his random instinct to bet on a dollar and a dream had just won him the lottery.

He had me sing the song several different times, trying out different beats: slow, fast, R & B, gospel style, pop cute, and finally, however the hell I wanted.

On that last take he said, "That was the one. Wonder style. Free and easy, natural."

"I have a style?" I asked.

"Now you do," he said. "Did you ever have vocal training?"

"Yeah, we had voice coaches on the set at *B-Kidz*. I sang on one of the B-Kidz Christmas albums. A really corny version of 'Rudolph the Red-Nosed Reindeer.' I'm so glad they don't play the record on the radio in Boston anymore."

"You're embarrassed to be on the radio?"

"No, I'm embarrassed to have a sucky song on the radio. It was so cheesy."

"Welcome to the music biz, Wonder." Tig asked me what female singers I liked. I named the usual suspects: Aretha Franklin, Janis Joplin, Janet Jackson and Madonna. He said, "No, what pop singers do you like—you know, young ones? All these pop princesses out there and boy bands, there's gotta be one of them you like."

"I guess I like Kayla okay. She's not as bad as most of 'em." When Lucky died so suddenly, Trina and Kayla had decided they couldn't continue their group, Trinity, without her. Trina's mom had been against the whole pop singing career anyway, and she was grief-stricken over Lucky's death. She forbade Trina to pursue a record deal again until Trina finished college. Trina, I think, was relieved that her mother had made the decision for her. Kayla, on the other hand, had gone solo and within the last two years had skyrocketed to become the queen of the pop charts, and the skimpiest bikini-wearer the music video channel had ever seen. She was an international sensation.

"You're not gonna go all diva on me, are you, Wonder?" Tig was Kayla's manager. He would know.

"Not if you're nice to me," I said, laughing.

"Girl," he said, "you don't even know what a natural you are, do you?"

Five

If being a natural meant fumbling lyrics, tripping on dance steps, and laughing hysterically every time Tig encouraged me to croon/wail/whisper the words "yeah" and/or "baby" in a song, then I was a natural-born superstar.

I often suspected the only reason Tig kept working with me after our first session was that I kept him amused as he juggled endless pages and cell phone calls from his divorce lawyer, Kayla and other artists, and record company execs.

Because school was let out for that week in September, I spent my afternoons at Tig's house, at his invitation. I don't imagine I ever thought our work would actually lead to a singing career for me, but it made my mom so happy to drop me off and to look into my eyes with hope instead of sadness. And excuse me, but the scene at Tig's—with the huge flat-screen TV to take in Will Nieves on *South Coast* while Tig answered phone calls every two seconds—was way better than the scene back home. If I had spent the week at home, I would have been stuck hovering over a black-and-white TV with bad reception to catch my soaps while hordes of townie kids reclaimed the beach outside our windows, and I would have passed that time hoping and praying that Mom and Dad didn't start a fight that would send Charles and me hiding out in my room and eating cold pizza for dinner.

A surprise awaited me at Tig's house on the second day. When I walked to the back of the house toward the studio, Trina Little was sitting on a lawn chair.

"Girl!" she exclaimed, jumping to her feet. She inspected me head to toe. "Look who seriously filled out that bikini top!"

My mom, her mom, and their sisters had passed on a distinct genetic breast code. Since growing into a C cup in the last year, I had become uncomfortably used to crossing my arms over my chest and looking down when people's eyes strayed across my new upper body. But Trina was like a long-lost sister, and I didn't care that she'd noticed that I was growing up—and out. I ran to Trina and gave her a giant hug.

She was wearing a Boston University tank top with side-button workout pants that swamped her tiny body. Trina Little *was* little—maybe five feet tall on tippy toes—but with a giant singing voice that could tear the church down. Just because Tig was her step-father's nephew did not mean it was nepotism that had almost landed Trinity a record deal—the girl was a powerhouse singer, Whitney plus Mariah times a million. She had the most beautiful dark skin I'd ever seen, coal black eyes, and long black cornrows hanging halfway down her back. When she moved, the

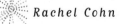
click of her cornrow beads seemed to have their own
rhythm, so even her walk was musical. I had never
understood why B-Kidz fan mail always favored Kayla.
To me, Trina had always been the coolest-looking and
the best singer, and Lucky the nicest and most genuine.

Trina held me tight. We hadn't seen each other
since shortly after Lucky's death. I was glad Mom
wasn't present. The sight of Trina—and the remem-
brance of Trina wailing out "Amazing Grace" at the
church funeral and the entire congregation shudder-
ing in awestruck tears—would likely have caused
Mom to break down on the spot.

When Trina let go of me, we sat down on the lawn
chairs, a luscious Indian summer ocean breeze filling
the air. Trina said, "So, you gonna be a pop princess?"

I laughed. "Yeah, right! Nah, Tig just keeps me
here for his entertainment, and I just need to get the
hell outta my house! Once that divorce of his is final,
Tig'll go back to his fancy Manhattan life and get lost
in Kayla-ness and forget all about ole Wonder Blake
singing customers' orders in the drive-thru at Dairy
Queen and failing Algebra 2 at Devonport High on
Cape Cod."

Trina said, "If that were true he wouldn't have
asked me to come out here today to work with you.
He wants me to work on some harmonizing and vocal
exercises with you, and check out your dance moves."

This was a shock. Having Trina as voice coach was
like getting Michael Jordan for a basketball teacher.

"You're so lying," I told Trina.

"I'm so not," she said. "C'mon, let's go get some lunch, and when we come back I am going to put you through some serious paces. Tig had to go into Boston for the day to sign some papers, but he'll be back later to check our progress."

We hopped into her cute little Honda. I recommended the local pizza place—just guess why. Hint: serpent tattoo. On the drive over, Trina told me about life in college. Trina was a sophomore at BU, a music major, and when she fulfilled her promise to her mom to get her college degree, she was going to go after that record deal for real—only she didn't want to be a pop singer, or a gospel singer. She wanted to be a country singer.

"Shut up!" I said when she dropped that bomb.

"Watch my dust, girl, I am going to be the first black female country singing superstar this candy-ass nation has ever known. I'm gonna be Charley Pride and Esther Phillips, Patsy Cline and Ella all in one."

"Who?"

Trina had always been like a walking encyclopedia of music history. She knew every obscure song from every important singer imaginable. *Beantown Kidz* was produced at a local public television station and did not, contrary to rumor, make any of its kid performers any kind of real dough, but Trina had invested what little B-Kidz money she earned to fund an incredible CD collection back when she was her little high school honor student self.

"Read some history sometime, Wonder. The Kaylas of today couldn't be around if not for the Petula Clarks of yesterday."

"Who?" I repeated.

Trina rolled her eyes and said, "Never you mind. Dig this. I am moving to Austin, Texas, when I finish college. Gonna hang out with the real songwriters, quality artists, see? None of that Nashville sellout bid'ness for me."

"I'll buy your records," I said. I would, too.

"Looks like I might be buying yours first!"

As we walked inside the restaurant, I muttered, "Check out the guy at the counter, Treen," using Lucky and my old nickname for her. "Major crush."

Trina eyed Doug up and down, then her gaze wandered across the tables, inspecting the customers. "This is sure one white town you live in," she muttered back.

"Tell me about it," I said, embarrassed. Cambridge seemed like a United Nations town in its diversity compared with white-bread Devonport.

"Hi, Doug!" I said when we got to the counter. I tried to act all casual but my voice had that annoying enthusiasm I seem incapable of squashing. I had a T-shirt on over my bikini top, but he was on instant guy cam—his eyes went right to my chest. Mine went right to his bicep-muscle serpent tattoo.

"Yeah—Wanda is it?" he mumbled.

A group of girls were giggling at a nearby table. I

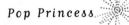
turned my head and saw Jen Burke, the new bane of
my existence. My first week at my new school had
been made miserable by her. For some random reason,
Jen and her clique of popular girls had targeted me as
their victim for the new school year. That I had been
a B-Kid was apparently the bug up Jen's ass.

Every kid from New England has seen *Beantown
Kidz* at least once, probably a lot more. I wasn't particularly great on the show—Kayla, Trina, and Lucky
were the real standouts—but I was known as "the cute
one" so I got lots of letters and one marriage proposal
when I turn eighteen from a movie star who's originally from Boston whom I won't name because I
thought the whole proposal was somewhat disgusting
and inappropriate. But since I had grown up and
moved away from the Boston area, people rarely recognized me anymore, for which I was grateful.
Unfortunately for me, Jen was not one of those people.
Furthermore, she seemed stuck in some B-Kidz backlash that looked to severely infect my junior year at
Devonport High. What is it about pretty girls named
Jen, anyway?

Worse, Jen and I shared a crush. According to
Katie, who knew every coupling in the town of
Devonport dating back to Molly Ringwald movie
days, Jen had been hot for Doug during the last school
year and had even hooked up with him at a couple of
parties. These groping sessions had never turned into
an actual boyfriend-girlfriend thing, but Jen was

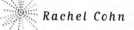

always making a play for him. That Jen had the major hots for Doug could be seen every day the past summer when she trounced from the beach to the pizza joint and suggestively slurped Diet Cokes and ogled Doug with her buds while Doug tried to work. She must not have realized Ms. Right—that would be me—had a history with Doug going back further than freshman year. Marco. POLO.

"Nope, not Wanda—Wonder, that's me," I babbled to Doug. I had known him since fourth grade! Why did he always pretend not to remember my name? "So can I have two slices of pizza, extra cheese and pepperoni?"

He started to write down my order but Trina interrupted. "Wrong. She'll have a turkey grinder with lettuce, tomato, and very light mayo. . . ."

"A Coke," I interrupted, but Trina plowed on.

"With two mineral waters and . . ."

"Fries?" Doug said, scribbling.

"We'll split a bag of baked potato chips. A Caesar salad for me, dressing on the side. Thanks, bub."

Trina laid a twenty spot on the counter and walked over to a table without so much as a glance back to Doug.

"Hey," I said, following her. "I don't like sandwiches. I wanted pizza."

"We're doing some serious dancing this afternoon, Wonder. You gotta treat your body with more respect."

I didn't have a chance to protest. Jen sauntered over to our table. "What, is this a B-Kidz reunion?" she asked. She had one of those nasty pretty faces: straight light blond hair and doll-baby blue eyes, but a nasty disposition, like if you took Barbie's teen buddy Skipper and turned her into Nellie Oleson from *Little House on the Prairie.* Jen was also like one of those size-zero girls that always had to wear cutoff shorts and tube tops to let everyone know how skinny and cute they were. Underneath the table, my hands nervously tugged at the T-shirt covering my flabby abs, the result of a summer spent eating pizza for lunch and banana boat sundaes on my breaks at the DQ.

Trina shot back her vintage I'm-not-taking-your-shit look. She stared Jen squarely in the eyes and said, "If it is, I don't remember the invitation that went out to you."

Point score: our girl Treen.

Jen flipped her hair and turned away. Her posse followed her out of the restaurant. As she left, Jen turned to face me at the door. She pointed at me, but said nothing. I was warned.

I wondered if Trina's coaching duties would extend to her becoming my five-foot-tall black country-music-singer-wanna-be bodyguard at Devonport High.

Six

On the drive back to Tig's, I asked Trina, "Do you stay in touch with Kayla?"

She shook her head. "Nope." I took the silence that followed for: Don't go there.

I wondered how she felt, seeing her fellow girl group member and friend go on to superstardom. From what I could see, Trina seemed genuinely happy and excited about her future. I wondered if the same was true of Kayla. You'd think so, since she had become so famous, but in the few days I'd spent with Tig, he'd spent half his time on the phone reassuring Kayla how great she was, how beautiful, how popular—as if she didn't know.

I did venture this question to Trina: "Do you think about her?" We both knew I meant Lucky, not Kayla.

"Every day," Trina said.

"Sometimes it feels like half of me is gone without her, and like I don't know what I'm supposed to do with the half that's left."

Trina said, "I miss her so much still it literally hurts. When songs she loved come on the radio, my stomach just turns over and I have to run to the bathroom. I bet Kayla feels the same."

I told Trina about the last year back in Cambridge, when Dad was forgetting to show up at the university and could be found wandering along the Charles River, Mom had been placed on disability leave from her law firm job because she couldn't make it through the day without falling apart, and my little brother had been caught spray-painting graffiti at the 7-Eleven.

"Sounds like this move to the Cape was what your family needed, Wonder," Trina said. "You'll get used to living here, trust me." Trina had such confidence that when she said those words—"trust me"—I believed.

For such a sweet-looking girl, Trina was a taskmaster. We spent the afternoon singing songs with mathematical precision, then drawing the songs out for depth and feeling. Trina's vocal stamina never wavered, but after a while my voice hurt from all the exercises, so Trina said, "Let's chug some Gatorade and then dance a while."

We went into Tig's living room and without speaking started clearing the furniture to the sides of the room, just like Trina, Lucky, and Kayla used to do when they rehearsed in the basement of our old house in Cambridge. Their determination had awed me back then. When I came home from school, I munched on junk food and watched *South Coast* and Oprah. Those girls came home and went straight to the basement, set up the speakers and microphones, and practiced singing and dancing for hours, with a precision that was fierce. People think that most pop

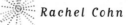
stars come out of nowhere and are just folks who got lucky to be born good-looking and with a decent singing voice. The truth is, if you look at the careers of most pop stars, even the really young ones, you will see that years of hard work, talent shows, failure, blind faith, and practice practice practice went into creating them.

That Trina could get me to dance at all was totally, simply, because I didn't want her to see that I couldn't do it. I had taken years of ballet, tap, and modern as a kid—I loved it, and was pretty good—but had stopped cold after Lucky died. In the time since, my muscles had turned to mush and I had to lie down on my bed to button my favorite pair of jeans. Feeling my body move again with fire and spirit might have been a welcome release if my body hadn't gotten so out of shape. And if anyone else besides Trina had been training me, I probably would have given up after the first misstep and said, "Hey, let's go see what's playing at the Cineplex instead." But because it was Trina, and I wanted to earn her respect and show her I could be talented and hardworking like Lucky, I stayed in the game.

I was sweating buckets and longing for a bubble bath and a really long nap when Trina said, "You know, you've got a great sense of rhythm. That's pretty hard to develop without having it to begin with. A couple weeks of rehearsing is all it would take to whip your slagging behind into shape."

I thought that backhanded compliment meant I was excused from working out after the hour of dancing she had just put me through. Wrong. Because I was *so* good, Trina turned on the music video channel and we danced through another hour of pop music videos, repeating the routines during commercials and stopping only for sips of Gatorade. Trina probably could have gone on all night if the Kayla video hadn't come on, silencing her instructions and—finally—getting her to zap the TV off and flop onto the couch.

"What do you think of those red streaks in Kayla's hair?" she asked.

Since becoming a pop princess, Kayla's long and curly black hair had been straightened and streaked with red highlights, her thick eyebrows reshaped to appear longer, slimmer, and arched, and her body had turned lean and taut, scary skinny, especially in comparison with her ample bosom, which I can assure you were not the real deal. Half the boys' lockers at Devonport High had posters of Kayla hanging inside.

I thought Kayla had been prettier when she looked like a real person.

Tig walked through the door, cell phone to his ear. "Yes, Kayla," he said, sighing. "The magazine is giving you a cover, not a feature. You know it's only covers or nothing now. Right. Out." He snapped the phone shut.

Tig looked at Trina and me flopped on the couch.

"Well?" he said to Trina.

Trina said, "Girl's got what it takes, if she wants to take it."

No discussion. Trina's opinion was law. He said to me, "Can you spend Saturday and Sunday here? We'll make the demo then. Trina, can you come back for the weekend to do some harmony with Wonder and choreograph some moves for a video demo?"

The whole deal felt like one big joke, but I was confident that ultimately nothing would ever come of it, so what did I have to lose? Plus, I liked hanging out with Trina again.

"I'm in," I said.

"Let's do this," Trina said.

Glamour? No. Excitement? No. Just business. And the business completed, this prospective pop princess hit the shower to get ready for her evening shift at the Dairy Queen.

Seven

That night, I was so exhausted from the workouts with Trina it was a miracle I stayed awake on the job. I wanted to go straight to bed and pass out. Fortunately for me and the DQ, I was perked up by the arrival of a select group of customers: Doug and his band members.

When I saw them outside getting out of their trucks I made a beeline to the bathroom for a quick lip gloss and mascara touch-up. Customers waiting on me? What customers? I made it back to the register just as Doug came to the counter.

"You again," he said. He was wearing denim jean shorts cut off at the knees and flip-flops. His upper bod was lean, a little hairy, absolutely perfect. The fire coming from that tattoo serpent seemed to be calling to me personally: *C'mon, Wonder, make a complete fool of yourself for us. Wouldn't be the first time, right?*

"Me again," I said with a sigh. I hoped drool wasn't falling from my mouth onto the counter. I heard Katie giggle from the kitchen. "What can I getcha?"

His buddies all looked stoned. The DQ experience must have been a munchie run for the band. "Coupla brownie sundaes and a strawberry soft-serve with jimmies on top and one fat-free chocolate froze yogurt," Doug said.

"Who's the froze for?" I asked, and flashed my glossed grin.

"Me," he stated, deadpan. "Gotta watch my girlish figure." It was not my imagination—he actually winked at me.

"Coming right up!" I said. I think I might have yelled. He jumped back a little. His gorgeous sea eyes were bloodshot and murky under his thick brown lashes, the kind of lashes that would have been almost pretty but for being offset by the stubble covering his jaw and chin.

"He's totally flirting with you," Katie whispered to me as we prepared the group's order.

"Sigh," I said.

"Tell him how you know Kayla! He'll totally want to go out with you then."

I shuddered at the thought. I would never name-drop like that.

I took Doug's order to his group's table outside and asked, "So, are you guys really playing at the Home-coming Dance?"

Doug looked embarrassed. "A gig's a gig, man. Yeah."

"Cool!" I said. *Cool?* Lame answer, Wonder. I wished I had on a short skirt so he could get a good rear view as I trounced back to my register, but no, I had on supersexy polyester uniform pants. Maybe my butt muscles had improved since that day's workouts with Trina. As I walked away, the guys were talking low and mumbling, but I caught these words: "new girl," "junior," and "B-Kid."

I returned to the register and, blissfully uninterrupted by more customers, watched them eat their ice cream for ten minutes. Gotta love the off-season. Just townies and the occasional Tigs to populate the glorious DQ.

My bliss was interrupted by the ninth circle of hell: Jen Burke—again—and her posse—again—this time arriving minutes before the store closed. I tried to pull my uniform visor over my eyes so she would not recognize me, but no such luck.

"Look, everybody, it's Devonport's own B-Kid, slumming it for minimum wage at the Dairy Queen," Jen announced.

I wish I could say I had a sudden dose of Trina empowerment, but I didn't. Truthfully, I was scared. Jen was someone who had the power to make my life miserable at my new school. So I pretended I didn't hear her and I focused on that Employee of the Month award I was coveting. Cheerfully, I said, "Welcome to Dairy Queen. May I take your order?" *May I shove hot fudge sauce up your big fat nose, bitch?*

Doug distracted her from whatever form of torture she was devising to spring on me. He poked his head inside the store and called to her, "Hey Jen, we got shit here." He gestured to Jen and her gang to join

him and his crew. Was he trying to save me, or score with Jen?

She squealed, "You guys are so fucked up!"

Jen snarled at me quickly, then strutted outside. Through the glass windows I saw her smush herself onto the bench next to Doug and light a cigarette.

I went to the supply closet to pull out the old mop and pail. What would Lucky do? I wondered. Grace under pressure—that was Lucky. Not someone to jump into a fight if provoked, like Trina, nor someone to enlist a group of love-struck guys to fight her battles for her, like Kayla. My heart pounded extra hard for missing my sister. Lucky would have figured out a way for me to make friends with the girl *and* get the guy.

The restaurant was empty and the outside benches cleared when I came out of the supply closet to close the joint. I had only waited inside there, chasing back tears over missing my sister and hating my new life, for fifteen whole minutes.

Eight

Dad and Charles picked me up from work. Charles said, "Mom made the worst meat loaf for dinner. Even Cash wouldn't eat it. Dad and I need to stop at Mickey D's on the way home. We're starving."

I was so seriously tired, but I said, "Okay." We had to use the drive-thru because the restaurant was about to close. Since they didn't want Mom to know they were sneaking food after her disastrous meal, Dad parked on the street and he and Charles ate in the car.

I leaned over from the backseat and reached into Charles's bag for a handful of fries. "Order your own!" Charles barked. I stuck my tongue out at him. Charles said, "That's not a pretty face for a pop princess."

We both laughed, but Dad got on his stern face. Dad said, "Wonder, you're not really serious about this business with Tig, right? I said okay to get Mommy off my back, but I'm assuming you're too smart to really take this seriously."

I lied and said, "We're just fooling around. Nothing will come of it—I don't have the kind of look or voice Tig works with. I can't sing like, you know, Lucky." I said her name low and soft, as had become our family custom, and then I diverted their attention from the name I had just spoken. "Guess who came to rehearse with me today. Trina Little!"

Dad and Charles both brightened up over their Big Macs. Trina had been practically a member of our family during the years she, Lucky, and Kayla had been like the Three Musketeers.

Dad said, "Doesn't sound like Gerald Tiggs is 'just fooling around' if he asked Trina to drive all the way from Boston for a day to work with you. How is she doing in school, anyway? Still a straight-A student?"

"She's good. Sassy and smart as ever. She's gonna be a country singer!"

This revelation prompted Charles to tune the car radio from the pop station playing Kayla's latest hit to the country station playing a lame sugary hit by a flaxen-haired, dull-voiced country queen. "Ewww," Charles cried out. "Trina's too good for this."

"I'm sure if Trina sets her mind to country music it will be a lot more original than this pabulum," Dad said.

Charles and I both asked, "'Pabulum'?"

Dad said, "Find a dictionary." From the backseat, I reached over and tousled the back of Dad's gray hair. He did have occasional moments of cuteness.

Later that night in bed, I tossed and turned. It had become habit that I had a hard time falling asleep. When I did sleep, it was only for a couple hours at a time, never for a whole night. Nightmares—Lucky bolting across the street, the sound of screeching brakes, me standing mute and shocked, Mom screaming—regularly struck me during sleep, so that I would wake up shaking and sweating, staring into the night, fearful of falling back asleep. Some nights when the lap of the ocean outside my windows was calm and quiet, I could hear Dad's fingers tapping a keyboard downstairs, or Mom's TV broadcasting Conan upstairs, and I knew they were struck sleepless too.

As I lay in bed wide awake that night, restless, I thought about the potential opportunity Tig was offering me, and the confidence he seemed to have in me. On the one hand, I didn't think for a sec that I had the kind of talent that could sell a million records; on the other hand, if someone of Tig's skills and experience thought I did have that talent, didn't I owe it to Lucky to give it my best shot? To complete what she had started?

I turned on the lamp and pulled Lucky's scrapbook out from under my bed, where I had it hidden from Mom. I flipped through the pages of first-place ribbons from talent competitions, honor roll reports, Girl Scout commendations, chuckling at the contrast between Lucky's roster of accomplishments and her handwritten notes. Lucky had the worst handwriting ever, an intense scribble that would have made you think she was a space case. Kindergartners who had written B-Kidz fan letters that Lucky had taped down throughout her scrapbook had better penmanship than she did.

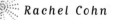

She had a couple of full pages devoted to pictures of just the two of us: as little kids in the bathtub surrounded by rubber duckies and plastic toys; wearing identical sailor suits at the beach one summer; playing dress-up with Mom's makeup and nice clothes; Halloween with Lucky as Dorothy and me as the Wicked Witch; and the two of us making faces at the photographer from the *Boston Globe* during makeup on the *B-Kidz* set. There was a shot of me performing a hip-hop dance on *Beantown Kidz* that Lucky had framed with silver star stickers, under which she had written, "Wonder Blake can be an annoying brat ☺, but the girl can dance!"

On one *B-Kidz* taping when I had been singing backup for Lucky, she had looked at me funny afterward, and I thought she was angry that my voice had been too loud behind her. Instead, Lucky said, "You know, you're the real singer in the family." I laughed because I thought she was kidding, but she wasn't. "Tell Mom you should take singing lessons with me," she added, but I said nah. I thought I had all the time in the world with my sister.

I turned on my side in bed, so awake I felt like my eyelids were bolted wide open. My front bedroom windows offered the beautiful ocean views, but my side windows, with the bird's-eye view into Henry's bedroom next door, offered occasional sideshow entertainment. Sadly for my insomnia, Henry's light was out, so tonight I wouldn't get to smile and laugh into

my pillow while Henry jumped on his bed and performed air guitar; nor would I be treated to one of his exclusive performances for my benefit, during which he played opera on his stereo and made wild operatic hand gestures out the window as he mouthed the arias, looking like Adam Sandler's "Opera Man."

My stomach grumbled. I tucked the scrapbook back under my bed and went downstairs for a snack.

Dad was sitting at his computer. The computer monitor and the moonlight reflecting off the ocean outside the living room windows provided the only light. I could hear Cash's tail wagging at Dad's feet.

I flipped on the kitchen light. Dad said, "It's three in the morning. What are you doing awake?" I heard the ring of an IM coming through on Dad's computer. His hand turned the volume down.

Mom must have heard me trudge downstairs, because she was right behind me. "Sweetie, what are you doing up?"

"Geez, I'm just hungry. Why all the interrogation?" The chocolate emergency at hand was making me grumpy.

I walked into the kitchen and pulled some stale Chips Ahoy! from the pantry. Mom and Dad followed me and sat down at the kitchen table, where Mom opened a bag of Doritos and Dad lit his pipe. Somehow I had stumbled into a family powwow.

Mom said, "How did things go with Tig today?" She had been asleep when I got home from my DQ shift. These days, when Mom wasn't eating, she was usually sleeping.

"Good. Trina came. She's gonna, like, coach me."

"Fantastic!" Mom said. Dad's eyes hardened but he didn't say anything. Mom looked at him and said, "Our baby is going to be a star!"

Dad said, "So long as she keeps her grades up. I expect an improvement over last year, Wonder. I'm not kidding."

"Sure, Dad."

Mom said, "Who cares about grades! Wonder has the chance to be the next Kayla!"

Mom was laughing, and I knew she was joking and I think Dad did too, but he shouted, "GOD-DAMNIT, MARIE!" He got up from his chair and went outside to the beach, slamming the screen door so hard behind him that it broke off its top hinges. Poor Cash whimpered under Dad's computer table.

Mom burst into tears. Again. I patted her hands to let her know everything would be okay.

Nine

Working with Trina over the weekend was worth switching my weekend DQ shift with Katie, even if it meant I had to work after-school shifts every day the following week. I knew that when Monday came, I would go back to my real life as the new girl at school with the broken-down home, the crush on the impossible guy, the B-Kidz backlash to live down, and the grades to bring back up to standard if I ever intended to get Dad off my case. I wanted to give Trina and Tig my all before I turned back into a pumpkin.

Mom came to Tig's with me on Saturday morning to co-sign the artist representation contract that Tig's lawyers had prepared. Sounds like a big deal, but it wasn't—yet. It was a standard contract—no money involved—that spelled out the terms by which Tig would represent me in any potential entertainment opportunities.

The really cool part of the day was that Mom didn't wig out when she saw Trina. Mom didn't cry, she just hugged Trina and sat down with her at Tig's kitchen table and asked her all about her life at Boston University. She told Trina how proud she was of her, and how she knew she had the smarts and talent to

make all her dreams come true. I had told Trina a little about our family life the last year in Cambridge, but she warmed to Mom right away and gave me a sort of look like, She's not doing as bad as you said! Mom had gained a lot of weight since Lucky's death, but on that Saturday, her larger size was the only difference from the old B-Kid mom Trina had known back in Cambridge. Perhaps it was seeing me with Trina and Tig, or signing the contract with Tig; maybe Mom just felt like our lives were getting back on track and there was something to be hopeful about again, and she could act normal.

Mom stayed at Tig's for over an hour and was going to be late for her shift at the grocery store, but she took her time about leaving. As she walked to her car Mom turned to Tig and said, "I know you'll take good care of my baby." I knew she'd spend the remainder of the weekend getting the silent treatment from Dad.

Trina had our weekend mapped out on a precise schedule: four hours each for song and dance rehearsals on Saturday, two hours' rehearsal time followed by two hours' recording time for each on Sunday. For the demo, Tig and I had chosen a song that Trina had written, "Don't Call Me Baby (Call Me Woman)," an awesome song about a girl demanding respect for being as smart as she was attractive. The song was a good fit for my voice because the melody had more of an R & B than pop flavor, and it was a funky empowerment kind of song that wouldn't have suited Lucky's soft and sweet demeanor. Lucky's shadow would not creep over my performance of Trina's song.

Trina worked me hard—very hard—but I have to say, by the end of Saturday night, when I collapsed in bed, I was twice the singer and dancer I had been even the week before.

The weekend was a sleepover occasion, as Trina wanted us to have maximum time together. Trina came into the living room and sat with me on the pullout sofa bed. She was wearing a stiff white nightgown against her dark skin, and her long cornrows were tied into two sets of plaits falling down over her shoulders. I was wearing flannel PJs with Oreos pictured on them, and teddy bear slippers. It was like the old days, when I used to join Kayla, Lucky, and Treen's slumber parties and we would sit on Lucky's bed and talk until dawn.

"You did good today," Trina said. "Tig was impressed. He thinks you have what it takes."

"Like Lucky?"

"Wonder, your talent is so totally separate from Lucky's. How come you don't see that? Don't do this for her—do it for you!"

"But Lucky was the singer!" I whispered. My confidence wavered continually, despite Tig and Trina's encouragement.

"I know you are not going to like hearing this, but let me lay one on you: You're a better singer than

Lucky. No disrespect intended here, but Lucky was presence, and you're the real deal."

If it had been anybody besides Trina speaking that way about my sister, I would have stopped them cold. I did protest, "But you and Lucky were in the same group. Why were you in the group together if you didn't think she was a great singer?"

"Lucky was my friend. I loved her—you know that. But Trinity worked because our voices together added up to a great whole. Solo, Lucky might not have had enough. She balanced out Kayla's hard voice and my overpowering voice. She softened us, evened us out. She also kept me and Kayla from killing each other. Lucky was a peacemaker. She did not have what you have—pure natural talent."

I knew Trina wasn't dissing Lucky. She was just being Trina: honest.

I had a sharp intake of breath. It felt so good to be around someone, besides my parents, who had known and cared about my sister.

It seemed I had barely fallen asleep when I felt Trina gently tugging my arm to wake me. Through the sheer living room curtains, I could see the sun rising over the ocean. In my dawn-struck squint I saw that Trina was already dressed and wearing a track suit. She stretched down on the floor next to me.

"Get up, lady! First we'll go for a run, and then we'll get busy."

"Have you ever thought about a career in the military, Trina?" My voice was whiny, but I was already stepping out of bed. I mumbled, "Wonder needs full-on caffeinated double latte."

"When we get back."

My voice came alive. "Now!" Trina shot me her *don't-speak-to-me-in-that-tone-of-voice-young-lady* look, and I whimpered, "Pretty please?"

"Yo, princess, be ready in five minutes and I'll have a regular coffee with skim milk and an Equal in a thermos for you."

Sigh. "Deal."

The early morning run turned out to be a good idea, totally energizing me for the day. By the time later that afternoon that Tig hit the "record" button in the studio, I was raring to go, and with Trina singing harmony, I admit, I sounded great—and confident. We were able to record the demo in five takes. Recording the video turned out to be easy too, especially when Tig prompted me to make faces into the camera. "Just be yourself," he said, advice that allowed me not to mess up the dance moves Trina had choreographed to the song. The moment of perfection came when Tig suggested we take the videocam out to the beach, and he recorded me dancing and doing cartwheels on the sand. I was psyched by how well the song recording had gone and how well I had performed Trina's choreography, so our takes at the beach were fun and carefree—exactly the mood Tig wanted.

When I left that night, Tig told me, "You did great

today, Wonder. Just remember, these things are so arbitrary. What Trina and I think is great might send dozens of record execs snoozing. But you'll hear from me if I get any positive responses. Meantime, I arranged with the dance studio in town for you to take dance classes. Three times a week after school, all paid up through Christmas. Think you can do that?"

I nodded and thanked him. I was feeling muscles reawakening in my body, and I wanted to ride that wave as long as possible, pop princess or not. And hopefully the classes would not interfere with *South Coast* airings.

Trina grabbed me in a hug. "It's been too long," she whispered in my ear.

"Can we still hang out, like even if nothing happens with all this?" I asked her.

She handed me a piece of paper with her e-mail address and dorm room phone number on it. "You know it. Work hard, Wonder. Lucky would be so proud of you." She added, "*I'm* so proud of you."

Tig said, "So, Wonder, think you're ready to be a pop princess? No promises, of course, but if I shop your demo around to the labels and they like it, your life could change . . . quickly."

I wasn't ready, but I wasn't worried. No way would any record company be interested in Wonder Blake. But thanks, Tig and Trina, for the fun weekend away from Chez Blake. Cinderella will turn back into a pumpkin now.

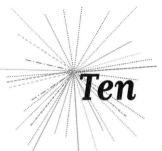

Ten

Autumn passed, with no word from Tig. Mom jumped every time the phone rang, but I was growing indifferent, feeling hopeless, not about the music career, but about our new lives by the sea. Charles was doing well in his school and had lots of new friends who didn't care that he was a summer who had become a townie. Charles rocked on a skateboard. That was enough. As for Charles's older sister, she was finding Devonport High to be hell on earth.

No matter what I did at school, I just didn't seem to be able to get it right. You'd think I went around school wearing a shirt emblazoned with the letter "L" on it—"L" for "Loser" and not for "Laverne." As far as I knew, I wore cute clothes, I was okay-looking, I didn't pick my nose in public, and I tried to be friendly to everybody, no matter whether they were a geek, jock, stoner, cheerleader, or brain. Maybe my loser status was because I had transferred into a class that had already spent two years together, or perhaps because I was a former summer who had been a B-Kid and Jen Burke had made it her mission to tell anyone who would listen that I was a stuck-up bitch. There was always my theory—that a secret memo had been circulated to the student body stating simply, *Wonder Blake: Nobody.*

Even Katie stopped associating with me at school. A summer spent practicing handsprings and pleasantly shouting back orders at the drive-thru window had prepared Katie for her dream—she was chosen as an alternate for the cheerleading squad. That, and cleared-up skin thanks to a Retin-A prescription, had granted Katie lunchtime admission to a cafeteria table of short-pleated-skirt girls and athlete guys. Now she was on her way. I would have been dead weight to her at school. We didn't talk about the fact that we were friends at work, but not at school. It was just something that happened.

The months of September and October found me roaming the halls alone, standing mute at my locker as kids who had known each since elementary stood around talking and laughing. When I tried to jump into a conversation, I got looks of contempt, or was just ignored. Lunchtime would have been torture if not for my unexpected savior, Science Project. Henry had a small group of geek friends he could have hung out with, but he regularly ditched them to sit with me in the darkest and farthest reach of the cafeteria and go over my algebra homework with me. Oh yeah, I could barely maintain a C average, despite my promise to Dad to get my grades up.

I begged Mom and Dad to let me drop out of school, or at least for us to go back to Cambridge.

They said no. They said, Making new friends takes time. Be patient. Join a club!

Easy for them to say. They didn't have to hear the whispers when I walked by people's desks: "That's the girl that was a B-Kid." "That's the girl whose sister died." "She used to be a summer."

I was missing Lucky something fierce. The time since she had died had been soaked up in basic survival. Now, in this new environment where no one really knew me, I hurt. I could see Lucky and me walking the school halls together, sharing a plate of fries at lunch, whispering in each other's ears when we scoped a hot guy. I thought, If Lucky were here, I could do this, I could deal.

Mom must have read too many of those empower-your-teen-daughter saving Ophelia whatever books, because she came into my room one night with this genius idea: "Have you thought about trying out for the school musical? I just *know* you'd make friends doing that. I happen to be sure you're the most talented singer at that high school, probably in all of Devonport. Give it a try, won't you?"

I said okay just so she'd leave my room but Dad followed right behind her. "Hey, kiddo, guess what Dad got you online. A subscription to *Teen Girl* magazine!"

Thanks Dad, that oughta solve all my problems. That'll get me right on track to being a well-adjusted teen!

Dance class was my one refuge. After the initial

OUCH that came from regular dance classes after two solid years as a couch potato, I was burning up the dance floor at the small studio in Devonport. The sweaty girl I saw in the mirror of the dance studio was not the outcast who never got invited to parties or didn't have friends—the sweaty girl I saw in the mirror was alive with power. The minute the music came on, whether it was hip-hop or modern or classical, I felt my body relax and I was able to concentrate in ways I never seemed capable of in school. As I pushed, pulled, tapped, swung, twisted, turned, stretched, and flew across the dance floor, I imagined myself liberated from Devonport, living on my own, bailing on school entirely.

But when the music ended, I went home to Mom and Dad—Mom and Dad who weren't fighting like they did in the Cambridge house in the year after Lucky died, but who now, in this big house, just didn't particularly bother talking to each other. Dad was more interested in obscure-Civil-War-trivia-dotcom, and Mom could not be separated from sad TV movies on the Lifetime channel starring just about every actor who'd ever been on *Beverly Hills, 90210.* Good thing Charles had that skateboard.

Alone in my room at night, I pretended I was a pop princess. With Kayla's latest CD in my stereo, I practiced lip-synching songs in front of my mirror, adding dance moves from the day's class. A rainbow of pop princess pictures—Kayla, Mariah, Kylie—plastered the mirror, thanks to Dad's *Teen Girl* subscription for me. In my room, in that mirror, I was anybody I wanted to be. For hours, instead of studying, I could pretend I was a pop princess. The mirror didn't know that at school I was considered a freak.

Eleven

Confident with my dance moves and sadly following through on Mom's advice, idiot-for-brains here really did audition for the school musical. I thought I could make a decent Miss Adelaide in *Guys and Dolls,* which would be so convenient, as Doug Chase was a shoo-in for Nathan Detroit. I sat through the auditions watching Jen Burke warble through *"The sun will come out, tomorrow,"* looking like a stick figure with fake emotive hand gestures and sounding like a tone-deaf Miss Piggy, I swear she was awful, but her whole clique of friends screamed and applauded when she finished and the drama teacher pronounced her performance "Very nice indeed!"

My name was called next, and even though Jen and her group were giggling and pointing at me, I didn't care—one thing I knew was that I was a better singer. My heart was beating very fast and my ears were ringing because I knew I was the object of Jen & Co.'s scorn and laughter, but I heard Lucky whisper in my ears: *You show them.* I didn't need piano accompaniment, I just stood there on the stage, closed my eyes, and tried to block out the laughter coming from the seats. I started out, *"Don't cry for me, Argentina,"* and was pleased that my pitch sounded right and my voice strong and pretty, when suddenly I heard Jen spew, "Some B-Kid here thinks she's Madonna!" I stopped singing.

The drama teacher shushed Jen, saying to me, "That's quite a powerful voice you've got there, Wonder. Sounds like you've had professional training. Would you like to try again?"

I nodded and closed my eyes, because I felt like I was going to cry from embarrassment. I went back into the song, but only made it to *"the truth is, I never . . ."* when I heard farting noises coming from a corner of the auditorium. Oh fuck it, I thought, why am I bothering with this?

I opened my eyes, looked upward quickly so tears would not fall down my cheeks, and, careful not to wipe at the tears, said to the teacher, "Ya know what? Between dance class and schoolwork and my job, I don't have time to do this."

I ran off backstage and out the fire exit. I stood against the brick wall of the school building, taking deep breaths, considering taking all my savings and running away, back to Boston—anywhere but Devonport. I'd figure out how to survive later, once I was out of this stupid town.

As if the situation wasn't bad enough, Doug Chase burst out the door just after I did. "Hey," he said to me.

I looked over my shoulders to make sure he wasn't talking to someone else, but no, it was just me standing there. I didn't say anything back—I was still choking back tears. Was he to be the last stage of my humiliation?

"You have an awesome voice," he said.

Shock-a-rooni! I sputtered, "Thanks." I sniffled.

Doug said, "We need a backup singer for my band. You interested in meeting the guys, hearing us play?"

I so almost said out loud, *If that meant getting to stare at your gorgeousness for one extra second, then yeah.* But there was that whole issue of my loser status; I couldn't imagine Doug's buds actually entertaining the notion of having an . . . UNPOPULAR person (NO!!!!!!!!!!!!) in their band. Then again, I thought, how much would Jen Burke be pissed off by the invitation?

"I don't know," I said.

Doug said, "We're playing at the Homecoming Dance. Come hear us, see what you think."

And just like that, he was gone, Doug and his serpent tattoo slithered back inside the school auditorium without a good-bye, as if they'd been a figment of my imagination. I didn't even have the chance to say, But I don't have a date to the Homecoming Dance!

So what. One week later, I dragged Henry to it, because I just had to hear Doug play. Of course, I didn't tell Mom and Dad I was going to the Homecoming Dance. The thought of Mom coupling Henry and me in front of the fireplace for pictures in our formalwear,

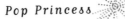
oohing and aahing over us when there was no "us" was just too . . . horrible even to think about. Mom and Dad assumed I had chosen to take a shift at the Dairy Queen that night. Instead, I snuck an old dress of Lucky's into my backpack, got dressed, and did my makeup in the bathroom at McDonald's. I slipped a coat over the dress and put on sneakers to walk the mile to school, where I met up with Henry. We had agreed to go to the dance as just friends.

"Wow," Henry squeaked when I took off my coat. Lucky's dress was a hot pink number with spaghetti straps and cinched waist. On her, the dress had looked sweet. On my curvy body, it verged on slutty. Henry's face turned the color of a tomato as I replaced my sneakers with a pair of slingback black pumps with three-inch heels.

"Science Project," I said, "it's just me. Don't get all weird." We were standing in front of the gym as people walked by, and I was on alert, hoping that Doug would show up and see my hot look before my glitter eye shadow and cherry red lipstick started to wear off. Through the gym doors I could see Katie and her cheerleader friends hanging out. Katie offered me a subtle, halfhearted wave, then quickly redirected her attention to her new friends.

I grabbed Henry's hand to drag him inside; his palm was all sweaty, so I dropped it right away. Henry and I must have made an odd sight. My getup made me look like I was about twenty-five, and Henry's awkward face and gangly height made him look like a prematurely aged twelve-year-old. How cool would it have been if Henry had worn an Opera Man cape instead of chinos and a white polo shirt.

The gymnasium was decorated with an autumn theme: Paper-cutout leaves covered the walls in golds, reds, and greens and strings of lights in fall colors hung from the ceiling. A giant banner across the stage proclaimed, "Go Devonport Lions, ROAR."

Jen & Co. found us straightaway. Her eyes appraised me head to toe and she exclaimed, "Oh no! What, is that a B-Kidz costume rejection you're wearing?"

Henry said, "Jen, go pick on someone who cares." My head did a double-take turn sideways at him. Go Science Project!

As they walked off, one of Jen's friends said, "Gawd, Jen, you are just gonna make the best Miss Adelaide this school has ever seen!"

Doug and his band stepped onstage, each of them wearing a black T-shirt that proclaimed "Doug's Band" in a goth Def Leppard–type print. Doug was clearly the center of their universe, so why bother to mine their brains for a clever band name when "Doug's Band" said it all? Jen forgot all about her victim to rush toward the stage and fawn over Doug. He did look awesome with his gel-spiked hair, tight black leather pants, and rock star T-shirt. Henry tugged on my arm. "Wanna dance?" he asked. I shook my head.

Although if I did want to dance, I thought, wouldn't Jen Burke be blown away! I was feelin' it. But really, I just wanted to watch Doug, which was better than listening to him. He wasn't much of a singer, and the band, though technically competent, was less than inspiring, not that anybody besides me noticed. The crowd was grooving like Bon Jovi was playing Devonport's Homecoming Dance.

I could have sworn that when Doug sang a punked-out version of "Isn't She Lovely," he was directing his leer toward me.

Hmm, I thought. Did that just happen? Weirdness. Potential.

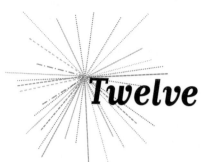

Twelve

An e-mail from Trina helped me get a grip. "So school sucks? Time to WAKE UP! Nobody can change the situation but YOU. Don't I remember you telling me that swoony white boy at the pizza place was in a band? Well, aren't you a singer? Do the math, Wonder. xo, Treen"

It took me a few weeks after the Homecoming Dance to get up the courage, but one evening I was walking home from dance class when I turned down a certain street where a certain Doug Chase lived. The band was rehearsing in the garage. I could hear the guitar wails halfway down the street, even over the roar of the nearby ocean. I walked right on in and said, "Hey." I never would have been so bold if we had been at school, where my outcast badge would likely have created invisible laser beams to bounce me away from the cool people had I dared approach them.

There were four guys hanging out: Doug on electric guitar, another guy on bass, a guy on drums, and one at a keyboard. "Wanda, right?" Doug asked. I couldn't tell if he was teasing. Despite the name mistake, his tone did not suggest I was the biggest loser he'd ever encountered in his garage.

Step 1: check.

"Wonder!" I said.

The guys were all staring at my chest. I realized I was still wearing my leotard under my short skirt and that my cleavage was spilling out. I untied the cardigan sweater wrapped around my waist and put it on. The past six weeks of dance classes were slowly turning my flabby figure into a lean, mean fighting machine, but if you're gonna be flaunting a leotard and tight skirt in front of your crush, excess boobage could be considered overkill.

The guys all looked bummed. Their sound had been loud, but apparently not pleasing to them. Doug shook his head. "It's just not happening for us today, Wanda."

"My name's Wonder," I stated again.

"Wonder," they all repeated. The guy on drums said, "The B-Kid, right?"

"Guess so," I murmured, deflating.

Doug perked up. "You ready to sing, Wonder? I told the guys about you."

"Sure. What song have you been rehearsing?"

"'Take Me to the River.' You probably don't know it. It's an old song by—"

"Al Green!" I interrupted. God bless Trina for the CD burn mixes she had been sending me so that I could listen to the singers whose vocal stylings she thought I should study.

The guys all nodded enthusiastically, at least as enthusiastically as a contingent of stoner musician guys could.

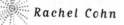

Doug tossed the mike my way and without saying a word the guys started playing the song. I didn't have time to think. I just started singing the first verse, and Doug's Band, with Wonder Blake at the mike, took off from there.

Step 2: check.

Thirteen

For the month of November, I forgot all about Tig and any hopes of becoming a pop princess. I even forgot about nagging Mom to take me to get a learner's permit. I was the new chick singer with Doug's Band, so good they sometimes let me sing solo along with backup for Doug, so good they even bought me my own "Doug's Band"-emblazoned T-shirt. I did have to wonder if they really thought I wore a "small" or if they just wanted to check out my rack in the wicked tight tee.

Word spread fast at Devonport High. Wonder Blake was no longer just a former summer B-Kid—she sang with Doug's Band. The revised secret memo might have read, *Wonder Blake: Okay not to treat her like a nobody. Tread carefully.*

Little things changed at school. Seats opened for me at lunch. Girls complimented me on my lip gloss in the bathroom. Guys stared dreamily at me in study hall when I sat at my desk and read song sheets, mouthing the lyrics to myself. Between Doug's Band and my part-time job, I wasn't studying much (at all), so my G.P.A. wasn't improving, but I couldn't have cared less.

What did not change at school was Jen Burke. If she

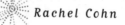

had disliked me before, now that Doug and I were hanging out, she hated me. She bumped into me in the cafeteria, saying, "If you think just because you're in Doug's Band that he likes you now, I know for a fact that you're wrong."

I had my Trina moment, and I said, "I know for a fact that I don't care what you think." That shut her up for the time being. Though she did purposely knock over my chocolate milk.

Doug was into me, I was pretty sure. How many times did I catch him smiling at me or scamming on me when I was belting out the tunes? By our tenth rehearsal, I had counted eighteen real times, though I was open to the possibility that five of those times were imagined.

But I knew I wasn't going crazy fantasizing his interest when I arrived early to rehearsal one evening and, as I approached the garage, heard the drummer say to Doug, "Man, she's got it going on. Don't fool around with her. You know that'll ruin everything. Do you realize how many gigs we could get next summer if she's with us? Dougie boy, don't do it."

"I won't!" he said, sounding defensive.

Way to eavesdrop, Wonder. Now I just had to figure out how to get him to go back on his promise to his bandmates.

I knew this much by now about Doug: His parents were divorced and he lived with his dad, who was a car mechanic; Doug's dream was that the band would buy

a van after graduation and move to L.A. and become rock stars; if he graduated from Devonport High, it would be just barely; his favorite band was Guns 'n' Roses (whatever) and his favorite artist was Bob Marley (much better); and the shorter my skirts got at rehearsal, the better his guitar played along with me.

Opportunity knocked one night soon after Thanksgiving. He was walking me home around nine in the evening after rehearsal, and we'd taken the route along the beach. It was one of those sickeningly beautiful Cape nights before winter hit hard: brisk, windy, moody. A half-moon hung over the water and if we'd cared enough to look, we probably could have seen all the way to Nantucket.

Doug lit a joint as we walked. He passed it to me. I'd never had one before. Square much?

We were about two blocks from my house; I could see it lit up in the distance. The nearby summers' houses were all dark. I plopped down on the beach and placed the joint between my index finger and thumb. I said, "Show me how. I've never . . . you know." What I really wanted to say was, Feel free to pounce on me at any time, Dougie.

"Really?" he asked. He took the joint back from my fingers. "Let me show you a better way to learn." He inhaled on the joint, and before I knew what he was doing, he had leaned right into my face and placed his lips on mine. I opened my mouth and he blew the smoke inside. When he pulled away, I coughed hard.

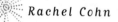

"What the hell was that?" I sputtered.

"Shotgun," he said. "Wanna try it again?"

I said, "Let's try it without the joint." The air was cold and the breeze whipping hard, the night sky dark and starry, but his lips managed to find mine, and mine managed not to fumble the experience too terribly worrying about nose positioning and breathing. I wouldn't say the earth moved or anything, but after a minute or two of awkward lip fumbling that was about as sexy as making out with Screech from *Saved by the Bell,* I got the hang of it. After five straight minutes of kissing, in fact, my lips were feeling quite competent. Hands, necks, hair, on to stomachs—I guess you could say we safely rounded second base, with an attempt at third. At last, I thought, Wonder Blake has her moment. It was the kind of moment so perfect that only a kid brother could ruin it.

"Wonder!" Charles yelled out in his loud Boston accent: Won-DAH! I could hear the wheels of his skateboard stumbling across the gravel road above the beach. "Ma's looking for you." Paranoia consumed Mom ever since Lucky's death. She wanted Charles and me to call her every two minutes to tell her where we were, and when we'd be home. If we were ten minutes late she sent out a search party.

I kissed Doug one more time, fast and memorably, and he escaped across the darkened beach. I stood up on the sand and shouted, "Shut up, CHAH-les!"

Fourteen

Strange that hooking up with Doug could give me a new sympathy for Jen Burke. Now I understood how she could get to be so mean. The guy could give some serious lip lock, but watch out if you tried to truly get close to him.

Rules for fooling around with Doug:

DO let him feel you up in darkened places when no one is around.

DO NOT attempt to hold his hand in public, or let on in any way, shape, or form that the two of you are an item. This fact is strictly a state secret, and the world order as we know it could topple should this secret come out.

DO fantasize about him during school, preferably during exams that will determine whether or not you pass.

DO NOT fantasize that Doug will acknowledge you as his make-out buddy to the band or at school, and for God's sake, DO NOT demonstrate any sign of affection for Doug in front of his buddies.

DO sneak out your bedroom window at night to meet him down on the beach. DO ignore Science Project's window surveillance of you sneaking out your

bedroom window and climbing down the tree outside the window. DO lie down on the blanket Doug's laid out on the sand and DO let him kiss you and touch you for hours on end. DO let him beg you to give it up.

DO NOT give it up.

Doug was not exactly fulfilling my ideal of having a boyfriend as part of my new life in Devonport. He was not the kind of guy like Science Project who offered to carry your books, or opened a door for you, or who talked to your parents when he was dropping you off after rehearsal like they were real people instead of morons whom you had to bail from as quickly as possible. When Doug and I passed each other in the halls at school he mumbled "Hey" and kept walking, and during rehearsals he snapped at me if I missed a note, or he would say, "Is this Wonder's Band or is this Doug's Band?" In private, he was a different guy. All the sweet nothings this girl wanted to hear, Doug was throwing bull's-eyes: "You're so pretty," "I want you so much," "You fucking rock as a singer." Yeah yeah yeah.

One evening after rehearsal we were making out in his basement while his dad was still at work. It was only about six o'clock, but the room was dark except for the flickering TV. My shirt was off and Doug was lying on top of me, his hand between my inner thighs, but not quite you-know-where. My jeans were still on, though the friction between our bodies as Doug rubbed against me told me the jeans were soon to be goners.

"Do you have, you know, something?" I whispered in his ear in that moment of heavy-breathing weakness. What the hell, I thought, why not just do it? Doug and I had gotten so close so many times in those stolen nights under the blankets on the beach late at night, maybe if we just crossed the line we could officially be boyfriend and girlfriend. But Doug's dad would be home any moment; if we were going to do this, it had to be soon.

"Yeah," he grunted. He jumped off me and raced toward his bedroom. "Be right back," he called out behind him.

His absence gave me time to reconsider. I thought, Is this how I want my first time to be, a quick shag in some guy's basement while Urkel pratfalls across the muted TV?

I was convinced Lucky watched me at all times. Ever aware of Lucky's spirit, I often kept naughty behavior in check—binging on Devil Dogs late at night, peeking at the smart girl's answers during chemistry, touching myself under the covers at night after groping sessions with Doug—for fear that Lucky was observing and scrutinizing me. In my mind, I could see her giving a thumbs-up when I was kickin' it at dance class, or nailing a song with Doug's Band, and when I wasn't being so good, I could see Lucky turning her blond head away from me in disgust.

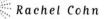

I thought of how I must appear to Lucky at that moment, splayed out on a basement couch, my shirt draped over its side, my bra unhooked but not yet off, my hair tousled over a pillow. What must Lucky think? Sleazy, that's what she'd be thinking. You know better, Wonder Anna Blake, she would say. Unlike Lucky, I had no intention of waiting for some mythical "true love," but I knew I didn't want the first time to be like this.

When Doug returned to the basement snapping a condom package against his wrist, he found me sitting upright, the lamp turned on, the TV off, buttoning up my cardigan sweater.

"Wha?" he said. He turned the lamp off and returned to his spot on the couch next to me, leaning in to breathe on my neck, as if he could somehow recapture the moment that had led to his running back to his bedroom for a condom.

I squeezed out from the embrace he was trying to lock me into. I said, "I don't think I want it to be like this." I started to say "I'm sorry" but then I thought, What do I have to be sorry about?

"C'mon, Wonder," Doug said. He patted his lap, as if beckoning me to jump onto it.

I averted my eyes from the partial woody going on under his boxer shorts. I said, "You won't even acknowledge that I'm your girlfriend."

"Man, is that what this is about?"

"Yes. Mostly. Maybe. I'm just . . . I'm just . . . I'm just not ready."

I expected to hear him say, I'll wait for you. I understand.

But what he said was "Get out."

"You're serious?" My heart felt like the Vulcan death grip had been clenched upon it.

"Yeah, I'm serious. I don't need this shit." Doug grabbed the remote from the coffee table and turned the TV back on.

I stood in front of him in shock, speechless. "I said go," he mumbled. He pulled an afghan over his lap, and I saw small beads of sweat on his forehead.

"Doug . . . ," I started.

"Don't bother coming for rehearsal anymore. You're out."

Fifteen

At school the next day, I walked around slouched over, dazed, feeling as if I had been repeatedly kicked in the stomach and smacked in the face.

Oops, algebra exam. Oops, spent all night alone in my room staring at the dark sky. Sorry, teacher, forgot to study, forgot to care. We both know I'll be failing this class, so you don't mind if I just stare mindlessly out the window while Jen Burke's pencil flies across her test paper in contempt of me, do you?

At lunch, Science Project found me sitting alone under a tree, shivering without a winter coat in the December chill. He sat down beside me and handed me a paper bag. "Here, I brought you some hot chocolate." Then he sang out, opera style, *"Here I come, to save the day!"*

I didn't laugh. I knew Science Project was just trying to be nice, but I wished it were Doug bringing me hot chocolate, Doug joking with me, Doug looking at me with the puppy eyes.

I felt tears stream down my face, and I wished my eyes could suck the tears back in so Henry would not see me like this. I looked into his brown eyes and thought, Why couldn't I be into a guy like you?

Someone nice and dependable and maybe a little geeky and not a gorgeous rock star wanna-be?

In that shaky voice that comes along when you're trying not to cry, I said to him, "I think I'd like to be alone right now, Henry, if you don't mind."

As I watched Henry slump off in the distance, I saw Jen Burke standing against the school's brick wall, a cigarette in her hand. Doug was standing over her with his arms on either side of her, leaning against the wall and pinning her there. She was at some distance from me, but I was sure I saw her glance toward me and smirk.

Screw school today. Screw Devonport High every day!

I jogged all the way to the dance studio in the center of town. I had to jog half a mile out of the way so I wouldn't pass by the grocery store where Mom worked during the day. When I got to the dance studio, I realized the difference in my body since the jog I had taken with Trina a few months earlier. Then, my muscles had ached and I had wheezed through most of the run. This time, I felt energized, ready for more, with no aching body parts and only a mild sweat on my brow.

As I sprinted up the steps to the studio, I remembered: Oh yeah, demo tape. Three months had passed with no word from Tig. I could only assume record companies had found my singing as laughable as I had found the prospect that Tig would even consider me worthy. The math skills that had eluded me that morning suddenly came into play as I equated in my mind: no Doug, no band, no passing grades in school. With no word from Tig, that meant that the last best thing I could possibly have going was also gone. Shit.

Jodie, my dance teacher, was practicing alone in her studio when I burst in. She stopped her moves and looked up at the clock.

"Aren't you about four hours early?" she asked.

I shrugged. "S'pose."

There was a pause like Jodie was considering whether to bust me or just deal. She let out a small sigh. "Well, if you're going to cut school I guess I'd rather you be here where you're safe than roaming the streets." Yeah, like boring Devonport could even dream of being that scary. Jodie said, "Go get changed. You've gotten so far ahead of your regular class that we can use this time to go over some moves the rest of the class will just never be ready to do."

Jodie took the hardest steps from each class I had taken over the last few months and lumped them into one session. It felt great. I felt like friggin' Janet Jackson and Madonna rolled into one superhuman dancing girl. The dancing freed my mind to think rationally. I realized: I had made a huge mistake with Doug. We could work this out. I couldn't lose him. He and the band were my only hope to survive Devonport High. Of course I was ready to go all the way—what had I been thinking? Anyone who could dance with the kind of abandon I was experiencing that afternoon was surely ready.

I watched the clock until I knew school had let out and Doug would be arriving home. I sprinted to his house, not caring that when I arrived he would see a sweaty girl with flushed cheeks and armpit stains from the day's workout overload. The band wasn't rehearsing that day, so I knew I would have Doug all to myself, to plead my case.

I knocked on his front door, but there was no answer. I could hear the television blaring from the basement and assumed he couldn't hear the doorbell buzzing. I entered the house through the open garage and crept downstairs, stopping to smooth my hair in a mirror lining the wall. When I heard squeaking noises as I walked down the steps, I figured they were coming from the TV.

They weren't. The sounds were coming from the couch, where Doug was naked on top of Jen Burke, going at it, all the way.

Sixteen

I raced the few blocks to the ocean and threw my shoes off. I headed toward the water but stopped right in front of the surf. The day was gray and cold, blurry, and the roar of the ocean and its stormy motion made me dizzy as I stood before it. I vomited on the sand, a chunk-free liquid heave that burned my throat as it came up. Within seconds, breaking waves had washed the mess away.

I crouched down for a few minutes, attempting to slow the swirls in my head. Home was about a half mile down the beach. I barely had the energy to stand myself upright. Images of what I had just seen pushed their way to the front of my mind: Doug and Jen, nekkid; me, an imbecile. I couldn't go back to school. Ever. I wished the sea would suck me in and turn me into a mermaid. Wonder the Mermaid would swim out to where the humpback whales ruled the North Atlantic coast and live with them and never come out again, not even to show off for the tourists on the whaling boats. I could never show my face again in front of, like, the whole island of Cape Cod, and Nantucket and Martha's Vineyard, too, and quite possibly the whole State of Massachusetts.

I started walking home, slowly. I bet this is what a hangover feels like, I thought, your head a ton of bricks

and your body like Jell-O. I had a plan. When I got home, I would call Trina and throw myself on her mercy. Surely she would let me come stay with her for a few weeks, till I could figure out how to permanently liberate myself from Devonport.

When I made it back to the house, it was silent, as usual. Charles would be out, Mom still at work, and Dad tapping away on the computer, probably IM'ing his little heart out instead of working on his great novel. Cash wouldn't even bother to bark. We might as well all have been ghosts with Lucky.

But when I opened the screen door to our house, to my horror, Mom, Dad, Charles, Henry, and Katie were standing in the living room. "Surprise!" they called out. Charles was holding a lumpy layer cake with sloppy pink frosting and burning white candles, but it was Katie I looked at: Did she know? Her smile was broad enough to glimpse her braces, but her eyes revealed no knowledge of my humiliation, just a slight twitch to indicate either that Henry had made her come or that she was looking toward the window to make sure no one she knew could see her inside.

As they sang "Happy Birthday," I glanced at the date on the pink Baby-G watch that Lucky had given me for my thirteenth birthday. Today *was* my birthday! Geez, file this incident away for future therapy, the mental girl who doesn't remember, or care, about her sweet sixteenth. I blew the candles out. I muttered "Thank you" and then ran to the bathroom, where I crouched at the toilet to heave again, though nothing came up.

Unfortunately, in my haste I'd neglected to lock the door, so who should follow me inside but Mom. At least she held back my hair as I attempted to throw up. When I was done, she sat on the ledge of the tub. "Oh God," she said. "You're pregnant. I knew I shouldn't let you sing with those hoodlums." Mom let out a soft chortle; she was kidding—mostly—but I didn't find the joke funny.

"Mom, eww!" And yo, Ma, relax—at the rate I'm going, the only way I'll ever get pregnant will be by Immaculate Conception.

"School called. You didn't show up for your afternoon classes. I would have been in a panic if Dad hadn't gotten a call from Jodie saying you were spending the afternoon there. Charles has been looking out the window for an hour waiting for you. He and Henry baked the cake themselves. Isn't that sweet? Henry said you weren't feeling well at school and that maybe you wouldn't want a celebration, but I insisted. Is that why you left school, because you weren't feeling well?"

"Yeah," I lied.

The ring of the phone distracted us. We were not the popularity house; the only time the phone usually rang here was when the firemen were selling raffle tickets or when Mom was moping around in her robe and slippers munching Nutter Butters and forgetting she'd taken the afternoon shift at the grocery store.

Charles knocked at the bathroom door. At least someone in our family had manners.

"WONDER!" he shouted. My head pounded again. "PHONE!" As I walked into the hallway, Charles shoved me lightly on the arm. "Dude," he said. "Thank Henry already, why don't you. I swear, you can be such a rude bee-yatch. The guy's not gonna hang around forever."

I shoved Charles back. "Shut up," I said, and took the phone from him. Please let it be Trina, I prayed, Trina calling to wish me a happy birthday. I could plead my case to her. I stumbled to the phone and said in major sick voice, "Yeah?"

"Wonder Blake?" a deep voice asked.

"Yeah," I repeated, trying not to sound so awful. What if this strange voice was like a radio station calling to tell me I'd won some cool prize and here I was, practically spewing into the phone for all the New England airwaves to hear.

"Wonder, it's Gerald Tiggs. Don't you even recognize my voice? Are you sitting down? Listen up, Cinderella. Pop Life Records wants to sign you up. Kayla's label! They want you to come audition this week. Think you can get to Manhattan tomorrow? I can have a ticket waiting for you and your mom at the airport in Boston."

Did I think I could? Uh yeah, I thought I could.

Hallelujah. Escape.

Part Two

Shades of Blonde
Dirty Blonde

Seventeen

Just days after signing with Pop Life Records, I received this e-mail from Kayla, who had agreed with Tig to "mentor" my new pop princess career.

Hey girl!
How To Become A Pop Princess, in Five Easy Steps:
Step 1—Hair. For the raven-haired like me, streaks of red, orange, or pink will do. For the mousy-haired like you, move on up, girl, to a dirty blond shade with streaks of gold. Tousle 'n' go go go.

Step 2—Dialect Coach. Your name is Won-DUR, not Won-DAH. Regional accents are forbidden for teen movie stars, but acceptable in a pop princess only if the accent is subtle and unaffected, and preferably Southern. If you are from Boston, you will have to work wicked hahd to unload that accent. Don't be a chowDAHhead. You prefer chowder, thank you very much.

Step 3—Diet. Expect rigorous dance and workout sessions, but don't expect those cal-burning sessions mean you can give in to the chocolate monster. Your outfits will be skimpy and so should be your meals. Skip the appetizer, dessert is a no-no, and you can forget you even know about the existence of pizza ("pizzer" to us Cambridge girls, hee hee). Learn to love your new best friends: grilled chicken and fish, and salads drizzled with fat-free dressing. The occasional Coca-Cola is acceptable, for a boost. The exception to Step 3 will be lunchtime interviews with teen magazine journalists, who will feel good about themselves when they can report to their readers that you gleefully munched down a double cheeseburger and fries dipped in mayo and ketchup, as you apparently do all the time. Throw in a slice of cheesecake to really make 'em feel extra good.

Step 4—Talent Manager. Tig is that rare com-modity: an ethical manager with killer instincts, who will protect your interests and instruct you in ensuring your financial future as if you were a corporation rather than a per-son. Don't ever expect to learn anything about him personally—he is all business and you are all product. Do expect consultations with top Wall Street financial advisers and brand-marketing executives.

Step 5—School. If you are under eighteen and maintaining a professional career as an entertainer, the law requires you to spend a certain amount of time in school, or with a tutor. Lucky for the pop princesses of the world, there's a nice little legal loophole called dropping out of school entirely. Go for the G.E.D. if you want, but you are a professional person in the working world now—and no one in the music biz cares whether you have a high school diploma or not. Your time will be consumed in rehearsing, performing, appearances, hair, and makeup. Try to ignore the look of sadness and disappointment on your dad's face as he watches your mom sign the form. You have a high-five-figure recording contract that could be worth millions if your album is a hit. His look could signal to you that for all your newfound success, your dad considers you a failure, a high school dropout. You know better.

See you soon in NYC!

Love ya baby, Kayla

Eighteen

The first single I recorded was called "Bubble Gum Pop." The song was about two kids who are making out and the girl's bubble gum goes into the guy's mouth and then they're in love. It was a pretty stupid song, if you ask me, with refrains like *"Chew it, blow it, lick it, I love my bubble gum, pop pop pop"* and you can imagine why all those religious groups later tried to have the song banned even though it really was just about bubble gum. It was a silly song, but a classic in that cheesy, catchy pop song way, the kind of song generations of teens would remember like they did "The Macarena," or "Whoomp! There It Is."

Within three months of my Pop Life Records audition in December, I had recorded "Bubble Gum Pop" to be released as my debut single, and I was working on a full album to be released by summer. Mom and I stayed in a small studio apartment in Manhattan owned by the record company. I slept on a futon on the floor crammed between a desk and a peeling wall and Mom slept on a pullout couch that took up most of the apartment when it was converted into a bed. Mom went back to Devonport every other weekend, but I was too busy to go with her; in fact, I made sure I stayed too busy to go home. Dad had initially said absolutely no way when the record contract was offered, but soon after that proclamation, my report card arrived: 1 C, 4 Ds, and 2 Fs, proving I had bested my last worst academic performance, go me! Dad said, "You just broke my heart"—but he let Mom sign the drop-out form. Even he couldn't deny that Devonport had been a disaster for me, that I was never gonna be the AP Everything golden girl that Lucky had been.

I was free of Devonport and the house of ghosts. Every day when I walked through the streets of New York, felt its massive whir of people and noises, excitement and danger, and its all-out living breathing vibe, I thanked Tig for having found me at the DQ, thanked Lucky for having passed on her dream to my genes. Every day when I danced and sang, I was grateful I would never have to prowl the halls of Devonport High again. A reluctant pop princess I may initially have been, but if it meant dropping out of school and leaving Devonport, I was completely on board.

In my eagerness to ditch school, however, I had not anticipated the other side of being a professional performer: work work work, all the time work. Tig and Pop Life Records had my time accounted for round the clock. Every day found me in some form of pop princess preparation: voice lessons with an actual opera singer; private dance workouts with a Broadway dancer who had choreographed videos for huge superstars;

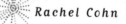
diction instruction from the acting coach who understudied some of the biggest names on Broadway; schmooze meetings with radio station program managers and publicity execs; shopping trips with wardrobe stylists; and regular visits to fancy beauty salons for hair and makeup consultations, facials, waxing, teeth whitening, you name it, all in preparation for making me over into the next teen pop star, the next Kayla. Sounds glamorous. It *was*—but also tiring.

Every night when I got home around ten in the evening to find Mom plopped on the pullout bed, watching *Law & Order* reruns and eating cookies, I asked her, "Did you remember to tape *South Coast?*"

If I had a dollar for every time Mom sighed and said, "Oh sweetie, I couldn't tape your show because I was watching something on another channel." That was the downside of sacrificing a ho-hum life in Devonport, Mass., for Manhattan, Noo Yawk. I no longer had infinite amounts of time to devote to Will Nieves and *South Coast.*

Tig found a way to make that up to me. He arranged for WILL NIEVES himself to be cast in my first video for "Bubble Gum Pop." I jumped up and down in his office for about ten straight minutes, screaming, "OH MY GOD!" when Tig told me.

Tig laughed. "Hold on to that enthusiasm and use it in the video! I figured you could use an incentive of sorts after the past three straight months of nonstop work, but I had no idea you'd be this excited! It's all good, Wonder. You've worked hard—now go have fun at this shoot."

Because of my *B-Kidz* days, I was comfortable with being on a film set, I knew how to hit my mark, I knew how to turn on for the camera. I did not, however, know how not to act like a complete imbecile the first time I met Will Nieves.

It was a two-day shoot and the first day did not involve Will. That first day was spent at a studio in Queens, filming slumber party dance scenes of me prancing around a girlie bedroom, smacking on gum and blowing big bubbles, jumping up and down on the bed, having pillow fights with other pajama-clad girls, all while we were staring dreamily at a poster of Will Nieves hanging over the bed. It was fun—but hard! Dancing to a complicated choreographed routine of steps with five other girls who are strangers behind you is one thing; now add in smacking and blowing bubble gum pieces large enough to make you choke, and trying to breathe while not getting out of step—not so easy.

The next day—Will Day, as I called it—we were filming scenes on a boardwalk at the Jersey Shore. Could have been a glam scene—the sky was a perfect blue, the sea looked beautiful and calm—BUT . . . the temperature was about forty-five degrees on an April day, and guess which prospective pop princess was wearing a polka-dot, bubble-gum-pattern bikini in

front of a film crew of about twenty guys? Because of the pop princess regimen of nonstop dance rehearsals and strict diet, I was as skinny as I'd ever been, but in that cold I had no desire to show off my new bod—especially with the wide-awake, very cold nipples under my bikini top. I kept running into the trailer between takes to throw on a robe and drink hot chocolate. I kept thinking, But I get to meet Will Nieves, this is so all worth it, better than a day of dodging Jen Burke's bullet glances at Devonport High.

A knock came at the trailer door, I opened the door wide, and there was Will Nieves, aka Roberto Perez, *Love Machine,* the scheming (but misunderstood) resident at South Coast Hospital, and also the illegitimate son and bitter enemy of chief surgeon and South Coast patriarch Robert Smithington. I about drooled hot chocolate out of my mouth in awe as he shook my hand and said, "Wonder Blake? I hear you're the next sensation. You ready to show us what you've got?"

My heart was beating so hard and fast I was sure Will could see its thump bursting out of my chest. My hands sprung to my mouth and I let out a small scream. Then I felt my face turning hot and red. Luckily, he laughed at my reaction rather than immediately shrugging me off as world's biggest dork. He said, "That's not the first time I've gotten that reaction from a fan, but it's definitely the first time I've gotten it from the costar on a shoot." I was all blubbery and my knees felt like mush. I couldn't form intelligible words to him as I passed him a magazine, but he found them just fine. "What are you trying to say? Oh sure, honey, I'll sign your *Soap Opera Digest* magazine. Got some extra hot chocolate in the trailer for me?"

I wanted to interrogate him: Was Roberto the father of shy Linda's baby? Had Roberto really been a guerrilla teen warrior in the Amazon before his greedy mother Heddy brought him to South Coast to claim the fortune of Robert Smithington? Were the show's producers looking to cast a new and improved love interest for Roberto (as Linda was too wishy-washy to ever command Roberto's attention for longer than a one-night stand)—and would those same producers be interested to know that up-and-coming pop princess Wonder Blake with the sexy new blond streaks in her hair and the worked-out-to-death new curves had been taking voice and acting lessons?

I felt sure I would never be able to complete the day's shoot without making a complete fool of myself in front of the camera. Tig's casting gift to me would turn out to be the end of my budding career—no way would I be able to lip-synch in front of the camera when Will Nieves was present. I would lose it, for sure.

A Kayla song was playing from the stereo as Will stepped inside the trailer. He snatched up the CD case on the counter and said, "Oh, Kayla! I love her!" Then he turned up the stereo volume and proceeded to perform a one-minute dance routine, mimicking the exact choreography of Kayla's latest video. He sang, too, imitating Kayla perfectly.

This was so *not* the behavior one would expect from haughty, macho man Roberto Perez, singing à la Kayla, "*You love me, baby, you know you do. Forget about her, she ain't one of your crew.*"

Mom and I gave each other a look like, *Huh?*

A knock on the trailer door told us it was time to start shooting. As Will walked out of the trailer he slapped the ass of the cute production assistant guy who had come for us and asked him, "What's your name, honey?"

Alas, my Will: swoon-height tall, black hair cascading down his shoulders, smoldering black wolf eyes, the chiseled looks of a god. Yet when he spoke, he sounded nothing like Roberto Perez of *South Coast.* In person, his voice was higher and his hips danced as he went over to the set and oh . . . my . . . God—he was so hot, and he was so GAY.

Sigh. Solved that little performance problem for me.

Will Nieves was like two different people. When the cameras rolled he was all over me, mister-hot-breathing-sweaty-muscular-lean stud, but the minute the cameras turned off, he was like Jack from *Will & Grace* though a million times cuter, singing back the "*Chew it, lick it, blow it*" lines with glee, while very thoughtfully wrapping me in a blanket as I sat in a chair in my skimpy bikini, goose-pimpled.

He said, "I can see it already, Wonder—is that really your name?—you're gonna be huge. You wanna hit the clubs with me tonight in Manhattan?"

I said, "I'm sixteen. I can't get in." How much would I have loved to go out with him? Maybe Will Nieves was no longer going to be a permanent fixture in my romantic fantasies (though Roberto Perez, *Love Machine,* would always remain my one and only), but he was—hello!—SO nice to look at, and fun and sweet, too. And after the months of hard work, I would have killed for a big night out on the town, dancing with a hot guy, away from Mom and the friggin' millionth ep of *Law & Order.* Not to mention how much backstage gossip I might be able to get out of Will about the cast of *South Coast.*

Will said, "Sixteen? You're ancient! I've been in the business since I started modeling in junior high, and trust me, you wanna go to the hot clubs in the city, you can. Your age doesn't matter if you're famous, if you've got the right look. And honey, you got it."

Mom came from behind him and said, "She's not famous yet. And she needs her beauty sleep." I sighed. This Mom-as-chaperone thing could get tired quickly.

When Mom wasn't looking, Will slipped a card with his phone number into my robe pocket, just before the director called us back to shoot. As we stood shivering in our skivvies in front of a board-walk saltwater taffy stand, he whispered in my ear, "After the song comes out, when you're ready to hit

the town, call me. Bring Kayla! We'll tear it up."

My fingers reached inside the robe and touched the rim of the card he'd slipped me. Wonder Blake was ready to have some fun—now she just had to figure out how to break free from Mom.

Instinctively, I knew the answer: Kayla. My mentor pop princess had been in California working on a new album during my first few months in New York, but now she was home.

Nineteen

A prime reason why the record company signed me, apparently, was that Tig had promised them I would tour with Kayla as her opening act. In the last year, Kayla had gone through three opening acts, each of whom had dropped out of her tour due to "scheduling conflicts." I may not have played an instrument, written my own songs, or had years of professional singing experience other than *Beantown Kidz,* but I had one ace in the hole no other prospective teen performer auditioning for Pop Life could claim: I had known and worked with Kayla since I was a ten-year-old B-Kid. Wonder Blake, sign here.

I also had a fallen pop princess to thank for my life. The record company had invested almost a year into building the career of a girl named Amanda Lindstrom, an apple-cheeked fifteen-year-old stunner from Minnesota who was being groomed by Pop Life Records to be the next Kayla. But when sweet little Amanda got pregnant and decided, against her parents' and her manager's objections, to have her baby and marry her sweetheart back on the prairie, the record company dropped her. The record company didn't want to completely lose the album's worth of songs and promotional work they'd

put into her, however; and don't think Tig's arrival with my demo tape in hand at Pop Life Records' offices just after Amanda's dumping was a coincidence—Tig's radar for opportunity is unsurpassed in the industry. While most albums take a year to be developed and recorded, my debut had been rushed through production. Pop Life Records was not known as a "pop factory" label for nothing.

Days after I completed shooting the video for "Bubble Gum Pop," I was in Tig's office going over my schedule. I had laid down most of the tracks for my debut album but I still had a few days of recording time booked, and Tig wanted to spend the afternoon with me and the vocal coach going over the remaining songs. Enter Kayla, all five-foot-two of legs, abs, boobs, hair, and charisma, bursting into Tig's office unannounced.

"Wonder Fucking Blake!" she called out.

Tig sighed. "Kayla, we didn't have an appointment today."

Kayla sized him up and down with her famous almond-shaped green eyes and said, "I don't need to make appointments with you anymore, right? Let's see, my last album sold, ka-ching ka-ching, I believe five million copies?"

"Diva," Tig said.

"Asshole," Kayla responded.

Kayla and Tig both laughed like they were having fun, but I wasn't sure they were joking.

I jumped up to give Kayla a hug. I hadn't seen her in more than two years. The brightness of her green eyes dimmed for a moment as she looked me up and down, and I knew that, just as Mom always did, she was looking through me for a piece of Lucky.

"So Tig here pulled you into this racket, eh?" she said. She ran her fingers through a strand of my blond-streaked hair and her eyes passed over the low-cut tight shirt given me by the stylist Tig had hired. "You're going to open for me this summer, right?"

I nodded, eager to please. It was so good to see Lucky's best friend again—and so strange to see her live and in the flesh of her new incarnation as reigning queen of the pop charts. She was a good fifteen pounds thinner than the last time I'd seen her, wearing low-rider jeans dipped down to there, with a halter top that left her tight, tiny stomach bare. Her raven hair was let loose in its natural curls, with red and pink streaks framing her gorgeous face.

Tig said to Kayla, "Aren't you supposed to be in rehearsal today?"

Kayla said, "Well, the music director didn't take kindly to me telling him he didn't know shit about my music. He threw a hissy fit and sent everyone home for the day. I expect you'll be getting a call from him any minute now."

You could almost see the tight little braids on Tig's head turning gray.

Kayla patted me on the back. "Don't worry, I got

your back, sister. I'll be watching out for you." Her tone was nice, but I wondered if something about her message was intended for Tig, not me. "C'mon, I got the driver downstairs, let's go play." She tugged at my hand.

Tig snapped, "We're working, Kayla. You two can have a play date later."

The thought of doing something *fun*—as I knew it would be with Kayla—overwhelmed my need to say what I knew Tig wanted to hear, that I wanted to stay and work. And work and work and work, as I had been doing for three straight months.

I whimpered like a puppy and begged Tig, "*Please please please.*"

Tig shook his head, but he let me go. "Oh, just play the cute card on me, sure. Yeah, I can see I'm not going to win this one. Wonder, go ahead and play, but the driver will be around at seven A.M. sharp tomorrow morning to take you to the recording studio. We gotta bang the rest of this album out quick. The record company is getting anxious, and they want that record out *now* if you're going to be touring with Kayla this summer."

I threw my arms up in the air and sang out, "Yeah! Fun day!"

Tig pointed at Kayla. "Bad influence," he told her as his phone line lit up from an incoming call. He slumped when his assistant buzzed in to announce Kayla's music director holding on line one.

"You love it," she answered, then she grabbed my hand to lead me to the door.

As we walked out Tig called out after us, "Kayla, her voice better be in prime shape tomorrow morning. You know what I mean."

"What does he mean?" I muttered to Kayla.

She slammed his office door behind her with the back of her foot. "Oh, he's afraid I'm going to corrupt you."

I didn't have a chance to beg to be corrupted before a giant ZZ Top-meets-sumo wrestler-looking dude pounced to Kayla's side. He was about six feet five million inches tall, with long thinning hair pulled back into a ponytail that fell halfway down his gorilla-sized back. He must have weighed three hundred pounds easy, and he wore bulky blue jeans, a leather jacket, and motorcycle boots. His ear had a cord attached to it that ran down inside his jacket. With hands that looked about as large and wide as soup bowls, he handed Kayla a baseball cap and a pair of large black sunglasses.

Kayla bunched her hair up under the cap as we rode the elevator down. "Wonder, meet Karl Murphy. Karl, meet my new protégée, Wonder Blake."

Karl the almost-sumo wrestler grunted something indistinguishable and reached to shake my hand. His handshake was so tight and strong I thought I would need an ice pack to relieve the pain when he let go.

Kayla said, "Karl is THE man. Stalkers beware!"

It was hard to tell under all that beard and mustache if Karl THE man let out a smile at Kayla's compliment.

Karl grunted into the mouthpiece of the cord hanging from his ear, "We're on our way down now. Outside thirty seconds, car in front."

"Girl," I said to Kayla, "you sure enough ain't no B-Kid no more."

Kayla laughed as the elevator opened at the ground floor. I started to step outside but Karl THE man motioned me back. He stepped out, scoped the area, and then gave us the okay.

We darted outside the building toward a giant SUV with darkened windows. Kayla took my hand to lead me to the car but was stopped by a pack of shrieking preteen girls who'd somehow recognized her under the hat and sunglasses.

"Kayla!" they shrieked. There was near-hysteria among the pack of girls as they screamed and jumped up and down.

Karl stood in front of Kayla. "Girls, if we can keep quiet, I think Kayla can do an autograph or two, all right? Line up here." His accommodating offer was grunted like a military command, and the girls snapped to respectful attention. Karl scanned the girls quickly. I do believe he was looking for any potential dangerous implements hidden in the pockets of their Brownie uniforms.

Once Karl had completed his inspection, he nod-

ded to Kayla, who turned on like a lightbulb. "Who first?" she asked, all smiles. Four girls extended pieces of paper that appeared out of nowhere. Kayla took a purple pen from Karl's enormous hairy hand and signed away, asking each girl, "Who's this for?" then inscribing the girl's name along with her signature "Love ya baby, Kayla." The girls were shivering with excitement and *ohmygawds* as Karl marched them away. One girl turned back and looked up at me. "Are you famous too? Should I get your autograph?" I shook my head a vehement NO, but Kayla handed me her purple pen and said to the girl, "Her name is Wonder Blake. Her first single drops any day now. She's your next false god." Even under all that beard and mustache, I saw Karl let out a chuckle.

As I leaned down to scribble my name below Kayla's on the girl's paper, I whispered into the girl's ear, "Not really."

Twenty

We hopped into the mammoth-size SUV. I recognized Kayla's grandmother sitting in the first row of seats. She was asleep, her head resting against the car window. Seeing her kind, wrinkled face brought back instant memories of hanging out in the kitchen at Kayla's house with Lucky and Trina during Kayla's grandmother's cooking lessons on how to make potato latkes with applesauce, pretending to listen but really just waiting at the table for her to dish out the delicious results. A young guy reclined across the backseat behind Kayla's gram, with an expression so hostile he had to be destined to become an unpleasant memory. The guy had a mess of brown hair with random, green-dyed spots throughout it, and hazel eyes that glared at me like I'd committed some form of atrocity by daring to step into the vehicle.

Kayla sat next to her grandmother, and with Karl in the front seat next to the driver, I approached the back row next to scowl dude. He did not relinquish the 75 percent of the seat he was occupying to make room for me.

Kayla leaned over and mock-smacked the guy on the hand-painted Converse All Stars that were resting on the back of her seat. "Make room for my girl, Liam!"

Liam, whoever he was, moved his baggy pant legs to sit upright and placed his feet on the floor. He wiggled around. When he'd found a comfortable position, he pulled a Tootsie Pop from his mouth and slowly turned his head around to me. He literally inspected me, inching his way from bottom to top, starting with my cotton candy–colored toes in their rhinestone-specked sandals, working his way up to my shredded cutoff denim miniskirt, stopping on the midriff sticking out between my skirt and tight shirt, then a long—*long*—pause on my chest, and finally up, up, up until his hazel eyes were meeting mine. I had never felt so violated by a guy's eyes before—who *was* this person? His eyes held mine in a dead-stare showdown until I couldn't help but look toward Kayla, like, *Save me!*

"Oh God," Liam finally said, "don't tell me you're the new pop princess. Tig must breed you all like rabbits."

Kayla leaned back and mock-slapped him again. She turned to me. "Wonder, meet Liam. He's Karl's son and an unfortunate hanger-on during college boy here's school vacations. See, it's his spring break, when most normal red-blooded freshman males would be in Cancún ogling drunk sorority girls in wet T-shirt contests. Instead Liam came here to New York with some lame excuse about needing to do research at the New York Public Library for an anthropology term paper,

but in fact just wanting to torture myself and Karl." Liam's scowl morphed into an ironic smile, as if he enjoyed Kayla's ribbing him. Then she added, "Wonder, you'll have to excuse Liam's bad manners. He's never gotten over the bitterness caused by his high school garage bands each sucking more than the one before it, reducing Liam to an embarrassing smarty-pants Ivy League existence at Dannon Yogurt University—"

"It's Dartmouth," Liam interrupted. He offered a dramatic sigh. "Not a place a high school dropout pop princess like you will ever see except from the window of a tour bus, isn't that right, Kayla?"

Kayla snickered, then Karl yelled from the front passenger seat like some dad on an agonizing road trip with bickering kids, "Enough back there, you two!"

This woke Kayla's grandma, whose head popped up and eyes sprang open. "Where are we?" she asked, confused. Then she saw Kayla sitting next to her and she smiled. She caressed Kayla's cheek. "There's my baby." Kayla moved over and snuggled next to her gram.

Kayla and her grandmother had always been close, much closer than Kayla was to her parents. Kayla's parents were both prominent academics in Boston: Her mom was a professor of women's studies and her dad a theology professor. Both of them were always being quoted and published in major newspapers and academic journals. You'd think parents would be ultraproud of a daughter with Kayla's talent and suc-

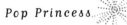

cess, but hers weren't; in fact, they'd always seemed embarrassed by her career, mortified that Kayla had chosen the B-Kid/pop star route and not turned into the classical music prodigy they'd expected when their brilliant minds had procreated. They sure hadn't protested when Kayla dropped their surnames for her professional performing career. It wasn't that Kayla went by one name only just to be like Madonna, but Kayla's mom was Korean and her dad was Jewish, and Kayla Kim-Chaimovitz was a whole lot of name for a prospective pop princess.

Kayla's gram—Mrs. C, as she had always been called by Kayla's friends—turned around to face me. "Is that . . ."

"Wonder Blake," Kayla said. "Yup. All grown up. Look at that."

Mrs. C's face was bright and sad at the same time—always the reaction I got from people who had known my family since Cambridge. "Look at her indeed," Mrs. C said. "Another beauty, just like Lucky, bless her soul."

Liam perked up from his slouch. "*You're* Lucky's sister?"

I looked back at him. It was too bad about his sorry disposition; without it, his stubble cheeks, hazel eyes, and scruffy mess of green-spotted brown hair could have passed for semiattractive. But oh my, with Liam's scowl of a stare, he looked like Angel from *Buffy the Vampire Slayer*—Angel from seasons one and two, when he was really skinny and moody, before he went off to his own show and got all into nasty Cordelia, before he started wearing leather pants and lost his street cred.

Kayla pointed her finger at Liam. "That's my best friend's kid sister. You're not nice to her, you have to answer to me."

He looked at me. "Oh, I'm so scared."

Karl: "*What* did I just say?"

Every tabloid and teen magazine that had Kayla linked with seemingly every hot young actor or teen prince of any European or South Asian royal dynasty had it wrong—Kayla and Liam clearly were a couple, even if Kayla and Liam hadn't figured that out yet.

I looked out the window as the car, caught in traffic, inched past the Plaza Hotel. A manure scent wafted over to us from the row of horse and buggies across the street. I had been in Manhattan for three months now, but I hadn't seen much of the city beyond studio spaces, offices, and salons. I tuned out Kayla and Liam's banter for a moment, fantasizing that I was the girl in the carriage, that some Will Nieves (but not gay) or Doug Chase (but not a jerk) fun great guy was treating me to a ride around Central Park. We'd laugh and hold hands and time would just stop for the two of us. I didn't care that the whole idea was about the lamest Disney romance scene a bored, boyfriendless, sixteen-year-old almost-pop princess could have ever imagined. I sneezed from the smell of the horse manure. Forget that fantasy—I could do

better. Okay, how 'bout me and unseen dream date guy go on the Staten Island Ferry like in the "Papa Don't Preach" Madonna video, only we don't dance around and worry about me being pregnant. Then maybe at the other end of the ferry there's a limo waiting to take us to some incredible Italian restaurant, and yeah, my guy is this unbelievably hot firefighter from Staten Island, ooh, that'll work, and . . . Yeah right, and maybe Tig would be text-messaging me every minute: *Where are you? Did you learn the melody yet? Did you lose those last five pounds yet?*

God, how depressing: Even my fantasy guys had reality checks. Shouldn't my *imagination,* at least, be off limits? "Where are we going, anyway?" I asked Kayla.

"We're here!" she said. The car was stopped in front of Bergdorf Goodman, only about the poshest department store in all of Manhattan, where Mom and I had gone window-shopping during the week we came for my auditions with Pop Life Records. Karl lurched out of the SUV and was met in the front of the store by two security types wearing smart suits.

Kayla turned around to wink at me. "Let's make this one fun!" She reached underneath her seat and pulled out a frizzy brown wig that had to be the ugliest hairstyle I'd ever seen. She placed the wig on her head and added a Burberry silk scarf over it, tying the scarf under her chin but pulling out several strands of electric mousy strands to frame her face. Then she reached into her handbag and pulled out a pair of wire-rim glasses. I couldn't help but laugh. She looked ridiculous, with her hot body and ridiculous head getup—like some trampy old librarian.

"Want one too?" Kayla asked me.

"Sure," I said. "Why not?"

Kayla reached underneath the seat again and pulled out a Cher-esque wig with thick long black hair and black bangs. She handed it to me along with a pair of large granny black cat-eye sunglasses from like 1955. I tried 'em on and knew my look was a success when even Liam laughed from his sulk beside me.

Karl came back to open the SUV door. He turned to Liam. "The driver will take you to the library. I'll be out tonight, so you're on your own. Don't get into trouble."

Kayla turned to Liam and flashed her megawatt grin. She pointed at him. "Yeah, Liam, don't get into trouble."

Karl helped Kayla, Mrs. C, and me out of the car. Then he sped off and the security guys whisked us inside the store, past rows of handbag and cosmetics counters I was dying to linger at, and into an elevator away from the crowds, who indeed did not recognize Kayla in her ridiculous disguise. We arrived in a private room where a tea service was set up and a personal shopper and several models were waiting to show us the latest line of clothes.

Nobody could ever say Kayla couldn't show a girl a good time.

Twenty-one

The clock on the wall in the private room at Bergdorf read 1:25. I thought, If I were trapped back in Devonport, I would be sitting through Algebra 2 literally watching the clock tick through forty-two minutes of torture, waiting for it to end, trying to ignore the fact that Jen Burke was passing notes to her chums that they always made sure my eyes grazed as it passed between their hands: *Some B-Kid bitch in this class couldn't sing and dance her way out of that blaring D- I saw slapped against her test paper!* Was this new life at 1:25 on a Tuesday afternoon school day better than the one I'd left behind? Hell YEAH.

In the short time I'd been in Manhattan, I'd been shopping with stylists for basic pop princess wardrobe—high-fashion jeans, short short skirts and tight tight blouses, cuter-than-a-teddy bear shoes—but nothing prepared me for the Kayla makeover. The shopping adventure with Kayla was like the Beverly Hills shopping scene in *Pretty Woman* where Richard Gere takes Julia Roberts to all the posh stores and makes the salesclerks totally suck up to her while showing her reams of gorgeous clothes, and she is laughing and smiling that horse grin and just having the best

time ever—except for that icky part about being a prostitute. And except for the part about Kayla's Sasquatch bodyguard hovering outside the showroom.

Stunning saleswoman: May I get you some more tea, Miss Blake?

Miss Blake: Why yes, that would be lovely.

Stunning saleswoman: What a figure you have! This Chanel dress is *the* one for you.

Miss Blake: Why thank you. I've been working out, like, A LOT.

Stunning saleswoman: We have scones too. Would you like a scone?

Kayla: No! (reaching into her purse and handing a protein bar to a famished Miss Blake) She can't eat bread. How do you expect her to fit into that dress? (She points to Miss Blake's dream dress.)

What looked on a hanger like a simple raw silk tea rose cocktail frock was, when on my body, a princess-in-waiting, *Vogue* cover wanna-be, unpronounceable Euro-name designer, Wonder Blake ECSTATIC dress. Seeing myself in the mirror with the dress on, I had to suppress the urge to twirl around like Belle in *Beauty and the Beast*—I couldn't possibly appear that uncool in front of Kayla. I stepped up on tippy toes instead, a ballet pose. Kayla snapped her fingers and BOOM, boxes and boxes of shoes magically appeared. Kayla chose the killer match: a pair of four-inch black spiked-heel pumps, cut in a triangular shape at the toes, with ribbon at the back to wrap around the ankles and partially up the leg.

Kayla stood up next to me at the mirror, pressing her hand into my upper arm. "Go on, flex," she said. I flexed for her and she felt around my new muscles. "Not bad, not bad." She flexed her own bicep: completely Halle Berry-worthy, sculpted to a lean work of art. "But you still have a way to go."

The saleswoman finished fitting the dress on me. "I wish I had a prom to go to!" I said to Kayla when I saw the reflection of myself in the mirror. The saleswoman was behind me, adjusting the hems while a tailor stuck pins into the dress.

"*Prom?*" Kayla said. "Wake up and smell the G.E.D. That dress is for like a movie premiere or a record release party. Paparazzi and shit."

"You think I can go to one of those parties?"

"Wonder! Snap to attention! This is your new life. You chose it. YES. *Live it, love it, wear it!*" Kayla sang that last sentence, jumping up to treat the room to a hip-hop dance grind accompaniment. "Ooh," she added, "I think I have a new song."

The dress didn't have a price on it. I asked the saleswoman, "How much does this dress cost, anyway?"

Kayla said, "This trip's on big sister Kayla. Think of it as a present from me and Lucky."

I knew better than to protest with Kayla. She always said what she meant; this was case closed. I smiled at her in the mirror. "Thank you so much."

Not like I could argue: Almost all of the advance payment from the record company had gone right into a trust fund for me, and the rest had gone toward a new living room ceiling and other home improvements for the house in Devonport. I was glad the money was being used to help my family, but at the same time, I wouldn't have minded having a little income available to me. I didn't even have a credit card. All Mom's and my expenses so far had been taken care of by Tig.

The saleswoman tried to be discreet, but she was ogling my boobs, adjusting them to fit into the dress properly. I'm like *Excuse me!* but I was too intimidated to protest. The saleswoman said to her assistant, "Call the lingerie department. Have them send up a line of (completely not understandable French name line of lingerie that sounded like a major spit) for Miss Blake." She looked at me in the mirror. "You're wearing the wrong bra size. Your . . . assets can be accentuated much better with the proper garments."

I turned beet red, but Kayla laughed. "Get used to it! I wish I had what you've got. Demure Lucky, you are NOT. I can already see the message boards on the Internet from every horndog high school boy in America. They're not even going to care about your voice—just look at you!"

"Ew!" I exclaimed. I instinctively crossed my arms over my chest. "That is so gross! Anyway, I don't see what the big deal is. These things always get in the

way, they're embarrassing, and my dance teacher says I have to work twice as hard just so their force of gravity doesn't keep me off half a beat. Guys writing about my chest on the Internet? I don't think so! That's disgusting—no way!"

Kayla turned to the saleswoman, the saleswoman's assistant, and the tailor. "Would you mind excusing us for a minute?"

They left without a word, and Kayla turned to me, eyes blazing Serious Moment. She said, "I think there's something you're not getting in this picture. Your first single is about to come out, and the people behind you are prepared to take it big time. This is not a school musical, this is millions of people seeing you, recognizing you, criticizing you. This is *it*. Public person—the good, the bad, and the ugly. Are you ready?"

In Kayla's voice I heard echoes of Lucky—without Lucky's sweetness, but with her natural concern. I muttered to Kayla what was my deepest fear. "What if I'm not good enough? This all happened so fast . . ."

Kayla said, "You ARE good enough. I didn't spend two years listening to you singing backup for Lucky—and drowning her out—on *Beantown Kidz* not to know that. And Tig would not have you here if you weren't. He played the raw tracks you've laid down so far for me. You sound great—and when Tig's record producer finishes with those tracks, I guarantee you're not going to recognize your own voice."

"But other people work so hard to get what I was just handed. What if I can't pull it off?"

Suddenly Kayla was no longer a concerned Lucky substitute. Now she was mad. "So you were chosen by Tig and Pop Life to be one of their factory pop prospects. So WHAT! Do you *know* how competitive it is out there? Do you *realize* that for every time you doubt your own ability there is another pop princess wanna-be cutting a demo, trying to knock you out of contention? So listen up now, because now might be your last chance. If you are in this, you'd better be in it all the way. I am NOT going to be putting my ass on the line for you, supporting your record and telling every veejay and journo out there about you if you're not ready to play in the big time." Kayla stopped, looked me dead cold in the eyes. "So tell me, Wonder Blake, are you in this or not?"

I said the right words. "I'm in."

Kayla locked her hand on my shoulder. "Mean it when you say it!" Her eyes were fierce, like drill sergeant Trina when Trina had been putting me through the paces the previous autumn. No wonder Kayla and Trina had always had such a rocky friendship, and no wonder Lucky had always been their intermediary. Kayla and Trina were both ruled by ambition; Trina had just opted to direct hers toward college.

I thought of all the time and energy Tig had invested in me. I thought of all the time and energy Wonder Blake had invested in herself. She had walked away from high school; she hadn't seen her dad or her brother or her dog since New Year's. Was she going to screw up those sacrifices with her own self-doubt, at the very moment that she was on the verge of something big? The Wonder Blake back in Devonport had dreamed of escape. This Wonder Blake, about to be throttled by a diminutive dragon of a nineteen-year-old singing superstar, *had* escaped—and she had a future, if she was ready to grab it. This wasn't about escape from Devonport anymore—this was about Wonder Blake making dreams come true: glamour, independence, singing her little heart out with the voice she'd never expected would be heard beyond a shower stall.

I said, "I mean it, sir, yes sir!" And this time when I delivered the line, I meant it. No more Wonder Blake, accidental pop princess.

"That's better," Kayla said. She opened the door to our private room and told Karl to bring the saleswoman back in. The saleswoman came trotting back, along with racks of sophisticated black couture dresses and piles of boxes with thigh-high boots and stiletto-heeled shoes. Kayla burst into song again. *"My turn!"*

Minutes later Kayla preened in front of me with a form-fitting black skirt that fell below her knees in the back and was slit open almost all the way up her thighs in front.

"Wowzamama!" I said.

"Wowzawhatever's right!" Kayla said. "This is what I'll wear tonight."

"What's tonight?"

"My place! You and me, some friends."

"But I can't go out tonight. I have to be at the recording studio tomorrow morning, and besides, Mom will never let me. . . ."

"Taken care of. I got Gram to call your mom and invite her to dinner tonight, to catch up, just the two of them. She told your mom you're spending the night at my house. I only get so many nights off work—we gotta make the most of it. And big sister Kayla gots to introduce you to some folks!"

"Does Tig know?" I asked.

Kayla pointed her words at me like she was gesturing in a music video. "*Tig?* Who cares about Tig? *I* am throwing a party for *you. Tonight.* My assistant has already made the calls." Kayla grabbed my cell phone from my chair. She switched it to off.

Twenty-two

*Kayla had stocked my coming-out party with prime-*time players.

But first guests had to make it past Judy, Karl's substitute for the evening, an off-duty NYPD cop originally from the Dominican Republic, raised in the Bronx, her hair back in a tight knot and her black eyes burning in a poker face she didn't seem to know was pretty. Cop Judy was one hundred fifty pounds of attitude and a Bronx accent so thick guests could barely understand her when she frisked them on arrival, looking for weapons or cameras.

Only after having made it past Checkpoint Judy could Kayla's guests stream into the living area on the third floor of the brownstone Kayla owned in Brooklyn.

Brooklyn? Uh, yeah.

Kayla had forgone the usual loft-in-Tribeca provision in the pop princess manifesto and opted instead to apply her small fortune to an old brownstone just a hip-hop away in the neighborhood of Brooklyn Heights, four full floors of refurbished wood mantels and staircases, spectacular furnishings, wide-screen TVs, and bookcase after bookcase, filled to overflowing—Kayla loved to read almost as much as she loved to sing. The

large brownstone had other advantages besides its proximity to Manhattan—it was big enough for a first-floor apartment for her grandmother, who had grown up in Brooklyn and whose wish it had always been to retire there; the second and third floors were all Kayla's; and there was a set of spare rooms on the top floor where Karl (who was out for the evening—hence Cop Judy) lived. That kind of spacious living arrangement would have cost several mil more had Kayla chosen to be based in Manhattan.

Kayla's dancers arrived first, on instant suck-up to Kayla: "Girl, you look GORGEOUS," and "Kayla, I got some new moves to show you—got some time for me tonight? These moves gonna be HOT on you," and "Wonder girl, you fill out Kayla's dress GOOD."

You knew a famous person had entered the room when the dancers, huddled in conversation, went quiet for a moment, then burst into excited whispers. Standing before Kayla and me in our receiving line was Freddy Porter, dreamy bleach-blond-haired, blue-eyed, six-foot-tall ex-B-Kid turned boy band member now turned solo singer—and he was all of eighteen years old. "Whoa—look what happened to Lucky's kid sister!" he said when he came up to Kayla and me. Lucky's "kid" sister was indeed all glammed up—wearing a she-can-barely-breathe tight black dress with a black lace corset top borrowed from Kayla, accessorized with the black spiked-heel ankle-ribbon shoes Kayla had bought me during our shopping adventure. My dirty blond-highlighted hair was ironed flat and my face was made up with pink champagne-colored glitter eye shadow and lip gloss, and big thick false eyelashes out to here, personally applied by Kayla's assistant Jules. Jules was a twenty-year-old beauty school dropout turned tornado-speed Edward Scissorhands celeb right-hand girl, the kind of assistant so talented she could arrange a house party stocked with a deejay, catered food, bar setup, and music industry celebrities on just a few hours' notice.

Freddy whispered into my ear, "You ready to pick up where we left off?" Why did he have to remember that embarrassing first kiss? Me age twelve, and him age fourteen, in a B-Kid dressing room. I saw myself in the large slanted mirror across Kayla's living room. My cheeks were crimson.

Luckily I didn't have to answer. J—simply "J"; no first name, no last name, no other letters in between—he of the syndicated morning drive time Top 40 radio program in the country, chimed in next to Freddy: "So you're the next sensation Kayla and Tig have been e-mailing me about, eh?" He scanned me up and down, head to toe—this seemed to be the new ritual for the day, inch-by-inch appraisal of Wonder Blake, commodity. With his black cashmere turtleneck and his discreet crew cut of thinning hair and his "eh?" J struck me as being like some prematurely balding Canadian newscaster for the teenybopper set. He grinned, like a bachelor uncle who didn't realize he

was checking out his niece's friends: "You gonna give us a show tonight?" He did a fake little bump and grind, and I quite possibly blushed even deeper; my poor cheeks felt like they were on fire. I managed only to shake my head. J said, "You're gonna give me an exclusive on debuting your song, though, right?" Kayla nodded her head at me; I nodded my head at him. Wow, two minutes into meeting two big industry players, and I hadn't managed to stammer out an intelligent sentence. Any sentence, for that matter. Way to go, Wonder!

Freddy and J had a small posse of rapper and actor types trailing in after them, most of whom I vaguely recognized from music videos or jeans commercials, and their group went right to the bar in the corner of the living room, where a hired bartender was mixing drinks next to a deejay laying out albums to get the party started. Freddy said something into the ear of the deejay, who nodded appreciatively, then wham! funksoul music shake it down now was blaring from the deejay's speakers. A bevy of Kayla's female backup dancers hustled to the center of the room right on cue, and Freddy and J and their crew admired them from a distance before joining in with the male dancers who formed Kayla's entourage. Within twenty minutes of guests arriving, the dance area was filled with people, and dang, these folks made the dancers in *Dirty Dancing* look tame. It wasn't pop factory Kayla or Freddy Porter-issue music blaring at this party, it was

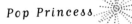

strictly R & B, and these folks could get their groove on. They had Mary J. Blige, followed by Parliament, then some Chaka Khan—artists I recognized because Trina and Lucky had swapped R & B CDs for years. The deejay blared some old-school '70s song and folks broke out into a *Soul Train*-style dance: Two sets of dancers formed a line to sandwich a solo dancer grooving down the center, as they all clapped their hands to the beat and sang out, *"We're riding on a groove line tonight, oh ooh!"*

Part of me wanted to join in, to show off my new moves. I could shake my ass down to the ground with my arms swinging in the air like nobody's business, except oh yeah maybe not in this way tight Kayla-size dress that I'd had to lie down on her bed in so that I could zipper up the side, and then be helped up by Jules while I sucked my stomach in and held my back straight as a board. Guests were dancing all over the living room now, beer bottles were popping open, chatter was rising, cigarettes were being lit, the music was getting louder and louder. Having introduced me to about everyone in the room, Kayla slapped my ass and said, "Sink or swim time, you're on your own, girl." She flitted off, a drink in her hand, to chat up a big movie agent.

I felt my suffocating figure retreat into a corner of the room, toward the stairs, panicked. Kayla had it right when she'd tagged me "girl." I shouldn't be here I thought—I was too young, in over my head, these

people were all college age and older, half of 'em famous. I was out of my league; I couldn't even get a date for the Homecoming Dance in Devonport. I saw Kayla lean in to the agent—were they about to make out? No, he was lighting a cigarette for her. Kayla smoked? That was surprising from a health fanatic like her who'd guzzled liters of water and had only eaten steamed veggies and sushi during our day together.

Kayla was no longer paying attention to me: This party was *on.* I bolted up the stairs. Sink or swim? I choose RUN.

I reached the top of the stairs, saw a bathroom light on, and retreated inside. Breathe, breathe, breathe, I told myself. I splashed some cold water on my face and all but fainted when I looked up into the mirror to see an angry alien face with a brown head specked with green spots standing in the bathtub behind me. I turned around, shocked—there was Liam holding a towel around his waist with one hand and a very tattered and wet copy of *Anna Karenina* in the other. How had I not noticed the steam in the room, the half-closed shower curtain around the tub, the candles burning on the tub ledge, the . . . Wow, Liam was really tall standing up and had a nice assemblage of chest hair over what appeared to be extremely tight abs.

"Do you not knock, pop princess?" he said. "Or perhaps you didn't notice the rope at the top of the

stairs which is *supposed* to signal to guests that this floor is off-limits?"

"I'm so sorry, I didn't realize . . . I thought Karl was out. . . . I didn't . . ."

"You okay, pop princess?"

"Excuse me, I have a name. That name is Wonder."

"You're looking flustered there, *Wonder.* Only half an hour of a Kayla party did that to you? That may be a new record. You're gonna need more stamina than that if you want to hold your own with the Kaylas in this business."

Like I needed to stand here and be insulted by his sarcasm dripping harder than the sweat down his stubble cheeks and framing his long brown eyelashes while I was trying to have a perfectly private panic attack. "Screw off!" I said. "What do you know anyway?" What a jerk! I marched back downstairs, ready to burn this party up.

Could I show that Liam!

I returned to the party from my little Liam encounter and headed straight toward Jules, who was carrying a tray of pink cocktail glasses. "Want one?" she asked, and I grabbed a glass brimming with a pretty pink liquid and a yellow lemon slice. I said, "Is that a pink lemonade?" Kayla chuckled from behind me and said, "Yeah, strictly Shirley Temples all around. No, dear Wonder, this is the great loosen-upper, the Cosmopolitan." I took a taste—oh-my-yum! I said to Jules, "Aren't you supposed to card me for this?" and Jules laughed and pointed to Cop Judy: "That's her job." Judy, having gotten the forty or so guests inspected and upstairs to the living area, acted immune to the blaring soul music as she stood guard at the door and protectively watched every move Kayla made from a discreet distance, but I saw her dowdy-loafer-wearing feet tapping up and down, back and forth. Cop Judy was feeling the groove of this party—who wouldn't, except possibly that awful Liam person?

I felt an arm around my waist. Freddy. He said, "Your turn to show us what you've got," and after slurping down Cosmo #2, I *was* ready. Freddy pulled me into a get ur freak on dance groove and I was feelin' it for real, dancing my little heart out, letting Freddy press up close as Kayla's dancers crowded around me saying, "Mmm, that girl can *dance.*" Two songs later, guess who was get-down dancin' through the middle of the soul train line in the middle of Kayla's living room floor, powered by her new best friend, the Cosmopolitan? That person would be Wonder Anna Blake, as two lines of dancers sang out, "*Go Wonder! Go Wonder!*"

After the fourth dirty dance, sweat running down my face, I needed a break. I plopped myself onto a sofa next to Kayla. Freddy plopped down next to me and draped his arm around my shoulder. "Wonder, Wonder, Wonder," he said. "I always knew you were going to grow up to be the hot one." I didn't know what to say to that—so I just didn't say anything. All of a sudden Freddy turned all respectful-guy serious, and said, as if to break the ice, "So tell me—college in your plans, or just hanging out with Kayla here and watching her hope you don't steal her thunder?"

I didn't dare giggle—though I wanted to, not because Freddy was funny but because my insides were now on full buzz. Kayla rolled her eyes at Freddy and said, "Wonder's not going the Dean route." She was referring to another ex-B-Kid, Dean Marconi, or Dean Macaroni as Lucky and I used to call him because he was so pretentious—even at age twelve, when Dean Macaroni was performing Shakespeare in the Park, he'd acted like he was above all us other B-Kids. In the past year, Dean Macaroni had been nominated for an Oscar for his star supporting actor turn as a heroin addict, but Dean Macaroni was too good even for the Oscars. He had forgone attending the ceremony because of his midterms at Yale— luckily he'd made sure every newspaper and magazine in America knew it.

Kayla took Freddy's arm from my shoulder and replaced it with her own. "Wonder's going the Kayla route. Superstar!" She spewed out that last word like the mental Catholic schoolgirl from the *Saturday Night Live* skits, and got a laugh from Freddy and me.

"College," I said. "Who needs that?"

"Yeah, that's my girl," Kayla said, "We're enrolled at the University of Life. Besides. I don't know about

you, Freddy, but after *Beantown Kidz* ended and I had to go back to school for a while, that was a rough scene. Once you've been on a TV show or whatever, you just cannot integrate back into a regular school, despite what any of them child stars from *The E! True Hollywood Story* say about how they popped right into high school after their shows were canceled and it was all hunky-dory. Gimme a roomful of shark agents and asshole record company execs with ice running through their veins before making me do another day of high school—snot rag girls whispering 'B-Kid' behind my back—"

"Whoa!" Freddy said. He looked at the square glass in Kayla's hand. "How many of those drinks have you had, old girl?"

She snapped, "Don't call me old!" and her tone change was so abrupt I almost jumped in my seat. Kayla removed her arm from my shoulder and was on her way to the bar for a refill before I could say, Hey, high school sucked for me, too, I feel your pain! Then Freddy got up and chased down Kayla, caressing her waist, telling her he was kidding, she was so hot, she was so . . .

I ran back upstairs and barged into Liam's room. He was sitting at his desk, a laptop in front of him, with only a small desk lamp for light. He took off monster-sized headphones from his ears and just looked at me in that intense, witch-hazel-eyes way that must have been embedded in his genetic code.

He grumbled, "I repeat, pop princess: Do you not know how to knock?"

I said, "Just because you have some weird unresolved or unrequited or I don't know what thing for Kayla does not mean you had to insult me before."

He said, "Kayla! What does she have to do with it? You were the one invading my space. And may I say, I had to put on the headphones to drown out the cheers of 'Go Wonder, Go Wonder' coming from downstairs, so I'm guessing you've relaxed a little since our last little encounter." He moved closer to me, right up into my face—why did he have to smell all nice Ivory soap? He touched my cheeks—what the . . . ?—then pointed his finger at me like a schoolmarm. "Your face is all flushed. You've been drinking!"

"One Cosmo!" I said.

"One?"

"Maybe two. Why, are you gonna give me some earnest speech about not giving in to peer pressure?"

"My dad's been in the music business since I was born, so I think I'm qualified to tell you—those people downstairs aren't your peers, trust me. You're so naive in comparison to them it's not even funny. So lucky you, no speech from me. You're sure you only had two drinks?"

"Two! And I'm having a GREAT time!" I'd finished gulping a third Cosmo on the stairs up to his floor—honestly, those drinks were so good, they *did* taste like a Shirley Temple, just without the fizz, none of that hard blech taste I associated with the annual New Year's beer or whiskey Dad let me sip to prove to me how much I wouldn't like alcohol. My head was a little dizzy, but I felt *good*. No punk Liam was going to ruin my party with his bad-ass attitude.

"If you're having such a good time, why are you in here?"

He really was just so annoying.

"Who are you to tell me I'm naive? What do you know about me? You just met me today! Maybe your bad attitude is from lack of fun. I think you should come downstairs and join the party." *Huh?* My mind was at war with my mouth: Shut up, Wonder! Pretty soon he'll think you like him or something! I added, "There's some video girls with big boobs wearing tube tops down there. You don't want to study up here when you could be like all the other guys down there checking those girls out, do you?" Yeah, great recovery, Wonder, well done.

Liam said, "I have better things to do. I have an anthropology paper I'm working on. And I've been to a Kayla party before, and 'fun' isn't the word I'd choose to describe them. What was Kayla drinking, anyway?"

"Why do you care?"

"I don't. I'm just trying to gauge the level of hangover tomorrow and whether I should spend the rest of spring break at my mom's upstate."

I sat down on his bed and unzipped the side of the tight black dress just a little—ah, nice deep breath.

My head was getting a wee bit woozy. "What does your mom do? Are your parents divorced?"

Liam reached his arms out, like to lift me back up. "Pop princess, I did not invite you in here. Don't make yourself comfortable."

I ignored his outstretched arms and looked at the pictures on the wall over his twin bed. The room was minimally furnished—just a bed, a dresser, and a desk; obviously Liam didn't truly live here—but the pictures showed that at least he was a part of this household. There were some skater and punk band stickers, an *Abbey Road* picture of the Beatles, a photo of—the Go-Go's?—waving from water skis, and there was a quote painted in green on the wall: "Baby we were born to run"—Bruce Springsteen. The stickers were surrounded by a little family assemblage of tacked-on pix: Karl and what must have been Liam's mom holding a baby Liam in front of a marquee that read "Aerosmith SOLD OUT"; an age tenish Liam and Karl at the Eiffel Tower; Liam with a mullet hair-cut and a T-shirt that said "Hudson Falls HS Swim Team" standing next to Karl on London Bridge; then a current-incarnation Liam and Karl holding up Kayla in front of the Leaning Tower of Pisa with what looked like a pack of screaming preteen girls behind them; and . . . a little photo booth snapshot of Lucky and Kayla, taken when they were both about fourteen years old—my sister still had her braces on—two years before Lucky died.

"How come you have a picture of my sister in here?" I said. "You didn't even know her."

"If I tell you, will you leave?"

"Maybe. Probably." Liam didn't need to know that my body's personal need to use the bathroom would in fact win out over his personal need for me to leave his room.

"Looking at that picture makes me believe in the Kayla that existed before, who just loved to sing, pure and simple, who had genuine friends who loved her. Makes me feel like there's hope for Kayla."

"You like Kayla!"

"You promised you'd leave. And yeah, I tolerate Kayla okay; she's the fourth pop princess Dad has worked for and she may be the most tyrannical but she's also the smartest—"

"No, you like-like her!" I said, but I didn't say it all accusing, I said it all sultry and deep as I stood up to walk out. I turned around and stood against his closed door for a sec and tried to zipper the dress back up, but the zipper jammed and I was too Cosmo-spacey to get it right. "Help me, please!" I said to Liam, exasperated that he was just standing there watching when he could have made himself useful.

He hesitated but then stepped over, practically right in my face. He played with the zipper till he got it up. Then his eyes honed in on my cleavage. "That's some dress you've got on there, pop princess," he said.

"Don't call me that, it's rude."

"Okay, Kayla Junior."

Grrrrrrrrrr . . . .

"You like-like Kayla," I teased again.

"Do not," he said.

"Do too."

"Want me to prove to you how much I don't?" He pinned his arms on either side of my shoulders so I was pressed against the back of the door. Then he leaned his body against mine, his legs pressed into my legs; I felt major warmth and a feeling of *uh-oh* spreading through my body. I closed my eyes without thinking—not that I was capable of thinking at that moment—and then his lips were on mine, oh wow, *nice.* Somewhere in that lip lock I mumbled, "What are you doing?" and his mouth only left mine for a sec to mumble back, "Proving to you I don't like Kayla." I let him kiss me for a minute more—okay, maybe two or three minutes more—ohmygawd he was the best kisser, yes there was tongue and it wasn't sloppy like Doug Chase, his was subtle and sweet and sigh he just smelled so good and his lips were so soft even with the stubble on his chin against my cheek. He let go for a sec to take a breath and in that moment I managed to shimmy myself underneath his arms and away from his Lee press-on lips before the urge to just completely jump his bones took over. I said, "Aren't you just proving to me the opposite?"

And I left his room and had that pee. Then I stood against the bathroom door for a good long while, taking deep breaths, promising myself I would not barge back into Liam's room to make even more of a fool of myself. Though the thought of attempting to steal more action with him did occur. Yikes, I wouldn't have minded making out with the Liam stranger all night long in that dark cavern room of his and forget about my coming-out party downstairs!

But with what little self-respect I had left, I headed back downstairs, thinking maybe it was time for me to crash before I got into more trouble, when the loud music from the living room zipped off mid-lyric, *"Start a love train, a lov—"* and Kayla yelled: "WHO THE HELL IS SMOKING DOPE IN HERE?" The air was indeed rife with smoke; it seemed everyone had a cigarette in their hand, even the dancers, who you would think wouldn't smoke. The smell was nasty but had, admittedly, just turned a little more pleasant and less pungent.

Cop Judy stomped to a love seat where a girl I recognized as being the gyrating thong-bikini girl in like five different hip-hop videos was about to pass a bong to Freddy. Judy lifted the girl by her collar and dragged her downstairs, where we heard the door slam behind her. I'm looking at Kayla thinking, You care about a little dope when I've lost count of how many vodka tonics you've downed this evening? Damn, she needed a rule sheet for her house parties.

Then the loud music turned back on just as suddenly—*"a love train, a love train . . ."*—and chatter and

dancing picked right back up as if Kayla had never laid down the law, but I needed a break and some fresh air. I repeated to myself: You are not going to crush on Liam, you are not going to crush on Liam. It was just a random make-out incident—the last thing this "Kayla Junior" needed was to start liking a guy who clearly had a thing for Kayla, whether he knew it or not.

The large space in the living room could barely contain the thick cigarette smoke whirling around, and despite my three Cosmos of the evening, cigarette smoking was not a vice I intended to join in on. Kayla's assistant Jules saw me wheezing and motioned for me to follow her out the balcony door for some fresh air. I stepped onto an outdoor patio that offered an illuminated skyline of Manhattan, which, with a full moon hanging off in the distance, appeared to be a legion of twinkling skyscrapers.

"Wow," I said to Jules, admiring the view.

"One of the benefits of living in Brooklyn," Kayla said, walking out after me. I could smell the hard alcohol on her breath even from a distance.

Freddy Porter joined us on the balcony. "Kayla's just trying to be hip, doin' the Brooklyn thang," he teased.

Kayla snapped at him, "Watch it, or you're on your way out the door too."

A very loud hiccup emanating from my body distracted Freddy and Kayla's hostile looks. Freddy stood beside me and playfully hit my back to stop the hiccups. Kayla rolled her eyes and turned to Jules. "Uh-oh, the hit man's found new prey"—she adopted a tone like she was a slurring commentator on the Discovery Channel—"let's go inside and watch the species from a discreet distance, shall we, Jules?" Freddy flipped the bird at Kayla. She flipped it back. From the large glass balcony doors, I saw Kayla trounce off to her bedroom, Jules in tow, and slam the door shut.

Then . . . was that Freddy's hand passing down my back, my spine, to—I spun around. "Hey, watch it!" I said. But I was giggling, too.

Freddy grabbed my hand. "C'mon, let's dance. Maybe we can have some fun now—I do believe your baby-sitter Kayla is officially smashed and retired for the evening. Jules has got her locked up for the night, I'm sure." Without Kayla standing at my side to nod yes or no to this request on my time and space, I just followed Freddy. My slurring brain was telling me, Hee hee, Wonder, you're DRUNK and you were just gettin' SOME and aww that mirror is so pretty and WOW your boobs are like totally spilling out of Kayla's dress, Go Wonder! Go Wonder!

Freddy led me back inside and tucked me into a discreet corner behind a large ficus tree. I stepped out just a little—wouldn't it have been nice if Liam had decided to join this party and seen *the* Freddy Porter putting the moves on me? Freddy put his arms around my waist. A slow song was playing—was it "Love T.K.O." by Teddy Pendergrass, Lucky's fave slow song? I could hardly pay attention. Freddy was grinding into me *real* close and that face that millions of girls adored was leaning into mine and . . . gross, his breath smelled like cigarettes and beer and Doritos and . . . ewwww, major stank!

I needed another drink! I grabbed a half-filled cocktail glass from a nearby table—anything to get out of firing range of Freddy's breath—and slurped the remaining drink down.

An antique grandfather clock standing next to us chimed two in the morning. The lights in the room were mostly either off or dimmed now, and couples were making out on the couches and love seats, beer bottles and heaping ashtrays scattered everywhere. And suddenly there was Freddy, all over me again, trying to dance with me, grinning. I wanted to yell GET OFF but my head was now literally spinning; I thought I was going to pass out. He grabbed me into a clench, and his wet lips came down on my neck. His hand actually grazed my breast but my head was spinning too much to shove him off. Thank God for Cop Judy, who came over, tapping—make that grabbing—Freddy on the shoulder and telling him, "Kayla said it's time for you and your crew to go," and even superstar Freddy knew not to protest Judy's hard clench.

I don't remember how I got out of that room, who was still there—whatever. I just know that when I found myself puking—and puking and puking—into the toilet upstairs, it was Liam holding my hair back.

Twenty-three

Pounding headache, pounding so hard dreams weren't even coming into my sleep of the dead. So why was someone shaking me? Maybe they were whispering but my ears heard a shout—"WONDER! GET UP!"

I squinted my eyes open. Mercifully, the drapes were drawn so there was no sunlight to throw my headache into pure torture. I opened my eyes wider. Why was Liam standing over me? Where was I, anyway?

"Car's waiting for you downstairs. Get up, pop princess."

I threw the covers over my head. "No!" Wasn't it like the law that after a night of partying you were supposed to be able to sleep well into the next afternoon? Hands on my waist now, shaking me again. Why, oh why? I hissed, "GO AWAY!"

"C'mon, get up!" The covers were pulled from my head and off my body. I looked down. I was wearing a large gray pinstriped pajama top that came halfway down my thighs. I reached for my ass—yup, undies still on; phew. No recollection whatsoever of changing into someone's jammies before I crashed.

Liam was standing on a sleeping bag next to his bed. I was in his bed! His hair was all tousled and his hazel

eyes were on full scowl. He handed my cosmetics bag to me, along with a new toothbrush. He pointed out the door, the door I remembered him pressing me against last night and me rather, uh, enjoying it. "I think you'll remember where the bathroom is," he said. He was wearing gray pinstriped pajama pants.

I hauled ass out of bed, all cumbersome and bloated, feeling like Mr. Snuffle-upagus from *Sesame Street* as I trudged my way to the bathroom. I saw my watch inside my cosmetics case: 7:15. Shit, the car to take me to the recording studio was supposed to come for me at 7! Hadn't I just fallen asleep, anyway? And wasn't the car supposed to pick me up at Mom and my place in the city? No time to think, had to get dressed and out.

I looked in the mirror—horror! My hair was stringy, my eyes all poofy. I tested my breath against my hand and it bounced back—so amazingly gross! Why were my clothes from yesterday, before the party, neatly folded on the toilet for me to change into? Do the math later, I told myself, just get going. I used the toilet, changed clothes, washed my hands and face, brushed my teeth (more like scoured them), twisted my hair up into a clip, and raced out of the bathroom.

Liam was standing outside his bedroom door. The door on the opposite end of the hall—Karl's room—was shut.

"Thanks, whatever," I whispered. We didn't *do* anything I don't remember last night, did we? No time to ask. Too scared to know the answer.

"8448," Liam said. Right, and the dog barks at midnight. What was spy boy talking about? Before I could ask him to decipher his code, Liam stepped back inside his room and slammed his bedroom door shut. Ouch on my head! He did that on purpose. I cursed him out under my breath as I tippy-toed down the four flights of stairs before putting my shoes on at the ground floor. Nobody was awake on floors 1, 2, or 3, though there were some passed-out bodies lingering on the sofas in the living area on the third floor where Kayla's party had been.

I stood inside at the front door. Security system! Aw man, the only way out would be either to trip the alarm and wake the household up, or wake up Karl the Sasquatch to help me. No, not that, please not that.

I could see the car waiting for me outside, the driver looking at his watch, annoyed. If he was annoyed, what would Tig be? Shit shit shit!

Oh. I punched 8448 into the security system, the light on the console turned green, and the door clicked open. Thank you, Liam! I un-curse you for your bedroom door slam!

I felt like a vampire when I stepped outside, the sun striking down on me so horrifically I thought my head would catch on fire. I covered my head with my arms and mumbled "Sorry" to the driver, who was holding the door of the Town Car open for me. I stepped inside. At least I could sleep on the way to the recording studio.

Think again.

Tig was sitting inside the car. He looked at his watch. "That's twenty minutes you've kept us waiting," he said. He looked into my squinting eyes. "WONDER!" he snapped, and my hands instinctively went to my ears to drown out his thundering voice. He took my hands from my ears and was kind enough to whisper, "Are you hungover? I don't believe this! I thought you were smarter than that, thought you could hold your own with Kayla's crowd."

I untied the sweater wrapped over my waist and placed it against the car window for a pillow. I leaned my head down against its softness as the car moved along the rough potholed street. "Please don't be mean, Tig," I said.

"'Mean'?" Tig said. "You *didn't* just say that."

I closed my eyes. Hopefully he wouldn't mind if I took a nap while he chewed me out. I felt some papers land on my lap and I looked down. Song sheets. He wanted me to rehearse in the car! Noooooooooo!!!!!!!!!!!!

"'Mean'," Tig repeated. "Me who arranged to pick you up here instead of at your mom's so you could have your fun night with Kayla. Me who trusted you enough to give you the day and night off yesterday to spend with your pal Kayla when the record company is banging down my door for you to finish this record by, like, tomorrow. Mean old Tig."

Rolling my eyes at him was not possible, as doing so might possibly have popped my eyeballs out of my

headache-struck head. I sighed and looked at the song sheet; I'd rehearsed these songs a million times already, but he wasn't going to let me off, he expected me to rehearse right now. I took a deep breath in preparation, surprised when my breath choked up on me. I sang, "*You and me baby, we were meant to be.*" Uh-oh. Bad bad bad. I hadn't been smoking last night but apparently the vestiges of about two hundred second-hand cigarettes were on my voice. I coughed, then tried to suppress a second cough, but that just made me cough harder. Tig handed me a water bottle; I gulped down a few swigs and tried again: "*You and me baby . . .*" Okay, now I sounded worse.

Now it was Tig's turn to lay his head on his car seat window. Make that bang his head on the window.

"You realize what this means?" he said.

"I'll be okay!" I said, trying to sound cheerful in my raspy voice. I coughed again.

"No, your studio time today is ruined. I can't let you record today sounding like that. And who is going to have to call the record company and make up the excuses? Me. 'Oh yeah, sorry, Mr. VP, your newest sixteen-year-old sensation couldn't make it to her recording session today because she's hungover.' No, don't think that one will go over well."

"I'm sorry," I said. I knew I'd screwed up bad, but Tig's words seemed harsh in comparison to the crime. Didn't everybody get hungover at some time in their life? And anyway, if I was going to get the "I'm very disappointed in you" speech, shouldn't that have been coming from, like, my dad, not my manager?

Tig tapped the shoulder of the driver and redirected him to drop me off at home instead of the studio. We rode in silence over the remaining journey, Tig sparing me a lecture until we reached the apartment building in the Theater District, a high-rise of corporate apartments from which a doorman was exiting the lobby to open the car door for me.

As I was about to get out, Tig held on to my arm to hold me back. He said, not all father-figure stern but just simple and all business, "Wonder, the car will be downstairs—HERE, not at Kayla's—at seven A.M. tomorrow. You will be down here waiting for it, on time, awake, and in prime form. You will rest today and drink lots of hot liquids. I'll cancel your dance rehearsal this evening." I nodded, causing my head to feel like a dam was bursting through it.

Then Tig added, "And Wonder, I know you're a kid and you have to act out every now and again—I understand that. But you're a professional now; there are people depending on you. You don't have the luxury to fool around that other kids your age have. That's the price you pay for this career, for a record deal. So consider this strike one. And three strikes and you're out."

Tig shut the car door and the Town Car sped off.

Twenty-four

I love George Clooney as much as anybody but I was like, "Mom! Turn off the TV already, would you?"

I was lying on the futon on the floor, a scarf over my eyes to drown out the flashing light coming from the television, trying to sleep. Did Mom care? No, she already knew that Dr. Doug Ross dawgs Nurse Hathaway through how many seasons, but God forbid Mom shouldn't relive the agony and the ecstasy again and again on the *ER* reruns all morning.

She said, "Well, I didn't expect you home this morning! I thought you were recording. Why does your hair smell like smoke? You look terrible! Were you smoking?"

I had arrived home and immediately flipped the futon mattress down and tried to slip under the covers for a nap, but no, she had to slam in my face with rapid fire interrogation: What happened last night? Why do you look so awful? Was there a party at Kayla's? Don't ignore me, Wonder Anna Blake!

I ignored her and was dead asleep within five minutes. Not two hours later—I know because the time was flashing on the cable box—she had an *ER* rerun blaring from the TV and my head was pounding

pounding pounding. I just lost it: "Mom, turn that shit OFF!"

Sharing a studio apartment with Mom was not my favorite part of the almost-pop princess arrangement. I love Mom almost as much as I love George Clooney but we needed more space BAD. I needed to have a hit single just so we could afford separate bedrooms! I thought of Kayla's four levels of luxurious space and reminded myself to sing my heart out in the remaining recording sessions if I wanted to be liberated from a small cramped one-room apartment with Mom. I wouldn't wish on Mom the heart condition that kept Kayla's grandmother confined to the first floor of the brownstone—and allowed Kayla to party on the third floor to her heart's content—but a few floors of distance between myself and my mother would be highly welcome.

Mom turned the television off. She looked down at me from her perch on the couch, an open box of Frosted Flakes on her lap. "Don't you ever speak to me like that again, young lady!" Tony the Tiger stared at me in reprimand as Mom ate some dry flakes from the cereal box.

And I wanted to say, Then why don't you go out and get a job or do something instead of lazing around this apartment all day when the family breadwinner is trying to take a friggin' nap to recover from her hangover.

Instead I said, "Sorry," because I kinda was, but

when I saw tears in her eyes, I am such a mean girl that I put the scarf over my head again so I could go back to sleep instead of making nice with Mom. I added, "Can you get me some Advil, Mom?"

I heard her turn on the portable phone and hit speed dial. She spoke into the phone like I wasn't even there. "Your daughter is being horrible to me. . . . Where were you last night, I was calling until eleven P.M. . . . You left Charles alone in the house to go do that? . . . Your daughter stayed at Kayla's last night— I think she was smoking!"

And I couldn't help but almost laugh underneath the covers. I wanted to say, I wasn't smoking but I did down a few drinks and I did consider having sex with Liam being I just discovered yesterday who's a GR-R-EAT kisser! Now, don't you wish I'd been smoking, Ma?

The scarf was snatched from my head. "Your father wants to have a few words with you."

I felt bad indeed but also glad—since I had dropped out of school to pursue this career, Dad had been giving me the silent treatment, not one e-mail or letter, just polite "How are you doing" chatter when he called to check in every week, and he hadn't come to visit us once.

"Hi, Daddy," I said into the phone. Are you going to talk to me for real?

"Were you smoking?" he said.

"No."

"What was going on at Kayla's? Was there a party?"

"Yeah, but no biggie. Just a couple people, some of her dancers—they were showing me new moves and stuff." That wasn't a lie, right?

"I thought you promised me that on your nights off you would be studying for the G.E.D. I'm not letting you off on your promise to take that exam. You're registered to take it in June. That leaves you two more months."

"Okay, Daddy," I said, but I'm like, Reality check, Pops! What am I going to do with a G.E.D. anyway? Clearly I am not college material! But this seemed to be the one issue where I could make him feel good about my future so I just lied every time and said that yes, I was studying. I hadn't cracked a single book since escaping Devonport High after the Christmas break.

"Try to sound more convincing next time, Wonder. And be nicer to Mommy. Here, someone wants to speak with you."

Dad passed the phone and I heard Charles go, "I don't need to talk," but he got on the phone anyway: "What's up, butthole?" His voice squeaked a little. My baby brother's voice was changing! What else had I missed?

"Same ole, frog face," I said. "Why aren't you in school today?"

"Spring break."

"Oh. Then why don't you come visit us. New York is really cool, you'll like it."

"What's so cool about it?"

Honestly, I had no idea. Its original main attraction to me had been that it wasn't Devonport. The coolest thing I had seen so far had been a private dressing room at Bergdorf Goodman and the inside of Liam's room at Kayla's house.

I answered, "Well, I'm here, and I can try to be cool?"

"Good luck with that, pop princess sellout," Charles said. He was kidding—he said it in a cute way—but also he was kinda not and the comment stung. Maybe he knew, too, because he added, "Henry came by, asking for you. I don't know why he even bothers with you, you don't even notice him. Like, are you so busy and important now that you can't even remember to stay in touch with your old buddy Science Project? Anyway, are you going to come home and visit us soon?"

"Doubt I'll have time." I almost hung up the phone on my baby brother. Like I needed him lecturing me about Science Project. I had a full-time *career* going on now—I barely had time to check e-mails, much less make chatty phone calls back home.

"Well, stop being mean to Mom and put her back on the phone so I can talk to her."

I handed the phone back to Mom. She started crying again. "I miss you so much, honey," and "A girl

asked you to a dance?" and then "Of course I'm coming to see you soon." I knew she was thinking what I
had been thinking—Charles's life was going on without us, and we weren't there to see it.

I swallowed the two Advils that Mom had placed
on my pillow while I was talking to Dad, and dozed
back to sleep. When I woke up, Mom was gone. She'd
left a note on the coffee table—*Went out for a walk,
back soon, Mom.* Not "Love, Mom," just "Mom."

My head was feeling better. It was three in the
afternoon already; I'd lost almost the whole day.
Except for the hangover part, it had been nice not to
work all day! I took a shower, then flopped down on
the couch to watch TV. I was home to watch *South
Coast*! How long had it been since I'd had that simple
pleasure?

But then Mom barged back in. "Turn the TV off,
Wonder." Mom said to turn the TV off? Either she'd
just had a lobotomy, or something was very wrong. I
clicked the TV off and Mom sat down next to me. She
took a container out of a paper bag and handed it to
me—hot soup.

She said, "Kayla's grandmother and I had a talk last
night. They have offered for you to stay with them at
Kayla's if you'd like. This apartment is obviously getting too small for the two of us, and I feel kind of use-
less here anyway—you're working round the clock, I
barely see you, you don't seem to even want me
around—"

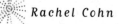

"That's not true, Mom!" I said. I wondered why I was defending our situation—because I really did want her around, or because I felt guilty that if I was honest with myself, I knew I didn't need her here any longer?

Mom played with a strand of my wet hair in that Mom kind of way. She said, "Thank you for saying that, sweetie. But let's face facts—Tig takes care of making sure you get to dance or voice class or the studio, you'll be leaving to go on tour in less than two months, and you'll be gone all summer. I'm just dead weight here." Mom tugged at the elastic on her pants. "And I think I've gained ten more pounds just sitting around waiting for you during your classes or waiting for you to come home from the studio."

I said, "But you could get a job here or take classes or something! You don't need to wait around on me. You're in New York City! Rumor is there's lots of exciting things to do here. You should do something for *you*."

"Wonder, I will stay here if you want me to, if you feel like you want me here with you. But I can see that for all intents and purposes, you're a working adult now. You'll thrive with or without me." Mom was crying now, her words came out in bursts between sobs and deep breaths. "I made a mistake—I wanted you to have this career for yourself and for Lucky, but what that's meant is that I've now lost *two* daughters. And I have a husband and another child back home—

and if I'm not careful, pretty soon they're not going to need me either."

I nuzzled Mom's head onto my shoulder for a good cuddle. She was shaking. I said, "Then go home. I'll be fine. I'm sorry about earlier." Suddenly I felt extremely old.

Her tears were getting my T-shirt wet but we held on tight. She said, "I can come back in the fall when you return from the tour—hopefully by then we can afford a bigger place. We can reassess as a family what we should do then."

I said, "Right." Sure we will, Mom.

And maybe my heart had just kinda broken. I did want her gone, I did want my freedom, and I did want Charles and Dad to have Mom at home.

But the feeling of emptiness in my stomach now was not from the hangover. I was truly on my own.

Twenty-five

Camp Kayla now in session. Floor one had Mrs. C's bedroom and a large kitchen and dining area; floor two had a guest room where Kayla's parents stayed when they visited, an office for Kayla's assistant Jules, and a rec room with a PlayStation and a giant TV with lounge chairs that were like something for a captain on any given *Enterprise;* the third floor was Kayla's master bedroom suite and the living area; and floor four held Karl's large bedroom and two small guest bedrooms— one for Liam, one for me. Totally the Barbie Dream House for the Brooklyn Heights pop princess set.

Tig wasn't thrilled about the new arrangement, but it did make his life easier. Kayla and I would be spending more time together rehearsing for the tour and promoting my upcoming record, so it was easier for Tig to have the two of us at the same starting point every day, and bonus, he no longer had to hear Mom's input about whether my skirt was too short or my shirt cut too low or whether I could stay at the studio round the clock instead of having to be returned home by ten each evening.

"Very clever," he said to Kayla when she announced our new living arrangements. We were on speakerphone. He said, "And Wonder, I trust you to learn how to play with the big girls now?" I said, "You betcha." My drinking days—so over. One day's worth of hangover was enough for me.

Just two days after Kayla's party, I had accompanied Mom to the train station. She held on to me tight as we waited for the train in the giant waiting area at Penn Station. As we stood under the big board that flipped arrival and departure times, Mom wouldn't let go of my hand. I asked, "Are you sure you want to go?" She said, "I don't *want* to go. I *need* to go." She squeezed my hand wicked hard; with her free hand, she reached into her bag and gave me a bank envelope with my name on it. I could feel a credit card inside. I knew I was supposed to feel sadder than I did.

I moved into the small bedroom next to Liam's on the top floor of the brownstone. When I say small, I mean small—there was only space for a twin bed, a nightstand, and a dresser—but I didn't care. I only had one large suitcase worth of clothes, shoes, and a couple CDs anyway. When I'd left Devonport, I'd really left it; no mementos or yearbooks or pictures came along with me. It was Kayla who took care of making the room feel like a home for me. The nightstand had a silver-framed picture of Lucky and me on it; I was a flat-chested Speedo-wearing Buster Brown-haircut tomboy and Lucky looked like a teen angel in her modest baby blue tank top bikini that set off her wide blue eyes and long blond curls. In the picture,

we were hugging each other as we stood on the beach in Devonport two summers before Lucky died. Kayla had taken the picture. Kayla had also placed a set of books on the nightstand, the *Anne of Green Gables* series, which Kayla and Lucky used to act out when we were kids and Kayla lived a few houses from ours.

Thankfully the new arrangement did not include me having to worry about being tortured over Liam in the next room. He was gone when I moved into Kayla's, visiting his mom for the rest of his spring break. I was relieved; I figured by the time he came back to Kayla's to visit his dad, I would just as likely be gone, and we would never, ever have to discuss our little incident.

I finished recording the last track for the album during a late night Saturday session. After a celebratory meal at an all-night diner with Tig and the recording engineers, I'd crawled into bed at five in the morning, grateful that it was a Sunday, which meant no voice or dance classes and, with no recording sessions left, just sleep, glorious sleep for me! Wrong. The clock radio glared 7:07 A.M. when I was awoken by this mad punk guitar and pounding drums blasting from the room next to mine, followed by Billie Joe Armstrong wailing about if his dear mother could hear him whining. D'oh, d'oh, double d'oh! Was "Welcome to Paradise" by Green Day so necessary so early on a Sunday morning, SO LOUD? I threw off my covers, got out of bed, and stomped to the bedroom next door.

Excuse me, but who does yoga poses while listening to Green Day? Apparently Liam Murphy, who apparently was not still at his mom's, does.

He had a yoga mat laid out next to his bed and he was in Warrior I pose. He looked up at me. "Nice outfit, pop princess," he said.

I looked down. Aw man, I had jumped out of bed so quickly and angrily I hadn't put on a robe, so there I was standing before Liam, wearing—braless—a white form-fitting cut off T-shirt that said "SKATER BITCH" in big black letters, a joke Christmas present from Charles that had become my fave pajama top. The charming shirt was complemented by a baggy pair of green flannel boxer shorts with yellow and red Santa elves pictured on them, a rejected Christmas present from Mom to Charles. Thanks, Charles, thanks a lot.

"Ha ha," I said. "I thought you were at your mom's."

"Ha ha," he said. "I thought the same of you. I came down to see Dad for the weekend before I go back up to school tomorrow."

"Well, would you mind keeping the music down?" I bowed, my hands in prayer pose. "*Namaste,* dingleberry," I said as I walked back to my room.

"Be up in time for dinner, snookums!" Liam said as I slammed my bedroom door shut. He turned the music down, but as revenge played Celine Dion in repeat mode in Green Day's place, so I had to suffer through Celine's heart going on and on, and on and on, for a good fifteen minutes till I fell back asleep.

So a nice advantage of staying on the top floor of a large brownstone, with no parental units present and an overseer who was a workaholic, spending her Sunday off in a marathon of dance classes, was that I could sleep until three in the afternoon and not have one trace of guilt or Dad coming in to say, "It's noon! Get up, lazybones!" I felt so good when I awoke late that afternoon. My recording time was finished—I could finally relax! Only one day of Liam till he went back to New Hampshire—surely I could deal.

I went into the bathroom and saw a shaving bag that must have belonged to Liam on the counter. I locked the door and unzipped the bag. Let's see, he had shaving cream, a razor, a worn-out Kurt Vonnegut paperback novel, the mandatory freshman-at-granola-university Tom's of Maine toothpaste, two condom packages—*a-ha!*—four crumpled dollar bills, a bottle of Flintstones vitamins (I tasted a Barney—very yum), a comb, and underneath all these treasures the major *a-HA*—a magazine cutout picture of Kayla, LAMI-NATED. I knew it: He was into her.

When I went downstairs after taking a shower and getting dressed, Kayla's parents were sitting in the living room with Liam, having an upstanding conversation about *Anna Karenina* and Liam's Russian lit class in the very place where Kayla and a bevy of hot bodies had been dirty dancing at my coming-out party little more than a week earlier. I had on normal girl clothes—blue jeans and a plain white T-shirt; no slutty pop princess getup, no makeup. Liam gave me a look like, Who knew?

Kayla's parents got up to give me a hug and we ran through the "Look who's all grown up" routine. They didn't ask anything about my beckoning singing career. "How nice that you're staying with Kayla for a while" was all Kayla's mom said. "She always wanted a little sister."

Kayla had total Birkenparents. They wanted nothing to do with the Mercedes convertible Kayla had given them as a gift—they had donated it to Planned Parenthood. Parked in front of Kayla's brownstone was her parents' prehistoric fuel-efficient Honda Civic with the Ralph Nader and UC-Berkeley bumper stickers. They had driven all the way from Boston to Manhattan to attend a symposium on Eastern religion where all kinds of gurus with multisyllabic names had been speaking over the weekend.

Liam said, "I can't believe you got to hear the rim-poche give a teaching. That is so cool."

Rimpo-what?

Kayla's mom said, "Oh Liam, next time you'll have to come. He was so empowering." She grabbed Liam's hand in a soul brother shake.

Kayla's dad wanted to know, how had Liam's class on religion and human rights gone last semester?

Liam said, "A," and Kayla's parents chimed in with

the same word: "Outstanding." Their heads were facing Liam, and I was standing behind them, so they couldn't see me. I frisked out my thumb and mouthed, "Aaayyy," like I was the Fonz. Liam smirked at me. What a suck-up. Kayla's dad said, "Think you can pass on some of this enthusiasm for college to our daughter?" Her mom added, "Oh Jesus Christ, good luck."

"Fat chance is right" came Kayla's voice as she bounded up the stairs and into the living room. She was wearing a pink leotard with armpit stains and pink tights and pink ballet slippers. Her face was a little sweaty as she entered the room, this pint-sized pink ballet fairy towing behind her lumberjack Karl the bodyguard, who was wheezing as he reached the third floor. Kayla gave each parent a peck on the cheek and then perched herself right in Liam's lap and wrapped her arms around his neck. She gave him a peck on his reddened cheeks. I knew it, I knew it, I knew it—there was something going on between them. Certainly Kayla's parents and Karl didn't seem surprised by the show of affection.

Kayla said, "I need a shower. Grandma said dinner will be ready in twenty." She turned to me. "You're having Sunday dinner with us, right?"

"Sure, thanks," I said. If Liam and Kayla were all PDA through dinner, I wouldn't have to worry about consuming too many cals—I'd surely spontaneously chuck them all before the meal was over.

"C'mon with me, talk to me while I'm in the shower, 'kay?" Kayla said to me. Maybe it was a relic of being an only child, but Kayla was one of those people who hated to be alone; she had to have someone with her at all times. Since Jules was tending to her own life and not her boss's that Sunday, I was the anointed company-keeper.

I followed Kayla to her bedroom, which was decked out in framed gold and platinum record displays, framed magazine covers of Kayla, and the largest king-sized bed I'd ever seen, draped in a rich gold-colored duvet. At her bedside were pictures of herself, Lucky, and Trina, plus pictures of herself with Karl and Liam, but not one of herself with her parents. She had a waist-high stack of books next to her bed.

Kayla blasted Eminem from the stereo, rapping about little boy and girl groups, how he'd been "sent here to destroy you"; Kayla giggled. She was dancing to the rhythm as she talked to me from the bathroom, throwing her dirty clothes from behind the partially closed door. She said, "Do interference with the parentals for me, wouldja? Just talk about . . . God, I don't know what, just do lots of talking, okay? Anything to keep them from going on the 'You Need to Go to College' rant."

I couldn't hold it back any longer; I said, "So are you and Liam a couple?"

Kayla popped her head from behind the door. "I don't think so! He's like a brother. He's like Charles

to me. I love him to death, but no . . . NO!"

She turned on the shower, so I don't think she heard me say, "But he likes you."

She said she didn't like him that way . . . and yet: She sat next to Liam at dinner, and she kept refilling his water glass without him asking. Her dad said, "Kayla darling, any boyfriend we should know about?" and Karl's bushy eyebrow raised under all those creases of forehead when Kayla said, "Daddy, you know I don't have time for that. And we all know I'm saving myself for Liam." Everyone around the table except me laughed, like there was some big joke I wasn't in on.

Her mom said, "Don't you have some wine for this meal?" and Kayla said, "Oh no, Mommy, I don't keep alcohol in the house," and I think Karl and Liam almost choked on their mashed potatoes right there.

Kayla's dad said, "What about that Dean Marconi? Isn't he at Yale now?"

Kayla rolled her eyes. "Yeah, he's a Yale man, but I do believe he hasn't determined whether he has a preference for the ladies."

"Really!" everyone else at the table said.

Kayla's mom said, "You know, Kayla, there's a wonderful young man in my feminist theory class this semester. He's a world-class cello player, from India I believe. He probably wouldn't even know who you are! What do you think, a fix-up?"

Now I almost spit out my string beans. Something

like the total male population in America fantasized about Kayla, and yet her mom thought she'd be doing her daughter a favor by fixing her up with a guy who wouldn't be prejudiced against Kayla, tragic sex symbol. Yeah, that poor chump.

Kayla's dad disagreed. "Bad idea, darling. It's already a miserable open secret at the university about Kayla—each semester I get at least two or three panting young men feigning interest in my modern Jewish history class who invariably end up dropping the course when they learn I don't intend to lecture on Kayla, Singing Superstar Who Could Have Gone to Harvard If She'd Wanted."

Mrs. C said, "Oh enough of that, eat your roast beef."

Kayla's dad snapped, "Mother, once again you've made a meal that chooses to ignore that we are vegetarians." And I'd thought the parents were just trying to leave more beef for Karl when they heaped their plates strictly with steamed veggies and mashed potatoes.

I said, "Kayla's debut album was multiplatinum-certified! How many gold singles does she have? Didn't you see the plaques in her room! Anyone can go to Harvard—they have an extension school that even I could go to if I wanted. But has anyone else at this table accomplished what Kayla has, all on her own? She has won how many Teen Choice awards? She works how many hours a day—like all of them? How

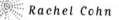
many Harvard graduates could afford a house like this, take care of everyone the way Kayla does?"

Kayla beamed at me. "Yeah, Mom and Dad! That's what I'm gonna tell Planned Parenthood when I send Jules to that auction to get back that Mercedes I bought you." Kayla gestured at me with her forkful of mashed potatoes that I knew were on display for show and would never meet her mouth. "Wonder, perhaps you'd like my mom and dad to explain to you the logic by which a rusty Honda Civic that's almost as old as you is a preferable vehicle to the brand-spanking-new Mercedes-Benz their daughter's hard work bought them."

Sister Wonder was in such good graces with Kayla for the duration of the meal, she didn't even get a reprimand from her for digging into Mrs. C's scrumptious pecan pie dessert.

Twenty-six

Later that night after dinner with Kayla's parents, because I had slept through much of that afternoon, I was wide awake at 2 A.M. after everyone had gone to bed. Unlike my floor mate on the other side of the wall, I tried to be quiet, so I sat up in bed with a Discman on, thumbing through a magazine. At least I thought I was being quiet, but there was Liam standing at my door. I took the headphones off. "Yes?" I said.

"You're singing out loud," he said.

How many times had this very habit gotten me busted—hell, that's how Tig had discovered me back at the DQ. I must sing really loud when I have those headphones on.

I said, "Sorry—maybe I'm not as good as Green Day or Pearl Jam or whatever you listen to—"

"I don't listen to Pearl Jam!" he whisper-shouted at me like I'd just laid the supreme insult on him. He left my room and returned seconds later, kicking my bedroom door shut behind him. He sat next to me on my bed holding a notebook of CDs. He flipped through the plastic cover pages, passing through Ray Charles to Ella Fitzgerald to Elvis Costello to the Clash to Aaliyah to Dead Kennedys to . . . "Okay, I get it, no Pearl Jam!" I said.

He slammed the book shut. "Thank you." He paused, gave me a *hmm* kinda look. "You sounded pretty good singing Janis Joplin across the wall. I wouldn't have expected you to like her."

I said, "Well, there's a lot of things you wouldn't know about me, seeing as how you've pegged me as this shallow pop princess without even getting to know me first."

He raised an eyebrow at me slightly. "Oh, I think I've gotten to know you a little, wouldn't you say?" He pressed his hand onto mine. Is that what he'd come in for—a booty call?

I grabbed my hand from him. "Last week, after the party . . . we didn't . . . you know?"

"No, we didn't *you know.*" He actually gestured finger quotes when he said "you know." "The only reason I was sleeping next to you in the morning was I wanted to make sure you didn't puke in your sleep. People can die from that." You sure know how to woo a girl, I thought to say. I felt my face flush deep. Liam added, "Still haven't heard the words '*Thanks, Liam*' from you."

"Thank you? Someone had also changed my clothes! I did not fall asleep wearing that tight dress and I have no memory of changing into your pajamas."

Liam leaned in toward me again. He whispered, "A fella's gotta get some privileges when he's saving the ass of the underage damsel in distress, no?" My eyes popped wide open. He let out a quiet laugh. "I'm teasing you.

You changed yourself—pretty poorly, I might add—and you kept saying"—here Liam inserted a thick drunken Boston accent—"'look the othuh way when ahm changin'. But it was all you. Give me some credit." His hand reached for mine again.

I said, "Your dad is just across the hall—what are you doing!"

Liam leaned in closer still; my mouth felt like it was being drawn to his like a magnet, and I was powerless against that force. "Dad's out. Kayla's parents were driving her crazy so she decided to go out. She called Jules; they're hitting the clubs in Manhattan about now." Was that why he was moving in on me, because Kayla hadn't bothered to invite either of us to go out with her?

I grabbed my hand back, pulled my face away to demagnetize where my lips desperately wanted to go. "You like Kayla. Don't even try to deny it."

"I don't like Kayla that way. We're just friends—we're practically family."

"You do too like her."

"Trust me, she doesn't like my kind."

"That's stupid—she's not a snob. She wouldn't care that you're her bodyguard's son, she wouldn't hold it against you that you're a college boy and not a celeb—"

"Maybe I like someone else," Liam said. Then his lips were on mine again and I knew it was coming and I was hoping for it.

Still, I had some dignity before I went right back

in. I pulled back and said, "What are you doing?" and he just said, "Getting you to shut up. God you look pretty without the makeup, without the pop princess clothes. . . ." and I put my mouth back on his to get *him* to shut up.

He stopped for a moment, got up to put a new disc into my Discman and attached the minispeakers to the machine, then turned out the lights and said, "Paul Weller, eighties British singer, bands like the Jam and Style Council, now he's like this soul singer," as some English guy who sounded sexier than Liam looked (annoying but true) started singing at a low decibel from the speakers. Liam lay down next to me; I felt his hands running through my hair, his nose feeling around my cheeks, then his lips on mine again, ah bliss, as we started to make out. And it was just that—making out, no urgent unzipping or unclasping, just hands wandering and lips touching, like some weird kind of soul kissing; it was so ridiculously nice. Except it only lasted about five songs, then he said, "I'm tired," and I was too and we just fell asleep in my single bed, fully clothed, me snuggled tight against his long lean body.

In the morning when I woke up, he was gone, his CDs were gone, his stuff was gone from his room, and he hadn't even left a note saying good-bye.

Twenty-seven

So did Liam like me? Or was he just using me as some kinky Kayla substitute? And why, oh why, not one phone call, no messages, nothing in the two weeks since he'd gone back up to Dartmouth? Was I a super-sized jerk for even hoping I would hear from him? And how many times had I listened to that Paul Weller CD he'd left in my Discman while replaying in my mind making out with Liam? Just listening to that Weller guy croon in my ears had the effect of making my body go all warm, my heart all fluttery, and my mind all racing, wondering if Liam was thinking of me like I was of him. Maybe he was flunking a Russian lit exam at Dartmouth right now because he was obsessing over whether or not he should call me.

"Wonder!"

I glanced at Kayla standing next to me. She grinned superwide and gestured with her hands toward the corners of her mouth—I was supposed to be smiling, not brooding, as industry executives stood between Kayla and me to have their pictures taken with us underneath a giant banner that proclaimed "WONDER!" We were at an industry function to promote the release of "Bubble Gum Pop" as my debut single, a showcase for radio and music channel programming executives, as well as promo and distribution executive types from the record company. As the occasion was in my honor, I was supposed to be a charming It girl and not obsessing over some granola punk in New Hampshire with whom I'd made out twice but who hadn't bothered to acknowledge me since.

I, for one, had imagined that a record release promotion would involve a late night club, surely at least one disco ball hanging from the ceiling of the room, lots of hipster dudes attached to cell phones and rock journo chicks with short skirts and bad-ass leather boots. I certainly didn't expect a Banana Republic–wearing corporate crowd who all seemed more interested in having their photos taken with Kayla before they tried to catch the 7:02 train back to Westchester than in meeting the junior pop princess, me. We were in a meeting room on the top floor of the record company's offices, with a stunning view of Central Park, now in prime spring foliage, sporting lush green lawns and white-bloomed trees, the western dusk casting red shadows over the stately apartment buildings lining the park. Waiters wandered with hors d'oeuvres and glasses of champagne and wine, which Kayla and I were under strict orders from Tig not to touch in the presence of these people. Two waiters approached Kayla, their quaking trays revealing their excitement at being in the same room as her. But Kayla wasn't eating—she was in freak-out mode over four pounds that had crept onto her body, and nobody was immune to her displeasure. On the car ride over, she had eyed the Power Bar that I was munching and snapped at me, "You could also stand to lose a pound or two, Wonder. That dress is awful tight on you." That was my cue to wrap up the rest of the Power Bar and place it in my bag and out of her sight.

At least there was one fun person at the reception: Will Nieves, *South Coast* hunk and my video buddy, who kissed my cheek on arrival and then gave up any attempt at being blasé upon sight of Kayla: "Worship you! I have all your records!" He turned back to me, said, "Love the dress." I was wearing the tea rose-colored raw silk dress that had been Kayla's gift to me from Bergdorf Goodman. It was tight on me, but not as much as Kayla said. I could breathe just fine. Even Karl, who never commented on those things, had told me I looked nice, like a "little lady." I think that was Karl's way of complimenting me for not choosing a basic slut outfit for my first official industry function.

Not like it mattered—all eyes were on Kayla. Folks said their polite hellos to me, then were fawning all over Kayla: "*Love* your work"; "You get more gorgeous by the day"; "If you keep selling records at the pace you're on now, you're going to need a full security detail to join Karl." For someone who didn't say much, Karl seemed to be known by everyone at the party. According to Kayla, Karl was the "Cadillac of security guys." Then why was his son such a d-a-w-g?

Kayla took in all the sucking-up like the pro she was, smiled graciously, remembered every executive by name, remembered their kids' names even, thanked them all for their support—"I'd be nowhere without you and the fans." At least she wasn't yet at the point of thanking Jesus every other sentence. She waited for the signal from Tig, then stepped up to the podium.

The crowd came to immediate attention when Kayla stepped onto a small stage that had been set up for us. She called me over, introduced me as "my friend, my almost-little sister, your next pop sensation, Wonder Blake." Luckily I wasn't expected to give a speech to the sea of adult faces. I just waved and said, "Hey, what's up? Thanks to everyone for coming out here this evening, and thanks to everyone for your support. I hope you like the record!" Dialogue provided by Tig. Simple, easy, natural—relief for me. Showcase events like this usually called for an artist to perform an acoustic set, to amaze the execs with an amazing voice or piano skill or whatever, but not in my case. Everyone knew that I was a last-minute substitute for Amanda Lindstrom, and that Pop Life Records was manufactured pop, so nobody expected me to belt out a few diva numbers. I was a product, and they just wanted to see what I looked like and whether I could deliver the package.

The guests offered polite applause, looked at their watches. I realized that what Tig had said was true— this video had only its first seconds to win or lose this

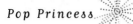

audience. My left pinkie went straight to my mouth—not a mock Dr. Evil gesture, but a nail-biting habit from since I was a B-Kid. Behind the podium, Kayla kicked my ankle. My arm fell back down to my side.

I still hadn't seen the video! Was I about to be exposed as the pop music scene's biggest fraud—and in front of a swarm of industry players who could make or break my career? The lights dimmed, and I was relieved when all eyes shifted away from me to a screen that came down against the far wall of the conference room. I was starting to sweat buckets. Kayla grabbed my hand in support—was she expecting I could slip her a few fruity Mentos that she knew I stocked in my purse?

I'd seen myself on television during B-Kidz days a million times, but nothing prepared me for the Wonder Blake that appeared on screen now. That girl on the screen now seemed totally separate from the prim frock-attired one watching her video image, wanting to chew off her fingernails and dying to step through the crowd for a little one-on-one time with Karl to interrogate him: WHY HASN'T LIAM CALLED ME? The lip-synching video girl prancing around in her polka-dot jammies, cut in with the girl strolling the boardwalk hand in hand with Will Nieves and wearing a polka-dot bikini, was like a whole other creature I didn't recognize. The audience in the conference room must have sensed the same thing, because the light chatter in the room completely died off, and distracted glances at the screen turned into intent stares. It almost didn't matter how good my voice did or didn't sound (for the record, it sounded good; not its best, but close)—the girl on the screen was breathing fire and life into the camera. I thought, Well, maybe I was a failure at high school, but apparently I am somewhat competent when a camera is placed before me.

I heard Tig mutter, "Yowza!"

Kayla dropped her supportive clutch on my hand.

There was a lot of applause after the video ended, and Will Nieves rushed over and grabbed me in a hug. If only I could have taken my miserable-at-Devonport-High self and transported her to this moment, wrapped in the arms of WILL NIEVES! So what about the big-time video debut. WILL NIEVES!

Interestingly, none of the record company people came over to congratulate me after the video. They all rushed over to Tig like it was him who had performed the song. The execs proclaimed: "Best Female Video of the Year nomination for sure!" "The camera loves that face!" "Top Ten radio single—it's bank!"

The one person I thought would be at my side congratulating me, Kayla, bolted to the other end of the room and into deep huddle with Jules and Karl, all of them with cell phones at their ears. She waved and smiled at me from across the room when a photographer stood in front of her, but as soon as the flash died

I could swear she was glaring at me like I had done something wrong. Then again, from weeks of living at her house, I understood that Kayla ran hot and cold toward a person. Minute to minute, she either loved or hated you, and in order to survive in her orbit, you had to learn to accept that behavior and not question it. If Lucky, my real sister, had been with me during this scene, she would have stood by my side, proud and clenching my hand.

Will said, "We're hitting the clubs tonight for sure!"

Like a good pop princess, I was about to say, "I can't! Aside from the underage-minor factor, I have to get to bed for an early call tomorrow morning," and I was glad Tig was standing nearby so he would hear that my work ethic was intact and I had no intention of having a night out partying. But before I could answer, Tig came over and said to Will, "Montana will be at Steam tonight, right?" Will nodded. Tig handed him a promotional copy of "Bubble Gum Pop" and said, "If you think you can get Montana to give this a spin tonight, I think Wonder's got herself a night on the town."

Yowza indeed! I asked Tig, "Did hell freeze over?" He tucked his arm into mine and maneuvered me into a corner while Will worked his cell phone. Then Tig said, "Just be yourself with Montana, okay? Don't go all Kayla with him."

I wanted to know who or what a "Montana" was, but Tig was called away by some record company

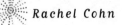
execs. Will came back over and said, "Let's go, star! I worked it all out with Kayla's assistant. We'll all meet up at Steam later this evening. Jules took care of getting us on the list."

"What list?"

"The VIP list!"

Twenty-eight

Here's what The List really meant—if you drop the right name at the door, and you're wearing the right outfit and you're sufficiently skinny and cute and famous, it doesn't matter if you're not of legal age—not even of legal smoking age. Welcome. Need ID? Uh, no. Your famous face—or in my case, Will's—gained you immediate access. There were easily a hundred people waiting outside the club, being kept at bay by the bouncers, but The List meant Will and I could whisk past the barricaded lines of wanna-be clubgoers, stomp right into that club, and be ushered upstairs to a private floor where the beautiful people congregated.

I'm not kidding about beautiful people. I never saw so many butt-dipping designer jeans and metallic gold halter tops, so much mascara, so many five-foot-ten blond Amazon girlies with fake boobs in my life! (Okay, I don't think I ever saw *any* before in real life.) I was glad I had changed out of the cute tea rose frock, but I was still strictly casual, wearing a short black skirt and basic black tee that was as eye-catching an outfit as your grandma's muumuu. Holding on to Will's hand as I trailed him toward Kayla's table, I was immediately intimidated by all the model and actress

types cooing into the ears of mogul guys in expensive suits. Again I thought of Lucky, thought of how a good night for her was curling up with a good book or sitting on her bed with a guitar and a notepad, writing songs; Kayla's world was totally not Lucky's scene, and when you threw Trina into their mixture, I couldn't imagine they ever would have made it through a year of being a girl group before splintering off, their friendships ruined.

The VIP lounge was actually a balcony that ran the square length of the dance floor, with sheer pearl gauze curtains falling from the ceiling to keep the regular folks downstairs from getting a good glimpse of the people upstairs. I'd caught enough *Miami Vice* reruns on TV with Mom to recognize that it was cocaine—and not sugar—on the first table we passed, lined up between two bottles of Cristal. I'm looking around thinking, Does Tig know about this scene? Thinking, If Mom checked this place out right now— techno dance music blaring, smoke rising, drugs and booze flowing freely, dancers bumping and grinding but serious—my ass would so be back at Devonport High in like a millisecond.

In the crush of people we might have had a hard time finding Kayla but for Karl, watching over every person, drink, and fleck of dust in Kayla's aura, his towering presence immediately letting us know where to find her. I thought it was interesting that when Liam was around, Karl was almost genial and fatherly, keeping Kayla and Liam from bickering, laughing at their antics together, but with Liam out of the picture, he was all business. I never heard him comment on Kayla's clubbing antics, her drinking, her moods—like he didn't care at all about her personally, just about her safety. I said, "Hi Karl!" but his hard face didn't even crack a smile, he just stepped aside to let us past to Kayla's table.

Kayla's power button was activated to full ON. She had on the designer jeans and the halter top, the designer mule sandals, her makeup so pretty and her complexion so flawless that she practically glowed. She was sitting on Jules's lap, a drink in one hand, a cigarette in the other, in conversation with none other than Dean Macaroni—er, Marconi—the ex-B-Kid who thought he was the next Robert De Niro, with Freddy Porter and some bleached blonde making up the rest of the group. I thought it was funny to look at the assemblage of youth entertainment power players gathered. Kayla, Freddy, and Dean looked so fancy and important behind the velvet rope, yet in my mind, I could still see them all as freckle-faced, buck-toothed B-Kidz preteens. Kayla slurred her words a little, gesturing toward me with the cigarette hand: "There she is, Dean! Lucky's li'l sis, my li'l protégée, the new *darling* of Pop Life Records. Bitch!" She stood up, laughed, kissed my cheek.

Dean was brown hair/blue eyes Joe Schmoe good-looking, but in an interesting, dorky kind of way, the kind of way that made you just want to swoon at the sight of him and have no idea why. I could see the cut of his pecs under a brown shirt that revealed his every muscle; the guy was just unbelievably hot, it's true. Out of respect to Lucky, who never liked Dean, I had to suppress sighing from the sheer nearness to his gorgeousness. Freddy stood up to greet me, but Dean remained in his seat, saying, "Oh God, not another pop princess? Don't tell me—you dropped out of high school, and the record company has sent you here tonight to whore for a mention in tomorrow morning's gossip columns."

That was the moment I officially retired my pop princess-in-training doormat routine. I went, "Well, nice catching up with you too, Dean! Pretentious asshole!" And I just walked off.

Damn, rude much, Dean? As I stomped off I wondered why I tolerated that kind of ribbing from Liam—made out with him for it—but from Dean Macaroni, I was compelled to walk off. Just because he was a capital-A Actor now, he had to judge me before even bothering to get to know me? What was I doing in this stupid place anyway?

By the way: Huffing away is somewhat difficult when you're totally out of your element, stranded in a too-hot nightclub, you don't smoke, don't plan to drink, don't plan on hooking up with any of the lecherous playas hanging around the VIP lounge, don't know exactly where you're stomping off to. . . .

I wound up hunched in a corner where a deejay booth was setup, standing there like, Oh, now what I am supposed to do? Good move, Wonder, going off to sulk when you have nowhere to go. I felt sure there was a giant banner hanging over me with an arrow pointing down at my head and big letters advertising "DORK."

But the music playing was good—the techno-blah had been switched to some ABBA disco meets Brit-pop sound that was fun and definitely had the crowd working on both levels of the dance floor. My Doc Martens boots—I'd never gotten the memo that this club was strictly *Sex and the City* fashionista shoes—were ready to jam to this music. The short guy grooving inside the deejay booth, who looked to be a mixture of Asian and Hispanic, wearing headphones over his bandanna-covered copper-dyed hair, was reading a comic book placed on the console as he spinned the tunes.

He saw me in the corner and said, "Don't you know this area is off-limits?"

I said, "Is it okay if I kinda don't care?"

He laughed, then yelled at me over the music, "You're brave. Don't you know that this deejay booth is a sanctuary? I play at this club only because everyone here knows not to talk to me."

I said, "Kayla's over there. I bet you would want her to talk to you!"

Kayla was slugging back her drink, laughing, now

on Dean Marconi's lap. Deejay guy said, "Kayla! That pathetic excuse for a singer? Her constant presence in this club is one of the reasons I almost didn't take this gig."

I said, "You must be pretty important if you can pick and choose your gigs like that, demand that no one talk to you while you're spinning and reading. . . . Is that manga? My little brother is really into Japanese anime, and that Hong Kong stuff too, but he'll kick your ass if you even *look* at his books, much less touch them."

Deejay guy said, "You're cute. Guileless."

"Thanks!" Note to self: Look up "guileless."

I didn't realize I had been dancing to the beat, when suddenly he said, "Are you a dancer? You move like one."

He already had a self-proclaimed hatred of Kayla. I figured it better not to speak up about my career, but Will Nieves took care of that anyway. He found me and said, "You just dissed Dean Marconi! I don't believe you!"

Deejay guy beamed at me. "I *like* this kid," he said to Will. Must have been Tig's lucky night, because Will said, "Montana, this is the girl I was telling you about last week, the one whose video I'm in. Her manager asked if you'd give the single a listen, see what you can do with it." Deejay guy was giving Will the I-hate-myself-for-finding-you-so-hot look. Deejay guy was crushing on my fave soap star.

I said, "So *you're* the Montana that Tig was talking about. Why does Tig care if you have the CD?"

Here's why. Turned out Montana (he had the thickest New York accent ever but spent a summer on a cattle ranch in the West, hence his deejay name) was not only the hottest deejay in NYC, and London and Ibiza (Ibiza? Ib-whata?), but he also produced on the side—he could take a basic pop track and turn it into a dance cult classic. He wasn't in the game to be rich or famous, however—Montana only worked with artists he liked personally, and apparently there weren't many of them. Tig's radar, the same radar that let Tig in on Pop Life Records' dumping pregnant Amanda Lindstrom from the label and finding the company desperately in need of a new pop princess to anoint, must have reported back Montana's crush on Will. Tig's okaying an all-access pass to Steam for this underage girl's night out with the hot soap star was no coinky-dink.

Montana had a portable Discman lying on the table. He threw the CD in and gave it a short listen on his headphones. "Not bad," he said. "Good voice, fun. The arrangement sucks, though. Shall we test drive this single, cute girl named"—Montana glanced at the CD package—"Wonder! Love it!"

He took the CD from the Discman and put it into the machine at the deejay booth. As the song that had been playing ended, I heard the opening chords of "Bubble Gum Pop" burst through the club. Wow! My

song! My voice! *Chew it, blow it, lick it, pop pop pop.* The crowd on the dance floor kept moving, but to the beat of the last song, as if to say, What is this? And new song it was indeed, as scratches, rhythms, and I don't know what else came from Montana's booth, turning this simple cute song into a kick-ass dance remix that soon had the crowd pulsing.

Kayla came up from behind me, pulled me onto the dance floor. "C'mon, it's your song! I can't believe what Montana did to it!" I hesitated for almost a second. Which Kayla personality was inviting me onto the dance floor—the one who considered me her li'l protégé, or the one who had dropped her supportive clench of my hand the minute the record company execs had pronounced my debut video a success?

But this was my moment too. I wanted to revel, whether Kayla was being nice or mean. I made my way to the middle of the dance floor, where I began a shameless grind with Will and Kayla; no Cosmos necessary for this junior pop princess tonight. Dean and Jules joined us—this song was *happening.* Dean gave me the pelvic grind dance from behind and whispered in my ear, "You sound good, Little Miss All Grown Up. Look damn fine too! Forgive me?" Kayla was on my other side, showing off the dance moves that had made her famous around the world. She was grinding so hard at my side it was almost like she wanted to push me off the dance floor. I swayed into Will, who danced a simple but smooth step, arms in the air, hips rocking to the beat. I could have danced with him all night. Jules and Kayla were dancing so provocatively together I think they could have turned all the gay men in the room straight and all the straight girls into lesbians. The club was jumping on both levels— my song was seriously working this crowd!

I thought about how Tig had masterminded this moment, how, from the vocal coaches and stylists to the song selection and video debut, he had been planning a series of plateaus to launch my career, not to mention his all-knowing radar that zeroed in on choice opportunities. As I danced, pressed inside a Dean Marconi/Will Nieves sandwich that made me what any girl with a pulse would have considered about the luckiest wench on the planet (if she didn't know I was secretly wishing it was Liam here dancing with me instead), I wondered, Where can I go from here?

The song ended; the crowd cheered. Montana pointed at me. He mouthed at me the words: "A hit."

Twenty-nine

Less than a year ago I was scrubbing down floors and toilets at the end of each shift at the Dairy Queen. Now, Cinderella was in full pop princess glory, in front of a television camera with microphone in hand, standing before the gigantic top-floor windows of a loft television studio in Tribeca to introduce "Bubble Gum Pop," her first single, which would be officially released on Tuesday. The full album, to be called *Girl Wonder,* would follow a few weeks later. In the distance outside the windows were views of the Hudson River and midtown Manhattan, but the closer view outside featured a giant billboard on top of a nearby building advertising a new line of sneakers targeted at teen girls—an ad featuring yours truly, bent over, her butt high (and airbrushed way thinner) and her grin wide as she laced up the shoes, with two guys smirking happily at the rear view.

Earlier in the dressing room, J, the radio/TV host whom I had met at Kayla's party for me, had come in to say hi. "You seem nervous," he said. Nervous about what? That I was about to be interviewed in front of a live studio audience of kids my own age, for a television program that was broadcast across the globe for millions to see? Me, nervous? Nah.

Kayla, sitting next to me having her makeup touched up, said, "This girl's a pro; she'll be fine." She patted my arm, which felt almost like a slap. She was still mad about a blind item that had recently appeared in the gossip column of her favorite tabloid newspaper: *WHICH underage prospective pop star upstaged her super-star mentor at an exclusive over-21 club hangout recently as she table-danced with not one but two of the hot young male stars who had been invited to keep company with the queen singer, but who instead spent their dance floor time fawning over the new princess?* Tig said Kayla was even more mad that Montana had agreed to produce an official remix of "Bubble Gum Pop." Kayla had been trying for almost a year to get Montana to work on one of her tracks.

The show was *J-Pop,* a live music video show broadcast every Saturday morning to the viewing demographic that had just graduated from Saturday morning cartoons but still needed a weekend morning TV baby-sitter to go along with their Cap'n Crunch. "This is it," Tig said to me.

"That's right," Kayla added. "This is the last appearance I'm making for you. I gotta be in Cali tomorrow to shoot a video, and we still have to hire more dancers and do tech for the tour. Wonder, you're on your own after this."

My nerves caught up with me in the form of my bladder; I always have to pee when I'm anxious. I excused myself from the dressing room, where Kayla,

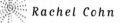

Tig, Jules, Karl, J, and an assortment of stylists and producers were hanging out preshow. Bathrooms—whether they were in Tig's offices, at Kayla's brownstone, the record company, or the recording studio—had become my haven, the one place I could be alone. As I was washing my hands I looked out the windows of the bathroom and saw the billboard advertisement featuring my picture. I stood up on the sink to climb into the window perch, where I nestled my body, legs against the wall, in a V shape to look out the window. *J-Pop* was set to go live in a matter of minutes. Tig's words echoed in my mind: *This is it.* No turning back now. I stared at the billboard advertisement, thinking it funny how the image looked in comparison to my strange lifestyle: I was splayed across a billboard representing the All-American Girl, pretty but not beautiful, innocent yet sexy, your basic cute and fresh girl at the mall. Yet how many All-American Girls graduate from high school outcast-slash-dropout to pop princess wanna-be, sixteen years old yet essentially living on her own, parentless—and crashing in the spare room of a pop diva's brownstone?

I understood now why Dean Macaroni had been so dismissive of me when we'd been reintroduced at Steam, why Liam had been contemptuous when I'd been introduced to him as Kayla's protégée: They immediately saw me as a product, not as a person.

My cell phone rang, Devonport calling. I said, "Hi, Mommy!" into the phone but it was Charles, not

Mom. "Hey, butthole, the whole town is tuning in to *J-Pop* this morning. Don't screw up or I won't be able to show my face in school Monday."

"Thanks for the vote of confidence." I could just see Jen Burke watching *J-Pop* this morning, then immediately starting an Internet smear campaign ratting me out as a Devonport High loser who should be shunned, not camping out with music industry A-listers.

"Don't be like that. You coming home to visit soon or what?"

"I hope so," I said, and I did hope so. After the months of work and preparation, I wouldn't have minded a nice weekend in dead-end Devonport. I'd sleep till noon with Cash lying at the foot of my bed, I'd be awakened by salty breezes coming into my room and Cash licking my face, Mom and Dad would take care of me, do my laundry and take me out for a lobster roll and a giant ice cream sundae (not from Dairy Queen)—man, that would be so nice. I wouldn't even care about running into Jen Burke or Doug Chase cuz I'd be telling Mom and Dad about this new guy in my life who goes to Dartmouth; Dad would be all over that.

Dad got on the phone. "Hi," he said. He was always so formal with me now, never offered a "honey" or a "sweetie," not even a "dear" when he spoke to me. "Good luck today—I'm sure you'll do just fine. We'll expect to see you in June for the G.E.D. test. Here, Mommy wants to wish you well."

Dad didn't wait for a response, which was okay with me—I dreaded the moment I would have to tell him I was backing down on my one sworn promise to him. I hadn't studied for the G.E.D. and had no intention of taking it. It seemed to me that now that my income was supporting myself and our family's home improvements, why should I be held accountable for that test anyway? Clearly I didn't need a high school education to make it on my own. I was doing just fine.

Mom said, "Hi, sweetie, I'm so excited and *nervous*! But I know you'll be great; I'm—*we're*—so proud! Henry and Katie are here. We're having a little celebration in your honor. I wish I could be there with you, but Charles has a skate meet later today."

I didn't bring up the fact that Charles had a skate meet like every other week, but how often was your daughter appearing on a famous TV show to debut her first record? I could only imagine that her absence was because of Lucky, that all the pain of our loss would hit her harder if she joined me on this important day, when she'd never gotten to see Lucky reach this point.

Mom said, "Here, someone else wants to say hi to you."

Katie's voice squealed, "OH MY GOD, Wonder! The whole town is talking about you; everyone at school just can't believe it! Are you hanging out with Kayla? What is she like? What other famous people have you met? I am so PSYCHED for you!"

How nice, Katie. I couldn't help but remember that our shared DQ experiences and years of knowing each other hadn't meant she wouldn't dump me at school the minute she got popular.

I said, "Is Henry there?"

There was a silence, then I heard Katie whisper, "But she wants to talk to *you!*"

Opera Man came onto the phone, singing, *"Is this the girl/who doesn't return my e-mails/doesn't/I suspect/even open them? I'm going/to slit my wrists now!"* I grinned wide, then worried that the smile might have smudged lip gloss onto my teeth.

I so suck. If Liam had sent me an e-mail, I would have canceled every voice and dance lesson, every business meeting, any recording session, just to spend the whole day composing the perfect response to a guy I barely knew, but I hadn't once bothered to e-mail or call Henry, whom I'd known since forever.

Kayla burst into the bathroom and locked the door behind her. I jumped down from the window perch so she wouldn't rag on me for scuffing my pants or not meditating or whatever she does before an important public appearance. And since there is no such thing as a private cell phone convo when Kayla is present, I mumbled "Sorry, gotta go" into the phone and turned it off. Now I double-sucked. I promised myself I would call Henry back later to apologize for getting off the phone so quickly.

Kayla went into the stall. "Swear to God, if anyone

follows me into this bathroom I'm gonna scream! Sometimes I just get so sick of people touching me all the time—can you sign this, can we take a picture of you with us, blah blah BLAH! The only place I can get any friggin' peace is the friggin' bathroom." Then, insta–mood change that was vintage Kayla. "Wonder honey, are you ready for your big day?"

She came out of the stall to wash her hands, telling me, "That outfit is adorable." I had on tight white capri denim pants and a tight white T-shirt with the Wonder bread logo across the chest, along with a pair of the sneakers whose brand I was now promoting, in colorful shoelaces that matched the blue, red, and yellow Wonder bread logo colors. Kayla touched my hair, fixed a smudge of my eye makeup. "Go like this," she said, blotting her teeth. "Now this," she added, rubbing her teeth with her index finger. I followed her instructions. She pulled a little tube of Vaseline from her pocket. "Put this on your teeth so they'll shine on TV." She patted my bum. "Good girl! The boys are gonna love you!"

I had a question I had been dying to ask her for weeks now. Since I seemed to be in her good graces at this particular moment, I took my shot. "Heard from Liam?" I put on my best *no big deal* voice.

"Liam! What the hell, you're asking about Liam when you're about to appear before millions of people on TV? What, do you like him or something?"

Very bad strategic move on my part. I knew I

should have trusted my instinct not to ask her about him. "No!" I said. "I was just curious. . . ."

Karl's knock on the other side of the bathroom door saved me the inquisition I know Kayla was about to put me through on why the hell I cared what Liam was up to. Karl's voice grunted, "Kayla, they're ready for you."

Kayla gave me a quick once-over. "Do great today. Liam? LIAM? Whatever! Think of Lucky, think of me." She headed toward the door, unlocked it, then turned back to me and winked. "Just don't do *too* great—I'm not quite ready to retire yet!" And she was gone.

Deep breaths, deep breaths. Jules rushed inside the bathroom calling, "Wonder!" When she saw me staring absently out the window, she snapped, "Showtime, girl! Get your ass out there, *now*! Kayla's just going on."

Jules hustled me over to the curtained guest entrance of the *J-Pop* set to wait before being announced. From the playback screen overhead, I saw J standing before the camera. He said to the audience: "We're introducing today a singer we think is going to be huge. But it's not me who's gonna tell you all about her. It's . . ." And then the cameras panned to Kayla as she burst into the studio, followed by a deafening roar of screams from the studio audience. The audience jumped on its feet, cheers and whistles and screams and high-fives all around.

"What's up NEW YORK?" Kayla said. The girl

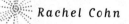

could work a crowd like no one else. In front of the cameras, with a studio audience, all of a sudden her attitude was all street, her language hip-hop, as if she'd grown up in the hood and not in a big Victorian house with an organic garden and Birkenstock parents in Cambridge, Mass. She chatted with J for a few minutes about her upcoming tour, the new video she was about to shoot, her possible movie career down the road. Then they got down to business—my business. Kayla turned to the audience: "So y'all *know* I am touring this summer, so now what I gots ta do is introduce y'all to my opening act, she's like my li'l sis, I've known her since we were coming up together in Boston. Give her a big shout out, awright? Wonder Blake!"

I rushed onto the stage, almost tripping over the soundstage wires, to where J and Kayla were standing. The camera zoomed in on the billboard outside the windows behind us. My heart was pounding a katrillion beats per second. But with the camera on, there was a comfort zone I'd known since *Beantown Kidz*. Somehow, the scene was less frightening than the nervous anticipation I'd experienced in the dressing room and the bathroom.

I could feel the excitement in the air, but I knew it came from Kayla's surprise appearance, not because of me. A frat dude type guy in the audience stood up and shouted, "Kayla, you're so HOT!" Kayla hand-gestured a phone signal with her thumb at her ear and her pinkie at her chin. She mouthed *Call me!* but to the camera, not to the boy in the audience. The crowd laughed.

J said, "Wonder, welcome, we're excited to have you here." He turned to the camera. "Everybody here knows about *Beantown Kidz,* how it launched the careers of Kayla, Freddy Porter, and Dean Marconi. Wonder's another *B-Kidz* alum—"

"She was like the baby of the group," Kayla interrupted. She put her arm around me in a sisterly grip. She even played with the ends of my hair, like Lucky used to do.

J said, "But now this girl is all grown up. She's got a debut single we're premiering here today." J turned to me. "Wonder, I first met you at a party at Kayla's house recently. The thing I noticed about you then— I think everyone at that party noticed—was how you dance. You just tear it up on the dance floor." Yeah, just gimme a few Cosmos, J, and watch me go!

Tig had told me to just be myself, not a Kayla clone. I said, "I love to dance! But mostly I was psyched that I got to dance with Will Nieves from *South Coast* in my first video. I have been crushing on him since seventh grade." I saw several girls in the audience nod their heads appreciatively.

J introduced an old B-Kid clip of me doing a hip-hop dance routine with Kayla. The audience was all "awww . . ." looking at our ponytail hair and awkward preadolescent faces and bodies. J said, "You've come a long way since those days, Wonder. What do you think of all this?" He gestured toward Kayla, the studio audience, the tall buildings of Manhattan outside the studio windows, the giant billboard of me.

What I was really thinking was not appropriate to say aloud, much less on national television. *Well, J, I think about sex all the time—when will I do it, with whom? (I'm, like, extremely curious about The Liam.) And my mind is so in the gutter that I'm in actuality wondering what your raw pecs look like without that tight black muscle shirt you have on, even though your attractiveness quotient gets severe demerits cuz I am fairly sure you wear a toupee. But I'm distracted because I have cramps at this moment and why did the stylist have to choose an all-white outfit for me during this time of the month, and this is the third day of my period and really what I am thinking is I COULD SCARF DOWN TWO BIG MACS RIGHT NOW!*

But I was a good pop princess. Instinctively I turned on for the camera, smiled wide, and said, "I'm thinking I can't believe I am on this show and that this is my life!" The audience offered a small trickle of applause, sincerity points.

J said, "We've got a game we like to play here—it's called Quick Questions. I'm going to ask you a few questions; just answer rapid-fire—don't think, just go. Question one: What is your favorite movie?"

"*Bring It On.*" My favorite movie is really *Heathers* but during the preinterview in the dressing room, J told me not to say that movie because advertisers on *J-Pop* would not appreciate a reference to a movie about a clique of nasty girls and dreamy Christian Slater who wants to blow their high school up.

"Best song to make out to?" This was a surprise question! The second question was supposed to be, "Who are your favorite singers?"

Without thinking, I blurted out, "Anything by Paul Weller." D'oh! Why did I have to say that? I prayed that Liam was too completely cool to ever watch a show like *J-Pop.* I saw Karl standing in the distance; I could have sworn his bushy eyebrow raised upward at my answer.

J turned to the audience. I think he was annoyed with me for referencing a singer obscure to the teen pop audience. "That was an interesting choice Wonder had; I didn't realize she had such eclectic taste in music. A lot of you here might not know who Paul Weller is. He's a British singer who—"

I interrupted, my face at full blush. "Next question please!" Everyone laughed.

J said, "I think Wonder speaks from experience! Well, that leads to the next question. First kiss?"

Okay, the last question was supposed to be, "Boxers or briefs?" (Boxers, fer sure.) I realized I had been set up. I didn't want to say "Doug Chase" because that jerk was certainly my first real kiss and no way did I want the whole town of Devonport knowing that, but J was laughing, and said, "No need to answer that

one, Wonder, we've got a clip here to answer that question, one that I think the girls in the audience will particularly be interested in." There it was, a New Kids on the Block–looking fourteen-year-old Freddy Porter asking me in a squeaky voice, "Wanna try?" and me bouncing my head like I was the genie girl on *I Dream of Jeannie* and then quite possibly the most embarrassingly bad lip smack in the history of television. The girls in the *J-Pop* audience squealed. Some girl shouted out, "You are so lucky!"

I laughed too. "How did you find that?"

J said, "We have our sources. Speaking of whom, we've got another surprise today, a very special caller on the phone. Freddy, are you there?"

More screams (LOUD! No wonder Kayla wore earplugs) from the girls in the audience as a current-incarnation video clip of Freddy Porter was shown, a close-up of the eighteen-year-old sex god with arms open wide on some tropical beach singing, *"Girl, I wanna get wit' you."* I looked at Kayla. Even she looked surprised— and Kayla *never* looked surprised. She whispered in my ear, "I have no idea. Just play along. Whatever."

"Wonder! J! Kayla!" Freddy's voice boomed out from phone speakers coming from I don't know where.

J said, "Freddy, what's up, dawg? So to Wonder's apparent mortification, we've been sharing with the audience—and all of the world—Wonder's first kiss, which it turns out was with you, dude. Care to share your memories of this magical moment? It's not every pop princess we get in here who has footage of getting her first kiss from Freddy Porter."

Freddy's voice blared: "She was a great kisser! A quick study!" Audience laughter and applause.

I played along. I went, "I was twelve!" Blech, my parents were watching this! How embarrassing!

Freddy teased, "Yeah, unfortunately there was no tongue. But you all want to know something?" The audience cheered. "That clip shows our kiss, right, on *B-Kidz*. But Wonder, do you want to tell everyone what happened *before* that take?"

The camera zoomed on me shaking my head vehemently. Freddy's voice again: "We had a practice session in the dressing room first! Her idea!"

The camera was on me again, this time my head nodding fast and embarrassed. "It's true," I said. Why did he have to remember that? I winked at the audience. "Practice makes perfect, I always learned." Cheers for Wonder from the audience. I saw Tig standing next to Karl, and if I didn't know better I'd say Tig's stone face had an almost-smile on it. I was doing good. I hoped Jen Burke *was* part of the Devonport contingent watching *J-Pop* this morning—I knew for a fact she had pictures of Freddy Porter taped all over her notebook.

Kayla ribbed me. "You never told me that!" How comfy-coze we all were, like a little B-Kidz reunion moment captured on *J-Pop*.

Then Freddy said, "Wonder, I'm . . . uh . . . wondering." (Audience laughter again, some screams of

"We love you, Freddy!") "Should we pick up where we left off? Maybe dinner sometime?"

And I swear to God, the shrieks and screams in that audience you couldn't believe. The girls in the audience apparently didn't know Freddy wasn't bad as a dance partner, but that he was a little . . . shall we say "frisky"? . . . with where his hands strayed. Not to mention that Freddy had a tendency toward bad breath and toward assuming all girls are easy. I doubted the swooning girls in the audience would have appreciated me reeducating them about the object of their lust, however.

J said, "Wonder, I think you've just been asked out on a date on national television by Freddy Porter. I think the screams in this audience can testify to the fact that a lot of girls wouldn't mind being you right now! So, does Freddy have a shot?"

I repeated Kayla's earlier hand phone gesture, thumb at my ear, pinkie at my chin, but instead of mouthing the words I sang out, "Call me, Freddy!" and the audience cheered and applauded again.

J said, "Wonder, care to introduce your video?"

I said, "Here it is: 'Bubble Gum Pop.' I hope you all—and Freddy!—like it!"

And I was officially launched.

Thirty

Kayla and I were in the monster SUV with the darkened windows riding back to her house from the *J-Pop* set when a text message flashed across my cell phone. From Liam! *Pop Princess:* J-Pop *makes me wanna puke, but even I will admit you were a star. Did I leave my Paul Weller CD in your Discman? ;> -L*

Oh, I couldn't take it anymore! I blurted out to Karl, sitting in the front seat, "Hey Karl, did you give Liam my cell phone number? Is he coming back to Brooklyn once he finishes finals?" I'd lost count of how many times I'd tried to give Karl a subtle hint to drop my digits on Liam. Karl was practically my suite mate up there on that brownstone fourth floor, and I didn't know how many more times I could pretend that I'd found Liam's book in the bathroom, or I'd heard about some awesome restaurant up by Dartmouth that Liam should know about, so maybe Karl could tell Liam to like call me sometime or whatever? Now that Karl had finally gotten the message, I felt like the universe as I knew it could not possibly go on any longer without me finally getting the DL on Liam. Who cared if Kayla was in the car? After my *J-Pop* performance, I was golden—for now.

I had read the CliffsNotes for that book Liam was studying when he visited during spring break, *Anna Karenina,* and I was primed to impress Liam with how smart and literary and shit I could be. I'd surely learned enough about the book to fake a conversation about it with Liam, hopefully a conversation that could end quickly with another make-out session while Paul Weller played from the Discman with the minispeakers attached.

You'd think a pop princess getting a huge launch from her record company would have better things to obsess over. You'd think.

Karl turned to face me. There appeared to be a squint under all those eyebrows, like he was on to me. "Maybe," he grunted. He pointed at Kayla. "Think you can behave?"

Kayla giggled. Weird how she loved to be called on her bad behavior. "Tell Liam he can crash at the brownstone all summer if he wants, doesn't bother me, Wonder and I'll be gone on tour. But Karl, don't break his heart too badly when you tell him I'm no longer saving myself for him." Kayla turned to me in the way backseat we shared. She grabbed my hand. "I wanted to tell you before but you have been dead asleep every night when I get home: Dean Marconi and I hooked up. We're like unofficially a thing and all."

I said, "But I thought you said Dean was gay."

"Not all the time," Kayla said, with this near-exasperated voice like, *Well, duh.*

Tig was sitting in the aisle seat in front of us. He said, "Kayla, this doesn't have anything to do with Freddy Porter's sudden interest in Wonder, does it? The press will love it if you show up at events with Dean, but come on, are you for real?"

Kayla said, "Dean's manager is going to give you a call. He thinks he can put some deals together for me."

I swear you could almost see smoke rising from Tig's head of tight spike braids. He said to the driver, "Stop the car, I'll take a taxi home from here." The SUV pulled up at a red light and Karl jumped out to open the back door for Tig, who didn't even say good-bye to us.

Karl hopped back in and said, as the driver proceeded down the avenue, "You'd better watch it, Kayla, or you're going to lose your manager."

Kayla said, "Tig had better watch it or he's gonna lose his star client." She turned back to me, her face all glowing and girl-talk-ready. "So, Dean. Ahhh!!!!!!!! Do you agree?"

"Lucky never liked him."

"Lucky's standards were impossible. You practically had to be certified by a bishop to meet her approval. I'm amazed she liked *me*! But dig this: Dean wants me to come out to L.A. with him next week, to read for a part in his new movie. It's a small role but there are some hot love scenes and like it could totally help me break out of this pop princess mold. Maybe I'm ready to move on to something new, something bigger, after the tour."

I said, "That's great about Dean, if you're happy

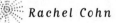

about it." It did seem weird that this superstar girl who was regularly named one of the sexiest performers in America never seemed to get around to dating. Here was a girl who guys literally drooled over, but then again, what guy had a chance, having to go through Karl or Jules or Tig or all the other record company and promo people surrounding her at all times? I guess it was no wonder the girl never had a real date. On the other hand, Kayla seemed more interested in her career than in any prospective love life. She worked like a demon, fourteen- and fifteen-hour days of rehearsing, dancing, and promoting, followed by nights out clubbing till dawn.

Kayla said, "What about Freddy! What was that all about? Are you gonna go out with him?"

I wanted to shout NO WAY! but a publicist from our record company had already arranged a date through Freddy's assistant before I'd even left the *J-Pop* studio. Not only was I told in no uncertain terms that I was to go on this date, but so would a photographer from *Teen Girl* magazine. When I protested to Tig he said, "So Freddy's a jerk, so what? Just go, have a quick dinner; you don't have to marry him, just get the photo op and be done with it. Not a big deal, just part of the job—the part ninety-nine percent of the teenage girls in America would kill to have." Yuck. Still, probably better than a date cleaning puke and crusted-on hot fudge sauce off baby high chairs back at the DQ—or was it?

I shrugged at Kayla, said, "Guess so."

Kayla said, "I heard he is like a major STD case."

"Nuh-uh! Who told you that?"

"I have backup dancers, you know. Guess what else? Dean told me. Freddy and his buddies, a couple other young male stars—you know, TV and movie actors, a few boy band types—they have this thing called the Pop Princess Club. It's like this contest to see who can . . . you know . . ." Karl was glaring at Kayla from the front seat. Kayla leaned over and placed her hand on my ear to whisper the rest: "It's like this contest they have to see who can take away the virginity of the most pop princesses or teen actresses or former child stars and whatever."

"That's disgusting!" I about shouted.

Kayla laughed. "I know!"

And I might have called Tig that very second to tell him the date was O-F-F not-gonna-happen, but something as exciting as Kayla's revelation was despicable happened just then. My song was on the car radio! My voice, singing "Bubble Gum Pop," blasting from the number one pop music radio station in New York on the radio program J deejayed after his Saturday morning television show. I jumped out of my seat, screamed, "That's my song, turn it up, turn it up!"

Karl must have witnessed this type of scene before because he smiled under all that beard and mustache and turned up the volume. Then he said to me, "You never forget your first time."

Thirty-one

My Stealth Date with Freddy Porter
by Teen Girl Reporter in Cognito

It's not every day a girl gets asked out on *J-Pop* by Freddy Porter. In fact, there's only one girl in the world who can claim that honor right now and that girl is Wonder Blake. But I got the next best thing: a reservation at the booth right next to theirs to eavesdrop on their date.

I stare discreetly over my menu at the dream team couple as they approach the table next to mine. Every pair of eyes in the whole restaurant is checking them out too. Personally, if I was on a dream date like Wonder, walking into a posh restaurant on the arm of a signature black Prada suit-wearing, quadruple platinum-certified sex god, I would find a better outfit. Ever heard of a stylist, Wonder? Hire one! Wonder is dressed—how to put this delicately—like a nun. Her perky head of blond-streaked hair is pulled back into a severe bun. With her long black skirt and loose black blouse with the collar practically choking the top of her neck, there is no evidence of the curvy body and generous cleavage that keeps my fourteen-year-old brother's face pressed to the TV every time Wonder's "Bubble Gum Pop" video comes on TV, which as we all know happens about every two seconds now.

Freddy is congratulating Wonder on her song's debut at number eighteen on the pop charts its first week of release. Could he be any sweeter? She just mumbles, "Thanks," like it's no big deal. Oh yeah, that happens to me every day, Wonder!

Plan: If I make myself choke on my asparagus right now, Freddy will jump to my rescue. He'll perform the Heimlich maneuver on my stomach, the asparagus will go flying right into Wonder's shocked face, and yippee, the pop princess is out for the night and Freddy's all mine. As extra thanks for saving him from one more minute of awk-ward first date conversation with a pop princess who apparently couldn't care less, Freddy leans over my prostrate body as I gasp for breath. Mouth-to-mouth resuscitation time . . .

The waiter comes for their orders. Freddy orders steaks for both of them, Wonder corrects him—she'll just have a salad, fat-free dressing on the side, and a Diet Coke. Oh, so she's one of *those* girls. I notice they both speak in thick Boston accents when they're together (I noticed the same thing when I saw Kayla and Wonder being interviewed together on TV)—must be something about being around your hometown crew that makes accents revert back in time. Freddy asks if Wonder plans to go to college—he thinks she's "wicked smaht." Wonder gives him this look back like: What do you know about me?

Ouch!

Is it possible that the Girl Wonder who graces the cover of this month's issue of your fave teen mag here would rather be elsewhere? She keeps checking her cell phone for messages, keeps looking at her watch like she's got a much better date lined up. Gorgeous women in slinky dresses are passing by the table clearly looking for Freddy to notice them, but his eyes are all on her, like he's on a mission, and Girl Wonder keeps turning her head from him like he has bad breath!

Folks, this is like watching the *Titanic* go down.

I am not happy with Wonder. This is *my* stealth date and she is ruining it with her bad 'tude. I want

her to ask Freddy if it's true a TV show is being developed for him, if we were on a deserted island together what CDs would he bring along for us to hear, I want Wonder to run her fingers through his blond locks so I can pretend her fingers are mine!

Their food arrives. Freddy lays into that steak like I wish he would lay into . . . never mind, mind outta the gutter. Wonder barely nibbles at her salad. At this point, they're barely talking, not after Freddy mentions a famous teen actress in Hollywood he used to date—*she* didn't mind enjoying a steak. Wonder glares at him. I give Wonder this: The girl gives good glare. "I heard about you and your club," she says, and whatever she means (Club Med? club sandwich?), Freddy's face has gone a little red and they both say "NO!" when the waiter comes by asking if they'd like to see the dessert menu.

Then Girl Wonder pops some bitter humiliation on Freddy! She slips the waiter her credit card when Freddy is distracted by a beautiful girl in a barely there dress who I could swear I've seen thonging her way through I don't know how many music videos. Freddy, if your date insists on paying the check, that's payoff money, that's I-don't-want-to-owe-you-nothing-no-time, no-second-date, nada money.

Hey, Freddy, cheer up. I'm free next Friday! And Dad won't let me use the credit card, so it's all you, baby!

Part Three

Shades of Blonde
Platinum Blonde

Thirty-two

There is no such thing as a bad day in the life of a pop princess. There can be days you are not happy, but never, ever show it. You've always got to be *on*. So what that I was in a nasty mood because I hadn't gotten a decent night's sleep after the barrage of appearances and interviews that had left my voice shot and my energy drained. So what that I was starving because of the 1,400-calorie-a-day carb-free diet of steamed veggies and grilled fish the nutritionist was demanding I stick to if I wanted to be the size-six girl my naturally size-eight body resisted but the record company demanded? The show must go on, folks. Do *not* stare longingly at the Cinnabon or Orange Julius counters in the distance.

I was at a shopping mall in New Hampshire, not far from Boston, waiting behind a curtain to perform "Bubble Gum Pop" to an audience of an estimated thousand screaming preteen girls and their parents. I peeked through a small hole in the curtain—had I really heard properly? A second-grade-sized girl was standing just on the other side of the curtain, singing to herself over and over, *"Wonder Blake Wonder Blake Wonder Blake,"* oblivious that the real Wonder Blake was standing right over her behind a curtain, some-what weirded out by the girl's aimless song.

The emcee welcomed the crowd, then introduced me: "You know her from her song 'Bubble Gum Pop,' which just hit number five this week. Everyone, please give it up for New England's own WONDER BLAKE!"

I burst out onto the platform, no longer shy about wearing the skin-clinging hot pants cut off just below the butt and the sequined bra top from the line of junior clothes I was promoting as part of the mall opening. I couldn't believe the decibel level of cheers and screams and cries of "Wonder! Wonder!" as I hit the stage. I scoped the audience, completely amazed by how many people were there to see me—just me, not Kayla. But I was immediately distracted by my audience scan because, holy shazam, was that Liam standing at the escalator on the second level of the mall in front of The Limited?

The recorded music came on and I went right into the dance routine, grateful I could lip-synch my way through the refrains of the song and just use my shot voice on the verse parts. I had a long way yet to go to reach Kayla level, with backup singers and dancers to carry the show when the star wasn't at her best. From the weeks of rehearsal for the tour, I had the routine down and was not intimidated about performing in front of an audience, which I'd done many times back when I was a B-Kid. So I easily went on autopilot through the performance as I checked out the lanky figure at the top of the escalator. That height! That snarl! It *was* Liam.

The music ended, and although I wasn't expected to perform another song, I asked the emcee, "Mind if I add something?" He nodded but shrugged his shoulders and pointed to the music console as if to say, What should we play? I shook my head: Nothing.

I sat down on the platform, my legs dangling over the edge, my go-go boots clanking against the backboard. I signed a few girls' Food Court napkins with one hand and with the other said into the microphone, "This song is for someone special in the audience."

With what was left of my voice, I sang Billie Joe's line asking if his dear mother could hear him whining—the line that had awoken me when it was blasting from Liam's room at Kayla's house. A cappella and at a slow tempo that turned the punk song into a soulful ballad, I sang "Welcome to Paradise" by Green Day, smiling wide and looking up at Liam. His snarl turned into a very large, appreciative smirk. I only sang the first verse; I knew the remaining verses were too depressing and out-there for this audience of first to seventh graders. When I finished off the verse with the line about the wasteland called home, there was a moment of stunned silence from the audience. Liam came to the rescue, skipping down the escalator and shouting out "Whoo-hoo" to jump-start the applause. The audience's clapping was polite but also scattered, mostly from adults in the crowd who probably never imagined in their lifetimes that they'd witness a hot-pants/go-go-boots-outfitted pop princess turn a Green Day tune into a love song on the stage of a New Hampshire shopping mall.

I stood up to hand the microphone back to the emcee, who announced, "Er, thanks, Wonder! Wonder will be signing autographs in front of JC Penney in about fifteen minutes. Now I'd like to bring out New Hampshire's number one morning drive radio team— give it up for those crazy guys . . ."

I walked off the stage and back behind the curtain.

Tig: "Interesting, but what the hell was that?"

I said, "Because girls, they wanna have fun."

Tig: "Don't do it again."

The mall security team led me to a table where a long line had formed for autographs. I was uncomfortable being propped up as a role model for these kids; I was, after all, a half-naked high school dropout who just happened to have a hit song that was a Greatest Gainer for Radio Airplay on this week's Billboard Hot Singles chart—but that was just part of the job. I went into smiley-happy pop princess mode, signing CDs and posters and magazine covers and sneakers, taking pictures with one after another of the shorties with shy little voices saying "Bubble Gum Pop" was their totally favorite song, was Kayla my best friend, did I want to marry Freddy Porter?

After about the hundredth autograph, I looked up

to see a basketball player-height Liam sandwiched among a uniformed soccer team of ten-year-old girls half his height and accessorized much better than he was. Liam held out a *Teen Girl* magazine cover with my face on it for me to sign. "So we're a full-on blonde now?" he said.

I tugged at a lock of my hair and looked at the platinum blond color. "Yeah," I said. "The song moved up three places after I appeared on the morning breakfast shows with the new color." I hated the new color, but it fit the new me, someone I didn't really know anymore, someone who performed on autopilot and starved herself because she was told to.

Liam said, deadpan, "Ah, your parents must be so proud."

Tig came up behind me. "Keep the line moving," he whispered in my ear. He gestured to Liam to join him behind me. I kept signing autographs as I eavesdropped on their conversation.

Liam told Tig he'd been on his way from Dartmouth down to a summer job on the Cape when he'd heard about the mall appearance on the radio and decided he had to check it out (Liam kicked the back of my chair when he said that). Tig told Liam we were heading back to Boston after the appearance to meet up with Kayla and Liam's dad, then sending me home for a few days' rest before the tour launched in Boston, did Liam need a ride? Liam had his own car. Well then, could Liam give Wonder a ride down to the

Cape? Tig had ordered a car service for her from Boston but Wonder was tired, she would probably appreciate not having to stop in Boston and just going straight home. Sure, Liam said.

Score! Cancel the pop princess's bad mood.

Thirty-three

Count on Liam to drive a beat-up old VW bus from like 1970-something. I took one look at the orange sherbet-colored monstrosity in the parking lot and asked him, "So what, is this your compensation to yourself for being too young to have followed the Grateful Dead around back in the day?"

"Very funny," Liam said. "It's a hand-me-down from my mom, who actually *did* follow the Dead around at some embarrassing point in her youth that we have agreed we should never discuss."

He opened the passenger door and held out his hand for me to hold as I lifted myself into the seat. I tried to ignore the electricity that passed through my body as our hands touched, this extreme tingle that had me scamming the back of the bus and noticing it had been stripped of seats and had only a blanket laid across the back. New Hampshire to Devonport was just a couple hours' drive. I made a pact with my hormones that together we would fight the natural urge to hook up with Liam during our brief interlude.

Liam hopped into the driver's seat and turned on the ignition. The radio came on, playing "Bubble Gum Pop." Liam banged his head on the steering wheel. "It's

impossible to escape this song; it's everywhere! It's not even safe to turn on the radio anymore." Maybe he noticed the downcast expression on my face, because he sighed and added, "The song is kind of a guilty pleasure."

I didn't want to talk about the song or my career. Since I'd left Devonport half a year earlier, my career had consumed my life. Even if our car ride would only last a couple hours, I was psyched just to spend time with someone my own age who wasn't a professional performer, or an adult who only dealt with me on a business level and always expected me to behave like an adult.

I said, "Fuck the song. How the hell is your life?" Please, tell me anything about you, I wonder about you all the time. It's SO unfair, liking you so much more than you seem to like me. "Could we just drop the banter and get to know each other like normal people?"

There was a slight upturn of Liam's lips, like he was flattered—and relieved. The VW bus ambled its way on to the interstate as Liam talked. His voice was really deep and sweet; I was surprised not to have noticed before. I could feel my heartbeat accelerating just from the sound of his voice, from the sheer nearness of him, his musky smell. "Well, whadya wanna know? I'm spending the summer in Woods Hole; some school buddies and I have rented this basic shack. We've all got jobs lined up, as waiters, cashiers, lifeguards, whatever. I tried to get a lifeguard job but I wasn't quite a strong enough swimmer. But Dad was nice enough to throw some bucks my way to cover my portion of the rent and I was lucky, I scored an internship at a marine biology lab, which is cool because I think that's gonna be my minor at school—"

"You must be really smart," I interrupted. "Like that Anna Karenina chick. She was wicked smart but kinda plowed on without thinking sometimes, right?"

Liam looked over at me. "Uh, yeah," he said. He did not look impressed by my literary mention, but his surprised look gave way to an indifferent one, which was better than a look of What are you talking about, idiot? "Why do you ask? Are you thinking about going back to school?"

I chuckled mightily. "Hah! No way—I am not school material. I'm at the University of Life."

"Spoken like a true Kayla clone."

I tilted my seat back and stretched my bare feet onto the dashboard. "I'm not sure if that's a compliment or an insult."

"It's neither."

Silence for a while, but a comfortable one. As we drove past Boston, I stared at the Prudential Building in the distance, knowing that I would give up every pop princess perk that had been thrown my way for just one more day back in our house in Cambridge, with my sister. What would Lucky think of Liam? I

could hear her assessment in my head: highly cute +
attitudinal issues = be careful, Wonder!

Liam flicked around on the radio until he settled
on a country station playing a twangy, sparse tune
with a male voice that was very hard and melodic at
the same time, full of emotion that didn't sound
Nashville-produced country-fake. "Merle Haggard,"
Liam said. "The guy's a fucking poet."

"My sister said the same thing about him, 'cept she
didn't say 'fucking.' But what kinda name for a guy is
Merle?"

"I don't know, *Wonder.*"

"Where did you learn so much about music?"

"My mom's a program director at a public radio
station in upstate New York. She doesn't make any
kind of money but she's that rare person who actually
loves what she does. She loves discovering new artists
and playing eclectic music and not having to work off
a playlist of corporate pop and rock chosen by advertisers. You'll have to meet her sometime; you'll like
her."

"I don't think she'd be interested in my kind of
music." Liam wanted me to meet his mom!

"Meet *you,* not the pop princess. Dad thinks you're
a 'good kid,' as he calls it, so you'll pass with Mom."

Karl said nice things about me? Wow. I always had
the feeling he only tolerated Kayla because she was his
job, that he didn't think she was a very nice person.
But I could never glean what Karl really thought; he

rarely offered opinions, was always just business. I said, "I thought your parents were divorced."

"They are. But they're still involved, if you get what I mean? Very strange relationship. They can't live together, but they never seem to stop loving each other. They date other people, but there's always like a few months at a time, whenever Dad isn't touring with whatever artist he's with, that he stays with Mom and it's like . . . just weirdness."

"That's nice!" I said. "My family needs a communal Zoloft prescription just to be in the same room together. So even if your parents are like sometimes together, sometimes apart, at least you know they always have this base with each other, and they obviously really love and support you a lot."

Liam shrugged. "Maybe. That's a nice way of looking at it."

Was I a fool to think that we were having an actual conversation, to think that maybe he could feel something for me if he was comfortable enough to let me in to his life like this?

As we got closer to the Cape I could smell a salty sea breeze. I was nervous and excited—I didn't know how my return to Devonport would work out, but the thought of the quiet and hanging out with Cash and listening to the ocean roar wasn't so bad.

I lifted my seat back up. Being in that comfortable reclining position was making me want to doze. Liam said, "You look tired. Should we stop?"

"I am sooooo tired, and hungry. You don't know what I would do for a nap and a lobster roll. But I can take care of both those things when I get home. I really appreciate you driving me and all."

"You're welcome, I guess," he said. He looked over at me for a sec. "I've never heard a pop princess say 'Thank you' before. Freaking me out."

I turned my head to face the window, soaking up the scenery as we crossed the bridge over to Cape Cod. When we were little, Lucky, Charles, and I used to scream with excitement in the backseat of our station wagon as it crossed over this bridge every summer to usher in our family vacation on the Cape. Now, the bridge felt like it was leading me to an alien place—or perhaps I was the alien returning to it.

Liam turned off Route 6 toward Woods Hole, not toward Provincetown, which was the direction for Devonport. "One amazing lobster roll coming up," he said.

"Oh, I was just fantasizing. I'm not allowed to eat that."

"So you're gonna be a too-skinny pop princess just cuz the record company says so?"

"You're right—fuck it, I want a real meal."

"At last, the protégé breaks free of the Kayla mold!"

Liam drove into a town I'd never been to. We passed by cranberry patches and rolling green fields and Snow White-pretty houses, just like all the other small Cape towns, until Liam pulled up at a seafood restaurant near the beach. He said, "Lobster roll and fries, right? You can come in, but you risk being tackled by a retainer-wearing army of Girl Scouts wanting autographs from the 'Bubble Gum Pop' girl."

"Don't care," I said. "Gotta use the bathroom." I tucked my hair under a baseball cap, still surprised to see the platinum color, and put on a pair of sunglasses. As further disguise, I had already changed out of pop princess slutwear and into a long flowing hippie girl skirt with a loose T-shirt.

I made it through the crowd of people at the restaurant and into the bathroom, my disguise fully working. But there was no escaping the pop princess. When I stepped into the stall, I saw a sticker plastered on the wall from a radio giveaway, a sticker with my face advertising *Wonder Blake, "Bubble Gum Pop" IN STORES NOW*. I sat down on the toilet, reading the graffiti that past toilet tenants had trailed below the sticker, each line written by a different pen and in different handwriting.

WONDER SUX.

OMG, Wonder is from Devonport!

No Wonder she SUX.

Shut up, WONDER is da bomb diggity!

She is a ho'!!!!!

Don't be mean, she's cute. She's not as good as Kayla, but who is?!? Kayla 4eva!

WONDER 'N' KAYLA ARE LEZBOS!

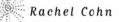

The bathroom stall criticism was not able to kill my appetite. Hey, this graffiti was kinder than the fancy music critics who had weighed in on my album, pronouncing it "pop garbage" and "addictively sweet and bad for you, just like the bubble gum of the song's name." Sometimes I wished I could meet one of those critics and just say, If you think my music is so sucky, why don't *you* go out and do it?

I found Liam at the front door of the restaurant holding two paper bags of food, the yummy smell of which was making my stomach turn over with wanting. Real food! We hopped back into the VW bus and Liam drove through a series of streets that dead-ended at a deserted beach spot. He hauled the blanket out from the back of the bus for us to sit on. Dusk was settling over the sky and the beach was absent the usual flocks of tourists—there were just a few people walking down the shore, barefoot, holding hands. I waited exactly no more minutes and dug into the food. "Mmmm, sooooo good!" Food, with taste! I remember. Enjoy now, pay later!

"Atta girl," Liam said. After we finished eating, we sat on the beach listening to the lapping of the water. Neither of us filled the air with chatter; we were both comfortable just sitting with our knees hugging our chests, the wind whipping our hair back, silent.

After the sun went over the horizon, I said, "I'd better get home or I am going to fall asleep right here."

Liam said, "I have a sleeping bag in the back of the

bus if you want to take a nap back there. I have a flash-light. I'll read a book on the beach while you rest."

I knew I should have said no, but Mom and Dad weren't expecting me until tomorrow anyway—I had never called to say the plan for me to spend the night at the hotel in Boston and take a limousine service to Devonport in the morning had changed. I didn't want this time with Liam to end, this time where I wasn't a pop princess or a daughter or a sister, I was just me, normal, hanging out with a cute guy, so I said, "Okay."

The back of the bus was a long space that was empty in the middle, with tools and CDs and food wrappers pushed to the sides. Liam laid the blanket down for me and placed the sleeping bag on top. I fell asleep within seconds.

When I woke up, darkness and starlight and ocean breeze were coming in through the windows. Liam was lying next to me, staring at me. A strand of hair hung in front of his face. I reached to tuck the strand behind his ear.

"What time is it?" I whispered.

"Just after nine. You've been asleep for two hours." His hand tugged at a strand of my hair, then stroked my cheek.

I wanted to say thanks for letting me sleep, thanks for the nicest day of my pop princess life so far, but I didn't. I placed my hands on his cheeks and brought his stubble mouth onto mine. So much for my pact with my hormones.

Thirty-four

I didn't intend for Liam to be initiated into the Pop Princess Club. It's not like I woke up that morning and thought, Hmm, today is the day the latest contender to be America's sweetheart will become not so innocent. It just happened—basic making out that turned into much, much more, fast. I kept remembering the Merle Haggard country song that had played during our drive down from New Hampshire: "It's Not Love (But It's Not Bad)."

Later, after he'd driven me home and we sat in the bus in front of my house on the dark street, where I could see Dad through the living room window sitting at his computer and my parents' upstairs bedroom window flashing TV light, signaling Mom's whereabouts, my heart literally ached from needing my sister. This was the one time I should have been rushing through the front door and running upstairs to our bedroom. I would lock the door and sit on Lucky's bed, and as I told her the story I would throw in spicy details that had never happened just to see the look of shock on her serious face. And I would listen to her lecture about my irresponsibility and appease her by indulging her in her favorite silly habit—brushing my hair until it crackled and then French-braiding it—and I would fall asleep with my Discman on my ears in the bed next to her as she read a book with her "Itty Bitty" Book Light clipped to it. Being able to tell Lucky about It might make the fact that It had happened feel less empty and ick and lonely.

For sure Liam didn't want to talk about It. Afterward, we rode in silence the whole half-hour drive up to Devonport. The only words we spoke were when I gave him directions to the house, and when I said "Could you please change the station?" when some random "Lite Rock, Less Talk" radio station had Foreigner singing about how it feels like the very first time. During the time of It, our only words had been "Do you have a condom?" from me and "Are you sure?" from Liam. *Yeah,* on both counts.

How could an experience you wait a lifetime to happen be over so quickly? In the moment, the experience was okay-nice, not earth-shattering, not scary, a little tender, a lot hurried. But then we stopped kissing right as It happened and we were just looking into each other's eyes and then suddenly It was so personal and weird and awkward and I would have done anything to turn back the clock on It, anything to remove his body from on top of mine.

It was over so fast.

For something supposedly so special, how come I felt so supremely sad?

I don't know what Liam and I weren't saying as we sat in the VW bus parked in front of my house later— *Gee, did that really happen?* or, *You'll call me, right?*—

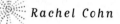

but the silence was unbearable, broken only by my teeth chattering in the cold ocean wind. Finally, words. "I have a flannel shirt there on the floor in front of your seat if you're cold," he said. Thanks, how romantic. I reached down to pick up the shirt, brushed the dirt from it. As I put my arms into the sleeves I tried to ignore the smell of gasoline and pure Liam-ness embedded in the green flannel material.

Maybe there really was nothing to say. I stepped out of the bus. Liam got out also, took my luggage out from behind my seat, and placed it on the lawn. Well, if he wasn't saying anything—not even "good-bye"— neither was I. Instead of going into the house, I walked down the wooden plank of stairs at the end of the street that led to the beach, not yet ready to face Mom and Dad. A group of kids had a small bonfire going on in the distance, and I could see a joint being passed around. And then I saw that Charles was in the group! Only Charles would wear a neon lime-colored skullcap that glowed in the dark. For a sec I had the urge to run across the sand and spring him from that group and give him some lame "Just Say No" lecture, but then I remembered what I had been doing in the last hour and thought, Hypocrite much?

Liam had followed me down to the beach, and the relief that positively flooded me when he wrapped his arms around me from behind was beyond comprehension. I turned around to face him, locked my hands around the small of his back. He leaned down and after all that silence, we at least had the perfect kiss, capped by moonlight shining onto the ocean. My heart was beating so fast I don't know how I lasted through that kiss, wondering what did he think of me, was this for real, when would I see him again? Why were we both incapable of speaking words to each other, about It, about Us, about anything?

Maybe the kiss wasn't so perfect.

Because for all that he caressed my hair and let me burrow my face in his neck, when he kissed me one last time before walking back up to the bus, somehow it felt like that last kiss on the beach had been a kiss-off.

I waited a few minutes until I heard the VW bus drive off, then I walked back up to the house. As I stepped inside, Cash barked at me like I was a stranger. I leaned down to pick him up, dying to pet him and slobber him with kisses, but he was having none of me. He sniffed me, then retreated to a corner and stared at me, accusing.

Dad looked up from his computer, did a once-over from my platinum blond hair to my skinnier-than-ever pop princess bod. He said, "Jesus Christ, I almost didn't recognize you." When I would inspect my reflection in the full-length mirrors at my daily two-hour dance classes, I sometimes didn't recognize myself anymore: ribs sticking out on my tightened stomach, an elasti-cized face. Dad did not stand up to greet me, hug me, kiss me. "I thought you were coming tomorrow."

"The plans changed." Great to see you, too, Dad.

Mom came charging down the stairs. "Who was Cash barking at?" She stopped at the end of the stairs and also did the once-over on me. "Wonder, what a surprise! You look so . . . different!" Mom, you have no idea.

Charles came in behind me. Someone had obviously sprayed him with Jean Naté or some drugstore perfume before he'd walked in—whoa, the stench. But whoa, he was like four inches taller than the last time I'd seen him and he had this baby soul patch on his chin and silver cross earrings dangling below that lime green neon skullcap. Not even a hello from him. Charles looked me up and down and pronounced, "You look fake." His shitkicker boots barely missed pounding my bare feet as Charles raced right by me, past Mom at the stairs, up to his room. Door slam.

When I went to my room and turned on the bedroom lamp, through the side window I saw Henry—with much shorter hair, I think—sitting at the computer by his dimly lit bedroom window across the way. Oh! I thought, there's someone who will be nice to me! For a sec I dared hope that Opera Man might make an appearance through the windows, but Henry just looked surprised to see me standing at my window. Then he pulled down his window shade. I'd like to think he was possibly just looking at porn on his computer and didn't want me to see, but I do believe that in fact the boy next door had just decisively dissed me.

Welcome home, Wonder!

Thirty-five

There's no place like home. Thank God. I couldn't leave fast enough.

I was still groggy when I went downstairs the next morning. Mom and Dad were sitting at the kitchen table, waiting for me.

"Good afternoon," Dad said. "I guess your record company doesn't mind if you sleep till noon."

Wide awake now, and p.o.'d! "Actually, Dad, they have me up every morning by six to work out and then I've usually got twelve-hour-plus days filled with pesky little things like vocal practice and rehearsals and appearances and interviews and photo shoots. It's called a job. At least someone in this family has one."

Low blow, I know. But when I looked around the house and saw the new washing machine and dryer, the repaired living room ceiling, the new storm-proof windowpanes, all long-overdue upgrades financed by my recent earnings, I was not about to take Dad's shit.

Dad struck back with, "The G.E.D. was yesterday. You didn't even have the decency to tell me you didn't plan to take the test! What are you gonna do, sing and dance your way through life? How long do you think this current lifestyle of yours can last?"

Mom stood up from the table. "Enough, you two!" She looked like she was about to cry. She faced Dad. "I thought we agreed not to start this again. Wonder will take the test when she's ready. Her career is obviously thriving—she doesn't need us to tell her what to do. Just be grateful she didn't pull a Kayla and threaten to legally emancipate herself from her parents. Just look at Wonder: She's fine on her own— maybe better off without us." Her eyes were a little teary as she turned to me. "Wonder, can I make you some eggs?"

I went over and hugged her. "No thanks, Mom, I just ate a Power Bar in my room."

"See!" Mom sputtered. "You don't need me."

"Actually, Mom, I wouldn't mind some eggs at all, but I need to cut the cals to make up for what I ate yesterday." I smoothed down her hair. Dad sat at the table, shaking his head, not making eye contact with me.

"CHARLES!" Mom yelled. "Get down here now, please!"

I'd already poured a mug of lukewarm coffee and added a Sweet 'n Low—what, fifty calories?—by the time Charles stomped into the kitchen. "What?" he grunted.

"Sit down," Dad said. "Mom and I want to have a family discussion."

"But where's Lucky? . . ." I let out automatically, before I realized what I'd said. I hadn't heard my parents convene a "family discussion" since long before she died. "Sorry," I murmured.

A sad silence hung over us, until Dad spoke up. "We wanted to wait until Wonder was home so we could tell you three . . . pardon me, you two . . . at the same time. There's no easy way to say this, so I'll just say it. Mommy and I have decided to separate."

If Mom and Dad were expecting whimpers and cries of shock and "No!" they were mistaken. "Good," Charles pronounced. "You're both miserable."

I said, hopefully, "Does that mean we're leaving Devonport?"

Mom said, "No. Dad will remain here."

Charles said, "I'm staying here too." Charles looked in my direction. "I like it here. Sorry."

Mom continued, "I've started looking for a job back in Boston. Once I've got a new position, I'll get an apartment there. Charles, I figured you would want to stay here, but I hope and expect you'll spend some weekends and vacations with me in Boston."

"Yeah," Charles said. "That'd be cool."

Dad finished off with, "We're not separating right away; we'll wait till Mom finds a job and is able to move."

I said, "You could come on tour with me, Mom."

Mom said, "No, Wonder. But thank you for asking. Letting you pursue this career was like opening Pandora's box. I regret encouraging you, but now that your career is ignited, there's no turning back. And I don't want to be the stage mom on the bus. I need to go back to Boston and get back into therapy and start my life over."

I didn't repeat my offer, though I suspected she would have liked me to ask her again. Mom's Boston plan was the most sensible thing I'd heard from her in years.

And that was that. My parents' marriage was over.

Thirty-six

After the "family discussion," I returned to my room. I sat in the window seat, looking out at the ocean, feeling blue about Mom and Dad, then feeling bluer that I truly must be a shallow girl if I was feeling sadder because I hadn't heard from Liam than I was about Mom and Dad's announcement. Was he not calling me because he thought I'd put the *hor* in *hormones* yesterday? What had I been thinking when I let that happen?

My cell phone ringer was set to its highest volume and the phone never left me, nestled in my pants pocket, yet I still bothered to check the voice mail every hour, even though there was no voice-mail message light flashing. It was nearly impossible that I would have missed his call.

I was putting on my running shoes to take a jog on the beach—payback time for yesterday's lobster roll and fries (and the bag of Oreos I snuck in my room last night) and the lack of dance rehearsal today—when Charles came into my room. A pretty, hippy-dippy-looking girl with long fine blond hair and a tiny frame under her wispy Indian sari-like outfit was attached to my brother's hand. My baby brother had a girlfriend! Charles said, "Amy, this is my sister. Wonder, Amy. Amy, Wonder."

"Hey," Amy said. She lifted her free hand in a wave to me. "I've, like, seen you on TV and stuff. You look different in person, like . . . bigger and all."

Thanks, Amy. I added one-pound ankle weights to each of my legs and laced my sneakers tight.

Charles said, "We're going to the DQ. Wanna come?"

"I'm going for a run, but I'll walk with you for a few." I followed them downstairs and outside the house.

When we were out on our street, Charles said, "So what do you think about Mom and Dad? It's about time, right? You know they've been sleeping in different bedrooms ever since Mom came back from New York."

I was thinking that maybe he shouldn't be talking about the family dirt in front of Amy, but her face had no reaction, like she already knew much more about what was happening in the Blake household than I ever would.

I said, "Were Mom and Dad like this back in Cambridge? It's hard to remember what we were like . . . before. If Lucky were here, this never would have happened, she would be so upset. . . ."

Charles stopped walking and just looked at me, hard and mad. "Wrong. Lucky once told me Mom and Dad would be divorced before I went to high school, and they'd be happier for it. You act like you're the only person who knew Lucky, like you're the only person who misses her. You make me sick sometimes! You use the memory of Lucky like a crutch. She would have hated that. Why don't you just go off and take your run, Wonder Fake—I mean Blake." He grabbed Amy's hand and stomped off, as I stood mute on the street, stunned.

What the hell was that about? I sprinted off toward the beach but didn't make it a quarter mile before I turned around and headed straight to the DQ. Charles and Amy were sitting at an outside table, sharing a sundae. I was grateful that I wouldn't have to go inside. I so wasn't up for a visit with my ex-DQ co-workers during this disaster "vacation."

I said to Charles, "I don't understand what I did to you to make you so mad at me." You'd think Amy might have realized Charles and I needed some alone time, but she stayed by his side and just looked down at the table, like *lalalalala.*

Charles said, "Dude, you act like everything bad that happens in this family just happened to you. When Lucky died, you acted like it happened to you personally, that you were the only person who loved her so you were the only person who suffered. Guess what? I might miss her more than you. She was cool; she wasn't like . . . you."

"What's that supposed to mean?"

"Well, for one thing, she wouldn't have sold out like you, she wouldn't have gotten so skinny you could barely recognize her, or dyed her hair a fake

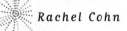

color, and she wouldn't have let herself appear in music videos half-naked, singing nonsense lyrics about nothing."

"She was going to have the same career I have now!"

Charles's voice rose. "No she wasn't! She played guitar, she wrote her own songs, she had her own life going. She would never have let herself become some Kayla puppet. Lucky cared about the music, not the image. It's like you only think about *your* loss, instead of the life ahead of her that Lucky lost. Maybe I wasn't a fuckin' B-Kid with you and Lucky, but I knew her a lot better than you ever realized. You act like everything that was hard for you after she died was because of Lucky instead of because of you, because you just weren't strong enough to deal, even though Mom and Dad would have done anything for you." Charles wiped at his eyes and took some deep breaths. For an about-to-turn-fifteen-year-old boy, almost crying in front of his sister and girlfriend at the DQ had to be some sore point of mortification.

Then it hit me, that in the three years since Lucky had died, we had never talked about her, not Charles and me, not Charles and me with Mom and Dad. We had just survived. And Charles was right—I did feel like Lucky's death was the greatest loss to me personally, and I'd never really thought about how much he loved her, how much he missed her. I didn't appreciate Charles bawling me out at Dairy Queen, but maybe he needed to vent, and if I was a good big sister like Lucky had been, I would be logical and calm instead of chewing him out in return.

I sat down on the bench opposite Charles and Amy. I took Charles's spoon from his hand and dug into the sundae and took a bite. Just tasting the soft-serve vanilla brought me back to my earlier life, wearing a DQ uniform and longing for escape. "Huh," I said. "Anything else I've done to offend you that I don't know about?"

Amy offered, "Ever since your video came out and you've been in all those magazines and on TV, Charles gets picked on at school. But he's, like, bigger than most everyone there so it's never gone that far. But people sing back the 'Bubble Gum Pop' lyrics to him in the cafeteria, they're all *'chew it, blow it, lick it, pop pop pop'* when he's passing by, and your house has been TP'd a couple times."

"I'm so sorry, Charles," I said. "And you still like this damn town?"

Charles shrugged, muttered "Yeah." Amy put her arm around his shoulder.

I said, "So if I were Lucky right now, what would I do with my career?"

Charles said, "For starters, dump those lame-ass songs and put some clothes on when you're on TV. And do something worthwhile with your fame; I mean Lucky was killed by a drunk driver, there's gotta be some anti-drunk driving cause you could support. . . ."

That would never happen, using my new status to become some anti-drunk driving mouthpiece. That subject was—and probably would always be—the most sensitive of issues to me, just too close to us. But maybe Charles had a point. Maybe I should use my new fame toward some form of charitable cause.

"Spoken by the boy I saw smoking a joint on the beach last night," I pointed out.

Charles's tense face opened in a small, sly smile. "That's different," he said. "I'm not driving a car, I'm going home and going to sleep. And anyway, before you bust me, who was the guy that dropped you off in the VW bus that you were playing tongue hockey with on the beach last night? Don't think I didn't see you. . . ."

Now it was my turn to smile and blush. Who knew my brother would turn out to be a cool guy, funny and complicated and maybe on his way to being a stoner, but, well, a brother I wouldn't mind getting to know a little better?

Then: Who but Jen & Co., along with Doug Chase and the members of Doug's Band, should emerge from inside the DQ and sit down at the table next to ours without even noticing me. I looked at Amy and Charles. "Excuse me for a sec, will ya? I just can't resist this!"

I let my hair loose from under my BoSox baseball cap and took off the tracksuit jacket I was wearing over my jogging bra. Maybe I had gotten too skinny,

but my muscles were *tight* and don't think I didn't want the party at the next table to notice. I stood up and stepped over to Jen and Doug's table. "Hi, guys!" I chirped. Jen's friend had a stack of magazines on the table in front of her, and there was my face on the cover of *Teen Girl,* with a caption that read "WON-DER-ful!"

Jen rolled her eyes. "What do you want?" she said, but one of her friends was all, "Hi, Wonder! Wow, you look great, how did you lose all that weight? Would you sign my magazine? I'm Christine, remember, from third-period gym class—" Jen interrupted her with, "Shut up, Christine!" Yeah, I remember you Christine, you were the girl making farting noises while I was auditioning for the school musical. And now you want my autograph?

Doug looked exactly the same, good-looking but in a bored kind of way, the kind of way that had to lead to premature balding and a beer belly by age thirty. Even his serpent tattoo looked bland on his bicep, like it had been demoted from fierce killer to bored onlooker. Doug said, "Check you out, Wonder! You here to play with the band again? You look awesome." He tugged flirtatiously at my hand, which I grabbed away from him and placed behind my back.

I shook my head. "I'm, like, going on tour with Kayla starting this week. We're going all over the country, that kind of thing. Hey, Jen, how did that

Guys and Dolls show work out for you?"

Jen huffed, stood up, and walked back inside the DQ. "Fuck off!" she called out before the door closed behind her. Jen's friends did not follow her. Christine said, "Freddy Porter! You lucky girl! What's Kayla like? Is it true she's dating Dean Marconi?"

I ignored Christine. "Is Jen your girlfriend now?" I said to Doug.

"No way!" he said. Doug got up from the table, but instead of going inside to soothe Jen, he dashed over to his truck, reached inside the passenger door, and rushed back to his seat. He held out a cassette tape to me, saying. "We made a demo tape. Think you could give this to your manager, or some record company people?"

AS IF!!!!!!!!!!!!!!!

I smiled very big, shamefully glorying in Doug's admiring look at me. "Sure!" I said. I took the tape and stepped back over to Charles and Amy's table. "See you guys later at home," I said to them. I did not resist the urge to kiss Charles on top of his head and give his shoulders a tight squeeze of a hug before I took off.

I made sure Doug was watching me as I sprinted from the DQ and tossed his demo tape into the garbage can that one year earlier it had been my responsibility to clean. The clanking sound the tape made against the metal can was SUH-weet indeed.

Just because I planned to consider Charles's desire

for me to upgrade my image didn't mean I was about to become a saint. There are some perks to the pop princess life, and a little slice of revenge on that day was one of mine.

Thirty-seven

I was walking back to the House from Hell—I mean home—when I saw this tall male figure with very well-defined shoulder muscles standing with his back to the street in the open garage at Henry and Katie's house. Before I could duck for cover and avoid talking to what had to be their studly cousin, *Science Project* turned around to face me! He was wearing jeans with no shirt and ohmygawd, what steroids had he been taking to get that new filled-out upper bod of muscle? Oh, I might be such a slut! For a split second, I forgot about the Liam being who had devirginized me just yesterday. It's not like all of a sudden Henry had turned into Brad Pitt, but last summer there was nothing on his chest besides skin and bones, and now he had filled out but good. There was definitely a grope-worthy experience going on there. This time last year, Science Project had a head of long, scraggly, dirty blond hair, and now he had a buzz cut that looked seriously Marine hot. Geez, first Mom and Dad separating, then Charles having a girlfriend, now Henry the Stud. What had been put in the Devonport drinking water since I'd left?

I almost felt all nervous and fluttery, and then my ego reminded me that *I* was the celebrity in this equation, not Henry who was all of a sudden so fine with the makeover. Henry who pulled his window shade down on me last night!

"Hey," he said to me, in this casual voice like he saw me every day and I was still the same ole girl from Devonport, not the Devonport escape artist–turned–pop princess with the hit song that I could hear right this moment playing from a car radio passing down the street.

"Hi," I said. "You look way different."

Henry looked at my head of platinum blond hair, then scanned my body. "*I* look different?" he said. "*You* look different!"

He walked farther into the garage, as if he had no intention of finishing our conversation. I guessed I did owe him an apology—make that apolog*ies*—for not answering his e-mails (that he'd long since stopped sending me), for jumping off the phone with him so quickly that day at the *J-Pop* studio, for never calling him back. Maybe I most owed him an apology for barely wondering how he was doing since I'd been gone.

Now I wondered!

I followed him into the garage. A small home gym had been set up inside, with weights, benches, and a punching bag hanging from the ceiling. Henry lay down on a flat bench and started to bench-press. I stood behind the bar, my index and middle fingers under the bar to spot him, but he didn't need me.

I said, "So, what's the Schwarzenegger deal about?"

Henry finished a set of ten reps. He pointed at a mannequin standing to his side that had pencil marks all over it, lines sculpting muscle definition on the mannequin where there was none before, and Post-it flags with numbers and mathematical signs all over them. Even if I hadn't failed algebra, I don't think I ever in a million years could have deciphered the meaning of the scribblings.

"I've only gained a few inches around the chest— I'd hardly call me Schwarzenegger. Anyway, it started out as a science experiment—when you were still living here, in fact, not that you were paying attention. I've been getting into robotics and I wanted to test certain physiological parameters in relation to an experiment on a crash-test dummy, so I started trying to bulk up with weight-lifting and carbo-loading to see how the theories applied to a human body. The buzz cut just made it easier not to have hair getting in the way when I work out."

"Go Science Project with the science project!" I said, impressed.

I was about to launch into a sincere attempt to apologize for my aforementioned friendship lapses when I heard Katie's voice approaching us from inside the house. "Oh, Science Project, there's another girl on the phone for you." She came through the door that led from their kitchen into the garage, and let out a squeal when she saw me. "WONDER!" She jumped up and down, then grabbed me in a hug. Then she turned to Henry and handed him the phone. "Don't hog the phone all day, again!"

Henry took the phone, said all sweet, "Oh hi, Andrea," in a voice that I feel sure was intended for me to notice, then he walked inside the house.

Katie said, "I have my *Teen Girl* issue with you on it upstairs! Will you sign it for me? And, like, tell me all about Kayla and FREDDY PORTER and Dean Marconi!" I almost envied her standing there, wearing cutoff denim shorts, a T-shirt and flip-flops, her hair in a scrunchie, looking like a happy, relaxed person. Some irony, I thought—Wonder Blake who once dreamed of escape from Devonport now had a mild case of envy going on for Katie's Devonport life of weekends and summer vacations with no responsibilities. She probably spent all day in her room, on the phone with her cheerleader friends, watching TV, or Katie's favorite activity, blogging on her Internet diary. Katie didn't have to worry about being bloated before a performance, or about showing up late at a meet-and-greet because the driver was stuck in traffic; Katie would never receive follow-up e-mails from Kayla after those experiences with Web links that contained mean reviews or nasty remarks about the new pop princess, Wonder Blake, who apparently was both a pudge and a diva. Stupid Internet—many curses on whoever had to go and invent that thing.

I lied to Katie and said, "I have a conference call

with my manager and the record company in a few minutes. I really gotta get back home." Fielding questions about Kayla, Freddy, and Dean was about the last way I wanted to spend my day off—especially with the new Mister Popularity, formerly known as Science Project, fielding phone calls from brazen little chiquitas—even though in fact I had nothing better to do while I was stranded in Devonport.

So I signed Katie's magazine, went home, and went to sleep. Devonport lacked anything to stay awake for anyway.

Very late that night, I sat in my bed staring at the dark sea, in major angst mode because Liam still hadn't called. Yesterday, he had been inside my body, and today, he couldn't even bother to call to say, *Hey, your technique could use some improvement, but not bad for a first time out* or whatever. With headphones around my ears, I was listening to that Paul Weller guy *again,* and replaying the scene in the VW bus with Liam over and over, when I noticed some flailing arms from the corner of my eye, outside the side window. I rolled onto my side, and there was Opera Man in the window across the way, wearing a cape over his chest, but with chunky biceps emerging from underneath the cape as his arms flailed about. Opera Man was performing the dance routine from the "Bubble Gum Pop" video.

I smiled. Maybe some people in Devonport weren't entirely a lost cause.

Thirty-eight

Philadelphia was the third city on our tour, and the City of Brotherly Love had a special treat for me in addition to my first (unbelievably yummy; who cared about Kayla's reprimand) Philly cheesesteak. I'd thought no city could offer a better welcome than Boston, where we'd opened the tour to an arena audience that went crazy for its hometown girls. But Philly had a huge video screen that played a surprise announcement taped that morning at the *J-Pop* television studio. Sounding like the Wizard of Oz, J helped close out my opening set by announcing to the arena audience of ten thousand people that "Bubble Gum Pop" would be the number one song on his Sunday morning, nationally syndicated radio countdown.

The crowd roared its approval as Kayla appeared onstage, unannounced and before her show, a microphone in hand. "Give it up for Wonder Blake, Philly!" she cheered. "Congrats," she said into my ear as she hugged me and flashbulbs went off like a light show. With an acoustic guitar player sitting on a stool set up next to us, Kayla sang one of her first hit songs, "Best Friend," directly at me. I added in harmony on the chorus, just because the moment was so sweet and why not? Kayla nodded at me, her way of saying it was okay to muscle in on her song.

Later, after the intermission, I stood on the stage sidelines watching Kayla perform her regular show, with a full live band, three backup singers, and ten backup dancers. She was truthfully a better studio singer than a live one, though her voice was always pitch-perfect, but to watch how she could match her dance moves to her song and connect to an audience was to watch a true pro at the top of her game. Technically, my voice was stronger than hers, and Tig said my phrasing and timbre were better, but she had an energy and pure love of performing I could never match. When it came to putting together the whole package—dancing, singing, and working the crowd— well, magic is a quality either ya got or ya don't, and Kayla had it in spades.

But sometimes watching Kayla could be a little intimidating, too, even for a newly crowned number one pop princess. I left the stage area and headed over to where craft services was set up for the road crew. The door to Kayla's dressing room was partially open as I passed by, and Jules's voice called to me from inside. "Wonder, c'mon in! Congrats on the number one! You must be stoked."

I stepped inside the dressing room, where Jules was sitting on a leather couch. I wondered if the road crew gossip was true, that Jules had slept with not one but two of the members of Freddy Porter's early boy band on her climb up the celebrity assistant food chain. Jules was hunched over the glass table at her knees, her long blond hair obscuring her face. "Thanks—" I started to say when she interrupted me with, "Ticket sales are sorta soft. Hopefully the newspapers all got pix with you, Kayla, and J on the video screen for tomorrow's papers to jump-start ticket sales a little, right?" Right, sure, thanks for deflating my number one song happy bubble, Jules.

Jules sat up, licking the rolling paper on the fat joint she'd been assembling on the table. Remembering Kayla's freak-out the night of my party at Kayla's brownstone when someone was smoking weed, I said, "Um, Jules, I don't think Kayla would approve. Her first set is going to be over in two songs. Maybe you oughta put that away."

"Yeah right, Shirley Temple, and monkeys are flyin' outta my ass," Jules said. "There's no off-duty NYPD cop to show off for here tonight. And doesn't the boss lady deserve a mellow-out treat, especially on the night that her protégé has knocked her off the charts? Right?"

How does someone respond to that? I couldn't! I just shook my head and walked out. I thought, Three cities down, seventeen to go.

Thirty-nine

Karl laid his last card onto the table, an eight of spades.

"Who wins again?" he smirked. "I believe . . . Karl does."

"Hey Karl," I said. "It's just Crazy Eights. Don't get too hyped on yourself. I recall a poker game yesterday afternoon in Minneapolis during Kayla's sound check that set you back, no? Remember Seattle and Portland, too?" Karl's eyes were dancing at me under those bushy eyebrows. I lifted my arm in the air and played with the five-dollar charm bracelet on my wrist. "Yeah, that's right, Wonder Blake won those games, and if you don't stop gloating, this poor bus driver who has driven us all night from Minneapolis to Chicago might have to stop the bus and kick you off. We've got three cities to go till we wrap up back in Boston, Karl, and I saw a nice locket to match this bracelet at that Wal-Mart opening last week. Watch the 'tude." Chalk up my tirade to lack of sleep mixed with two straight cans of Starbucks double espresso drinks from the refrigerator on the bus.

Karl chuckled. "Someone needs to downgrade to decaf."

Out the tour bus window, I could see the skyline of Chicago emerging. Karl and some of the road crew guys had promised to take me to a Cubs game—more fun for Wonder. But I was distracted from the view of the Windy City by the radio song blasting from the overhead speakers built into the tour bus. "Bubble Gum Pop" had slipped to number nine from last week's number five from the previous four straight weeks at number one, which could only mean one thing. . . .

Kayla slammed open the door from her private bedroom at the back of the bus. Her cell phone was in her hand, a mouthpiece attached to her ear, her PJs all rumpled, her hair wild and her eyes demonic. "Could you turn the radio *down* already?" She stepped back inside her room. Jules was on the chair next to the bed, also in PJs, a PlayStation console on her lap. Kayla slammed the door shut.

When was Kayla happy? When she was shut in her private bedroom in the back of the tour bus with Jules or one of her dancers, playing on her PlayStation and letting herself believe they weren't just letting her win. When was Kayla not happy? When through her bedroom door she could hear "Bubble Gum Pop" from the speakers in the front of the bus, particularly on Top 40 countdown Sundays when it turned out "Bubble Gum Pop" was number one. Again.

An appearance on *J-Pop,* constant radio play, and my much-publicized date with Freddy Porter had been enough to get "Bubble Gum Pop" into the Top 20. What had brought the song to number one—and kept it there—was a dance remix by deejay Montana that was a piece of genius, a completely remastered song that took my vocals and laid them over a dance beat that was old school funk turned into techno hip-hop. The new beat overwhelmed the fact that the song relied heavily on a catchy chorus and had minimal—and silly—lyrics. "Bubble Gum Pop" was just that fun song you can't stop singing along with and love grooving to in the clubs or on the beach or in the shower, but its summer dominance at number one was wholly the result of the musical strokes of Montana. I was just the cute girl on the record cover, the babe dancing with His Most Formidable Babeness, Will Nieves, in a new remix-version video hastily shot during an all-night filming session at a warehouse converted into a rave scene after a show in Atlanta.

But summer was officially over. We were at the tail end of September, the tail end of the tour, which meant that while "Bubble Gum Pop" was losing its chart dominance, perhaps Kayla's cross-country commentary to me as the song climbed the charts would disappear with it. Miami: "Wonder, could you drag that note out any longer? Who do you think you are, Celine Dion?" Dallas: "Excuse me, Wonder, I loved your supersincere speech to Tig about how you weren't going to diet anymore just because the record company said so, but that jumpsuit is way tight on you. Maybe next time pass on the Popeye's run with the stage crew?" Denver: "Oh my God, Wonder, did you know some horndog put up a Web site totally devoted to pictures of your boobs? It's called 'Bubble Gum Trollop.'"

If Kayla thought her comments could make me drop out of the tour like my opening-act predecessors had, she was mistaken. Nasty as she could be, Kayla was a very small fraction of the tour time; half the time she didn't even travel on the bus, but opted for private limo rides. She usually only took the bus when we had to travel all night between cities and she wanted to sleep in her tour bus bed. I actually liked when Kayla traveled on the bus, because that meant I could hang out and play cards with Karl.

I barely checked in with my own family; the tour crew felt more like family now. Traveling on tour was like an extended nationwide road trip, with TVs and music blaring and first-class hotels, as if I had won the deluxe camper in the Showcase Showdown on *The Price Is Right,* and set off for adventure with an all-access backstage pass. My list of adventures included: riding an alligator swamp boat in Key West, Florida; *laissez les bon temps rouler* in N'Awlins; singing the national anthem at a Texas rodeo show; hiking in the Rockies, personally escorted by a babe of a Park Ranger; helicoptering over the Grand Canyon; sneaking over to Tijuana with some of the road crew for after-hours partying following a San Diego show; and enjoying primo Cali beach time—roller-coaster rides in Santa Monica and sunbathing in Santa Barbara—

with dancers from Kayla's crew. I'd had to buy another suitcase just to accommodate all the plush white robes I lifted from every posh hotel room in every city.

I no longer minded the hectic pace of the pop princess lifestyle: traveling, rehearsing, grooming, performing, appearing. This was the life, sorta, that Wonder Blake had dreamed of back when she was working the Dairy Queen counter, and she rather enjoyed it.

My time on tour was booked solid. Not like I was gonna go all Little Miss Goody-Goody, but I did take Charles up on his challenge to do charitable work, and made sure that Tig scheduled free appearances by me at the local Boys & Girls Clubs in whatever city we toured; sometimes I even managed to snare Kayla for appearances, when I could guilt-trip her out of bed—and get to her before Jules could nix any request. Then there were the daily local radio station interviews to promote my album, *Girl Wonder,* followed by sessions recording promo spots for the radio stations. *Hi, this is Wonder Blake, and you're listening to . . .* I also had regular mall appearances where I would perform "Bubble Gum Pop" and sign autographs at a local record store. Still, I always managed to sneak in sightseeing time. Who knew when I would get to experience the world like this again?

Even opening up for the Kayla monster was enjoyable. I only performed twenty minutes' worth of songs, always ending with a "Bubble Gum Pop" finale, but it

was my important job during that short period to rev
up the crowd, to ignore the fact that people were just
streaming into their seats, overloaded with popcorn and
soft drinks, and viewed me as a performer to tolerate
until the real deal, Kayla, came on. Winning over the
crowd was my nightly challenge, and I was up for it.
"What's up, HOUSTON?" Insert name of city and
local fave deejay, mention the town's favorite dive diner
where you ate breakfast, then sing sing sing. A formula,
but it worked. Performance anxiety was not a problem,
especially not when I looked out into the sea of faces
and reminded myself, Screw this up and you have
nowhere else to go. I never experienced that moment of
looking out into a crowd of ten thousand–something
people and panicking. I psyched myself into thinking
of the crowds as one big blob of light, and once I was
able to do that, I could burst into performance. By the
time the light dissolved, I was halfway through the
song and the kids were dancing and screaming in their
seats. I remembered what Charles had said about the
true loss—Lucky not getting to live out her life—and
I vowed to relish the privilege of the experience for both
of us. After a fourth city called me back for encores,
Kayla cut my performance time to fifteen minutes, saying I needed to save my voice for all the daytime
appearances I was required to do (she was too big a star
for those appearances; her days were her own, and she
usually spent them sleeping or on her cell phone with
Dean Marconi). Kayla was not able to convince the

stage manager that "Bubble Gum Pop" was the song that should be eliminated from my act.

The Windy City approached as Karl stood up to turn the radio speaker volume down and "Bubble Gum Pop" faded into a soft whisper. Then he returned to his seat opposite me. Sometimes sitting opposite Karl while we played cards was like being in a stare showdown, and not because we were each trying to gauge the other's poker face. Karl had a way of look-ing at my eyes, then glancing at the green flannel shirt that I constantly wore because the bus was always freezing (yeah, that's why; the smell of Liam on the shirt, even after it had been washed, had nothing to do with it), and I had a habit of hugging myself to keep warm, looking at Karl's eyes and wondering: How much do you know?

Karl's cell phone rang, and I knew Liam was on the line because Karl said, "What's up, Punk?" From overhearing plenty of their phone conversations while pretending to doze against the bus window but really doing surveillance on Liam's life, I knew that Karl always called him "Punk." But Karl's "Punk" grunt to his son went down with great affection, like, "Hey Punk, Mom said you made dean's list. What's the matter with you—your old man is a dropout, you're making me look bad," or "Yo, Punk, sounds like a carburetor problem. Take it to Sal's in Quincy on your way back to school. He's expecting you. No, don't worry about it, the cost has been covered. Don't say

'Thank you,' Punk, just get it taken care of."

If Dad called me "Punk," would I like him more, would I be compelled to call him every few days to check in? Probably not.

Kayla was screaming for Karl from the back of the bus. He handed the phone to me. "You talk to the Punk a minute," he said.

Yikes, why did Karl always do that?

"Hi," I said into the phone. Why did my heart have to pound so painfully when I talked to Liam? In the time since It—three months, during which I had left two voice-mail messages on his cell that just said "Hey, it's Wonder" and he had called me back exactly ZERO times, though he never seemed to mind when Karl put me on the phone to him—I had accepted that It had just been some fluke fling for him, but It had meant a lot, lot more to me.

"So you made it to Chi-town?" Liam said. Why did even the sound of his voice have an effect on me? It so wasn't fair. "Good blues there. Make sure Dad takes you to hear some decent music, pop princess." He spoke very quiet, and monotone-slow, like he was hungover.

"Yeah." If I had any guts, I would have said what I really felt: You are the most interesting and smart and hot guy I'd ever want to be with, I could fall in love with you if you gave me half a chance, and I'm lucky to have been traveling and performing nonstop these months you haven't called or tried to see me, so that I could think about something other than how much you hurt me by acting like It never happened.

"I hear you're going back to Boston after the tour, no more camping out at Kayla's in Brooklyn. Maybe I'll see you there sometime—I go through Boston a lot back and forth to school."

"Yeah." What was that supposed to mean? Does that mean you want to see me or are you just being polite because you wish your father would stop handing his phone off to me when you call? State your point, Punk!

Should I bother to tell him I was only going home to Boston for a brief period, to check in on Mom and prepare to shoot a new video for the follow-up single to "Bubble Gum Pop," but otherwise I had no real plans? Tig said I was in danger of overexposure and the end of the tour would be a good time for me to take a little break before shooting the video and setting out on another promotional blitz for the new single. I would be completely free for Liam to haul ass into Boston anytime and sweep me off my feet.

"WONDER!" Never did I think I would be grateful to be saved from further conversation with Liam by hearing Kayla demanding my presence.

Karl walked past me. "Your turn," he groaned at me. He took the phone back. "Guess whose shrill voice that was, Punk. . . ."

I wandered back to Kayla's room. "Shut the door behind you," she said.

What the? . . . I kicked the door behind me. Jules

continued to play on the PlayStation, not bothering to acknowledge me.

"You have to listen to this voice mail I got last night. You're not going to believe this," Kayla said. She took my hand and guided me to sit on the edge of her bed next to her. She pressed some numbers into her cell phone and then passed off the phone to me.

I heard Liam's voice, drunk and slurring, sounding like he was in a loud bar: "Mmmm, K, whassup? So are we gonna finish what we started anytime, or what? I know we only messed around that one time, but I think about you all the time. Like . . . all . . . the . . . time. You're . . . torturing . . . me. I know you know I have feelings for you, so why do you have to treat me like dirt, ignore me? I gotta move on. There's this other girl in Boston I like. She's no you, but she's different, cute. I don't wanna be wasting my time waiting on you, Kayla." He started singing, *"Quit playin' games with tearin' up my heart* . . . or what's that stupid fucking song anyway?" There was a loud clank like he'd dropped the phone on the floor, then a background voice proclaimed, *"Dude,* you are *wasted.* You got anybody to drive you home?" and then the message cut off.

I looked up at Kayla after the message finished. Her emerald eyes were positively gleaming. She might as well have just thrown me into a WWF smackdown on the floor and jumped all over me for how dead I felt inside.

Kayla's finger latched on to my charm bracelet, like

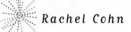

Lucky used to do. Kayla said, "Can you believe that shit? I mean, you've seen us together, you know I just think of Liam as a friend, like a brother, right? We never even really hooked up! We just made out one night when he was visiting during his spring break, right before you came to New York, but it was no big deal. And it was so long ago! I am so freaked out. I mean, ewwww! Do you think Liam's a stalker? I just called in Karl to tell him but then I chickened out. But I think I'm going to have to tell Tig to fire Karl—it's just too weird now. Right? What do you think?"

I snapped my wrist from her and stood up. I said, "I think you can be a real asshole sometimes, Kayla."

I returned to the front of the bus, but sat on the other side of the aisle from where Karl was sitting, yakking with Liam. I put sunglasses on so no one would see me cry. Fuck the Windy City, fuck the Cubs game, fuck the pop princess good life. I wanted to go home to Massachusetts, to see my mom, to be anywhere but here, where I felt like my heart had literally been snatched from my chest and stomped to bits.

"Later, Punk," I heard Karl say. He snapped his phone shut, then looked over at me. He said, "The Punk, you know. He's young, he's stupid. Give him time."

Forty

I was standing in the empty living room of Mom's new apartment in Cambridge when Charles walked through the front door and plopped two boxes in the middle of the floor.

"Put the boxes in the corner," I said to Charles. "You're blocking the middle of the room and the furniture movers are coming any minute."

Charles said, "Why don't you shut up and help instead of just standing there, lazy."

I said, "I am *directing* this move, not moving this move. I'm shooting a new video soon and I can't risk getting any injuries."

Henry came in and dropped some more boxes in the middle of the room. He patted my arm. "You just go on letting yourself believe that, Wonder." *Wonder.* Not *pop princess.* How refreshingly not Liam.

Charles repeated: "Lazy."

My hormones had Liam to thank that Henry could not penetrate my new anti-guy force field. I paid no mind to Henry's lanky shuffle through Mom's new kitchen as he checked out the appliances and inspected the thermostat. Henry's sweaty T-shirt, which said something in Klingon on it, negated any desire to inspect his Schwarzenegger muscle progress. My eyes were blind to Henry's postsummer head of sun-kissed dirty blond, newly shaved hair.

Since listening to the Liam message to Kayla, near the end of the tour, I had vowed to go off men, perhaps for good. I could either become a nun or a lesbian, I hadn't decided. If the major objects of my lust thus far in life had included Will Nieves (gay), Doug Chase (jerk), and Liam Murphy (dawg), I clearly needed a time-out to figure out what the fuck.

Henry said, "We've got all the boxes upstairs and in here and in the bedrooms. Want to go downstairs and grab a cold drink?"

I blurted out, "I can't, I've decided I'm not dating!" How my face could be turning hot in embarrassment in front of Henry of all people, I don't know.

Henry looked at me, confused—and like he was looking at the pop princess with the world's biggest ego. "Good," he said. "Because I wasn't asking you for a date. And now that I'm coming into Boston twice a week for a chem class at BU that Devonport High has given me a special dispensation to take, let's get this straight right now so we don't have the awkward moments when your mom invites me over for dinner." Henry's words came slow and with precise articulation, "I said, *'Let's get a cold drink,'* not an intimate dinner for two at Chez Red Lobster. Over?"

I laughed. "Over," I answered. "Over" had been our tree house sign-off word when we played World

War II ham radio the summer after third grade.

Henry bowed at me, like a Jeeves or someone. "Then, madam," he said, in an affected British accent that was all Cape Cod, "perhaps you'd like to join me for a little stroll along the Chah-les."

I slipped my arm through his. "Why, yes sir, I would." I stuffed my hair under a baseball cap and grabbed my big black Chanel sunglasses. The props were mandatory for any pop princess with a smash single under her belt who dared take a stroll through the neighborhood with the boy next door and dared further to hope to not get asked for autographs.

My cell phone rang as we were walking. "It's Tig— I have to take this," I told Henry. Henry popped into the video store on the corner while I sat down on a bus stop bench.

"Are you sitting down?" Tig said.

"Matter of fact I am!" I was hoping Tig was calling to tell me the good news that my new video could be shot in Boston. I was looking forward to spending more time in my real hometown.

"First," Tig said. "The record company has decided to release 'Baby U R Tha 1' as your follow-up single. I know you wanted 'Don't Call Me Girl (Call Me Woman),' and believe me I pleaded your case, but this unfortunately isn't about your personal preference."

Yeah, I was just the artist, who was I to have a vote on the song selection? Only an idiot like me would prefer a follow-up single with substantive lyrics and

my best vocals on the whole *Girl Wonder* album over another cheesy dance track that probably sounded a lot better performed by Amanda Lindstrom, the disgraced pop princess who'd penned the dumb song.

To my silence, Tig added, "It gets a little worse. You sure you're sitting down?"

"Yeah," I grunted. What could be worse? Would I have to perform the video with the Kayla monster making a cameo, playing that Liam message over the track like a rapper cutting into a pop song, with maybe a cute little dance number thrown in?

Tig said, "There are major rumors that Pop Life Records is about to be bought by a larger entertainment conglomerate. The marketing folks are panicked about their jobs and aren't freeing up the bucks for the budget that the director they hired for your video expected. Marketing got into a fight with the creative side who got into a fight with the director and as a result . . . I'm so sorry to tell you this, but they canceled the video shoot. The record company has decided to focus the video budget this quarter on Kayla's new album."

"Oh" was all I could say. Why did I feel a little happy over this news? No video meant less dance rehearsal and no week of starving off a few pounds before shooting began. No video meant I could help Mom unpack and be truly lazy: watch TV and go to all my favorite old haunts in Boston and ignore all the hot college guys because I was off guys now.

"It's just a small setback, kid," Tig said. "Why don't you give Trina a call—I know she'd love to catch up with you. Take a month or two off. Take a class that's not about dancing or singing. I'll let you know when the record company has decided what kind of promotion they want you to do for 'Baby U R Tha 1.' I'm sure this whole company buyout thing will blow over. Always does. Just lay low for a while, have fun."

Henry came out of the video store carrying a stack of Buffy DVDs. Why waste any more time getting to the "laying low" part? "Signal's running out, Tig, gotta go," I said. I snapped the cell phone shut. Way shut.

Forty-one

I celebrated the arrival of my seventeenth birthday in December by jumping out of my chair at a Cambridge coffee house when Tig announced that the record company was dumping me.

I hadn't expected for Tig to show up in Boston, I hadn't expected the record company to drop me—and I certainly hadn't expected to be as pleased as I was surprised over the news.

Pop music was cyclical, Tig said, and the tide was changing. Rock and punk were hot now, bubble gum pop girls—not. Pop Life Records had indeed been bought out by a bigger label, and the parent company was trimming its artist roster, consolidating its management structure. Big words for: Wonder Blake, expendable. Music downloading on the Internet and a weak economy had made profit margins slim—and as an "artist," I simply hadn't been that profitable. While "Bubble Gum Pop" had been a smash hit, credit for that was given to Montana, not me, and one successful single was not enough; I needed to have a smash album in order to be viable in the pop music circuit. Radio programmers hadn't liked my follow-up single, "Baby U R Tha 1," and with radio not having lined up in support of the song, neither had the record company—it was that simple. The song had tanked. The album sales for *Girl Wonder* were respectable, but not close enough to gold-certified. The new label was keeping on only artists who were platinum status or who fit into the rock/punk niche that was currently riding the charts. Sorry, kid.

Tig said, "You've got to be the first artist I've ever known to yelp with joy at news like this. And to think I was dreading having to tell you."

I said, "I'm sorry I'm such a disappointment to you, Tig. I know you were hoping for a bigger future for me."

Tig looked years younger since his management agreement with Kayla had expired and she had opted to sign on with Dean Marconi's manager. Or maybe it was Trina Little sitting next to him at the table, adding a sugar to his latte and brushing a speck of dust from his suit jacket shoulder. Gone were the Kayla-era bags under Tig's eyes and the tense jut of his jaw. He seemed . . . relaxed? Tig?

Tig said, "Hold on, you're not down for the count yet—don't be discouraged. We can change your image, easy. Trina tells me you've been working on your own songs. I love the hair back to its natural color. I can get you a new deal elsewhere, I'm sure of it. Or if you want to go out to Hollywood, we can line up auditions for you. I know a lot of people out there who like your look, love your voice. . . ."

"Can I think about it?" I said.

"What's there to think about? You've proved you've got what it takes to make it in this industry; this is just a setback. Don't give me that look. Okay, you can think about it, but not for long. The life expectancy of a pop princess's reign is short enough as it is. If we're going to change your image and reinvent Wonder Blake, we've got to do it while you've still got the name recognition." Tig looked at Trina. "What's she need to think about? This is your influence. Now what am I gonna do?" But Tig was smiling.

Trina nuzzled her nose against his: Eskimo kiss. It was almost disgusting. She cooed, "You can do what I've been suggesting to you for a long time now—start producing instead of managing, hear? Maybe that Montana guy oughta be your first collaboration. The guy owes you—he'd never have gotten the exposure for that number one without you."

Trina placed a kiss on Tig's cheek. She was all but sitting on his lap. I said, "If you two are a couple now, isn't that practically incest?"

Trina looked up from her Tig PDA. "If you recall, we were related by marriage, but that marriage ended in divorce anyway, so nope."

I asked, "How long have you two been . . . you know?"

Trina said, "You're such a good Bostonian prude, Wonder, with the *you know* instead of saying it out loud. Tig and I have been *you know* for a long time, but not seriously until that *person* freed up his time and his soul and did this man the biggest favor of his career."

I teased, "But Tig, you're a manager—you're supposed to be a slave to your artists and to the record companies, you're not supposed to have a life."

Trina waved her hand in the air like a low-flying airplane. "He's been slipping one in under the radar for a while now." Then they full-out kissed. I had to look away; it was just too much. It was like that time when Buffy saw Giles kissing her mom—great for them, but not something you want to witness.

Wonder Blake, Pop Princess wasn't supposed to have a life either, but somehow one had slipped in under her radar too. I'd come home to Boston at the end of the tour in late September with indefinite plans made more indefinite by Tig's advice for me to take a hiatus, and right away Cambridge was where I knew I wanted to stay. The leaves began changing color to brilliant reds and golds, the air got colder, and just like old times, the students were practically knocking me over on Mass. Ave. as they argued over existential something-or-other. Even riding the T felt right; for all my time in New York, I'd never ridden the subway, never felt part of the place.

When I arrived at Mom's, I never said, Look, I am completely freaked out because I slept with this guy and I kinda coulda been falling for him but it turned out he liked the Kayla monster and I feel like such a jerk, please can you just take care of me for a while so I can be sad and the biggest loser in the history of the world in private instead of in front of the whole music industry back in New York? I did tell Mom, Oh yeah, the tour was great, here's some trinkets and programs I saved for you, whatever. Congrats on your new job, Mom. You doin' okay?

I didn't intend to stay with Mom for long. I fully intended to get my own place. I had the bank account for it and maybe I wasn't a legally emancipated teen but I knew Mom would co-sign a lease for me, however reluctantly. She had signed the form for me to drop out of school, after all. But a week at her new place turned into a month that had now turned into almost three months and somehow the spare bedroom that was supposed to be for Charles had my bed in it, my CD collection, my TV, and my videotape collection of the *South Coast* episodes I had missed during the summer on tour (thank you, Mommy), and somehow Charles was sleeping on the pullout sofa in the living room when he visited on weekends. And as much as I had fantasized that staying with Mom would mean she would do my laundry and make dinner and be all-wise with the Mom advice, that's not how the living situation worked out. The fact was, my days were free and Mom often came home tired from work, so I ended up doing the wash. I wanted to learn to cook, so I ended up preparing dinner. And it was me who told Mom that leaving Dad had been the smartest thing she'd ever done to get her life back on track after Lucky's death. It was me who urged Mom to join Weight Watchers if she really wanted to feel good again, me who bought Mom the membership at the Y so she could go swimming in the mornings.

Somehow the pop princess had lapsed back into being a regular girl without even realizing it. The Boston accent was back wicked thick. So were the natural brunette hair color and the size-eight body and the four-times-a-week dance classes instead of the psychotic daily workout regimen and protein bar diet. And future pop princesses beware: A simple get-together for coffee with Trina Little could change your life. Not that I would ever let Dad know, but I was sneaking into classes with Trina at Boston University. The school thing started as a dare from Trina, who claimed I was full of it when I said I didn't need to go to college, and before I knew it I was enraptured in her history professor's lecture about how music had affected the course of the civil rights movement. Now the professor was up to the sexual revolution and my girl Janis Joplin was getting her freak on with the movement in San Francisco in the late '60s, and I was hooked. Every Tuesday and Thursday—at eight in the morning, no less—I was sitting next to Trina in that lecture hall, chugging caffeine and hanging on the professor's every word. And I wasn't just there cuz the professor had that tweedy, glasses 'n' frazzled hair intellectual look—very hot for a friggin' *teacher*—I was legitimately interested in what he had to say, though glad it was Trina and not me who had to write the final exam paper.

At BU, nobody recognized me as the "Bubble Gum Pop" girl. When I snuck into classes with Trina wearing a baseball cap and big ole sweats, I just looked like every other student there. It was great. There was no system of cliques I had to maneuver, no B-Kid backlash to overcome. Students there seemed to want to learn, to hang out, to grow. College was a world away from Devonport High.

The one place I was not safe from being the "Bubble Gum Pop" girl was the mall. I give full props to the middle school–age girls of the world. They can spot a pop princess, even one in sweats, no makeup, and natural hair color, from a level away at Claire's Accessories, and before you can say *text pager* a horde has swarmed you at the Danskin store, taking pictures with you and having you sign their sneakers, whose brand you were promoting six months earlier, and asking who is hotter: Will, Dean, or Freddy. Will, of course! And somehow, so long as no parent used those dreaded words *role model,* the experience counted as silly but fun. I oughta write a song about those girls!

Maybe my talent development was too little-too late for Pop Life Records, but I had come around to working on my own songs during my hiatus. Double-dared by Trina, I slipped into her songwriting class one day, a class that inspired me to take a look back at some of the songs Lucky had written. When I got over the shock of realizing, Huh, my sister wasn't that great a songwriter but her melodies were ace, I decided to try my hand at adapting her tunes for myself, a coauthoring project of sorts. Just an experiment.

Now here I was at Trina's favorite coffeehouse, poised to take the stage as "Anna Blake," undercover pop princess, unrecognized by the stream of college students and neighborhood residents streaming into the cafe for Amateur Open Mike Night. Surrounded as I was by an assortment of comedians in suits and Jewel wanna-bes with guitars and cowboy boots, I believed it a safe bet that I would be the first performer at this coffee house who'd had a number one national phenomenon hit record.

Mom arrived at the coffee house exactly at eight, while I was biting my pinkie nail nervously. She took my hand from my mouth and placed it on my lap before wrapping me in a big hug. There's a light in Mom's eyes now that's been missing since my sister died—a faint light to be sure, but a light nonetheless. At least the switch is flicked to ON. Charles and I no longer find her in her room with the drapes shut and the TV going, with a blank stare on her face and tearstained cheeks. She's made some friends at the new law firm where she's gone back to work as a librarian, she's counting those Weight Watchers points, and she's not living her life through *Law & Order* and *ER* reruns. At least she's trying.

Charles and Henry trailed behind Mom and joined

us at the table with Trina and Tig. Henry teased, "Well, this coffeehouse is no match for the Devonport High musical stage, but I think you'll do fine. If I fall asleep during your performance, just play a really loud note, that'll wake me up."

Between commuting to Boston for classes twice a week, finishing out his senior year at Devonport High, and holding down a part-time job to help pay for college, Henry hasn't kept up his Schwarzenegger workout routine, but even with his rapidly atrophying muscles, the boy's gotten some mad confidence happening. It's cute when it's not directed at all the science geek girls who trail after him at the end of his class at BU as I stand right there outside the classroom waiting for him. His new mad confidence could almost make me break my no-men vow, but we're not there yet. For now, I'm settling for baby steps, holding his hand while we take long walks along the Charles River, snuggling up against him in his car while we wait for it to warm up. At some point soon, this friendship is going to have to graduate a level; there is heat between us now that will have to be acted on, but I know he won't make the first move. I owe it to him.

I almost didn't hear the Amateur Night emcee call "Anna Blake" to the stage, I was so lost in another trance stare with Henry, this stare of anticipation and of I've known you practically since I was born, how did you suddenly get to be so interesting?

I stepped up onto the stage platform and looked

out into the crowd as the folks from my table hollered high for me. Why was I so much more nervous about sitting on a stool, a guitar in hand, in front of maybe a few dozen people, than I ever had been about lip-synching and gyrating half-naked in arenas with thousands in its audience? This whole scene was so intimate. Yikes! *Now* I was getting stage fright?

I looked over at Trina; her eyes were wide, like, *Go on, start now . . . NOW!* Was I frozen on the stage? Why all the painful silence? Oh, because the crowd was expecting a performance, not some faux Anna Blake chick staring back at them like Bambi in the head-lights. Trina nodded at me. *Sing,* she mouthed. I looked up at the ceiling, focused my mind on the mantra that had carried me through frazzled opening number nerves during the Kayla tour: big blob of light, big blob of light. Yes, good, my hands were moving on the guitar, strumming the few chords Trina had taught me. I opened my mouth, reminded myself, Relax, relax, relax. The song had to come, a new take on Lucky's song "I'm Ready," the first song I had sung to Tig back in Devonport a million years ago. I whispered into the mike, "This is a song my sister and I kinda wrote together. It's called, 'I'm Ready (Except I'm Not).'" Whew, polite laughter—solid gold.

And I sang, folk-sweet:

> *I barely knew you, but I just knew*
> *I wanted you, and I wanted you to want me too*

I didn't think, so we just did
But you wanted us, wanted It, to stay hid
Cuz you didn't believe in us, or in me
I didn't understand then, there was another she
I'm telling you, I'm Ready
Except I'm Not

(Tempo change, hard strum on the guitar, moving into a wail, watch out Alanis . . .)

And now I want It back
My time, my heart, my longing
Cuz I said I'm Ready
But I'm not!

Sweat was coming down my cheeks by the time I finished the song. To my surprise and extreme relief, the audience burst into major applause. I grinned like Ferris Bueller's best friend and stepped off the stage and walked back to my seat.

Mom, Charles, and Henry all congratulated me, but it was Trina's opinion I wanted, not Mom's "What was *that* song about, Wonder?" Trina got on her *American Idol* judge face and said, "Songwriter—maybe; helluva voice—yes! I mean, you could sing before, but now! Hard to believe that's the same voice that made a cute pop demo little more than a year ago. You just get better and better. There's feeling and phrasing to go along with that voice—it's a totally new ball game for you."

Tig said, "Exactly! C'mon, Wonder, what's there to think about, now's not the time to drop out. You *have* to let me shop another deal for you—you're ready!"

Trina gestured the "shoosh" sign with her hand at Tig. "Except she's not," Trina said. "Do you ever actually listen to lyrics, Tig?"

"What's the rush?" I asked. As a songwriter, I had a long way to go. Was I supposed to rhyme? Or focus on the story? Or on the melody and the way it fits the lyrics? Just how does a catchy chorus spring out of thin air and onto the page and then into song? Maybe . . . sigh . . . practice, patience, time, and . . . *grr* . . . some official schooling would help.

A few amateur acts later, our group got up to head over to Mom's for birthday cake. I was the last out the door, halfway out the exit, Henry's index finger latched to the index finger on my left hand, when I felt someone grasp my right hand as I passed through the doorway. I let go of Henry, stepped back—what was that? The coffeehouse was lit with candles, so the room was very dark. I could hardly tell who the person was sitting alone at the back table but then I recognized the smell, the same smell as a certain green flannel shirt I treasured.

Liam.

Forty-two

*I can't say that when I recognized Liam in that coffee-*house I had the same feeling as when I saw Doug Chase at the Dairy Queen so many lifetimes after we had hooked up, this feeling of Eh, you look major dumb and not at all attractive to me anymore, what had I been thinking lusting over you? No, with Liam I had that unfortunate old feeling of my heart sinking into my stomach, and that chemical, hormonal rage of wanting to straddle him on his chair, press my chest onto his, suck my lips on him and run my fingers through that mess of his hair and . . . Oh no, Wonder, not this all over again.

I sent the gang on their way to Mom's and told them I would meet back up with them soon, then I returned to Liam's table after the gang was safely down the street. "Hi" was all I could say. Could his timing possibly have been any worse? My thighs practically had a cell phone imprint on them from having had that phone in my pants pocket, waiting and hoping on random repeat for months and months for him to call me, to express a desire to see me. And only now was he here, when I was finally starting to feel, like, over It?

"Some song you performed there," he said. "Dad told

me I could find you here tonight, but he didn't say to look out for 'Anna Blake.' I never heard a pop princess sing like that, *Anna*."

So over the sarcasm. "Is Karl back from his Harley adventure across Canada?" I asked. "He sent me a postcard from Calgary, said he would drop by if he came back through Boston, but he didn't say anything about sending you ahead of him."

"He's back. Staying at my mom's." Cute! Karl and his true love, together again.

"Does he have another security gig lined up?" Kayla had fired Karl at the end of the tour. One of the happiest days of his life, Karl said, right after the birth of The Punk and Nixon's resignation.

"Not yet, but you know those pop princesses, they grow on trees."

"Oh!" I rolled my eyes, not teasing. "Enough with that! Say what you want about my so-called career but it helped my family through some lean times, allowed me to see something of the world, got me out of a town I hated—"

"You don't have to be so defensive; I know you worked hard. I'm sorry, I was out of line." He waited for me to respond. When I didn't, he offered, "You look really great. Like a different person."

"Who cares how I look?" He looked the same, all scruffy gorgeous, though the green spots in his hair were gone and he now sported a shag of chestnut hair and wire-rimmed glasses instead of contacts over his hazel eyes.

He said, "You seem kinda hostile. Was this a mistake for me to come here? Should I leave?"

I had positively no idea what to say to him. Since It, I had composed e-mails to him but never hit Send, had hundreds of conversations with him in my head, and now he was sitting before me, and my mouth just wasn't forming words. Why now? *It* happened in June; we were in December now. I could only shrug at him.

He said, "I don't know what you want me to say."

What did I care anymore, truly? Now the words came, fast. "I want you to say you were crazy in love with me, that it wasn't all some big joke on me, that you knew I was so into you, you knew I wasn't ready for what happened even though I wanted it to happen, but you used me, it was Kayla you wanted and that feels like shit! Even pop princesses have feelings, Liam." My voice had grown louder and people at tables nearby were staring.

Liam whistled. "That's a lot. Feel better now?"

"No." A little, actually.

He covered his hand over mine on the table. Stop tingling, skin, stop! "Look, I got the bus parked out on the street, and it's hard to talk in here with all these people. Wanna take a ride, talk, whatever?"

I'm not falling for that one again, sucker! I couldn't help but laugh. "You've got to be kidding," I said. I took my hand away, but my laugh had broken the tension.

He smiled. "Yeah, maybe not the best idea."

I said, "Punk, why don't you say what you mean. Are you here because you want to fool around with me, or you want something more?"

Liam's hazel eyes looked downward at the candle on the table. "I dunno," he mumbled. "What's 'more'?" His eyes looked back up, into mine. I was shaking my head *no*. "No to which part?" he said.

"Both."

"Because of that whole Kayla thing? I think you misunderstood about all that."

"Then maybe you owe me an explanation. If you liked Kayla so much, why didn't you just go for her?"

Deep exhale from Liam before he started in. "Right before I met you, see, there had been this night with Kayla and me; we were both drunk and we started fooling around but it never went any-where. The next morning she acted like it never happened—I don't know, the way she drinks, maybe she didn't even remember. I was into her, I admit it. I mean, she's not just gorgeous and talented—even though her music sucks. She's *smart,* like smart in a really hot way. But the whole thing was just too much of a *Chasing Amy* situation. And then you came along and things just . . . happened between us and then Kayla got involved with Dean and I was confused about who I—"

"What are you talking about, '*Chasing Amy* situa-tion'?"

"You know, that movie with Ben Affleck, about the

guy who falls for a lesbian. What's that look for? Kayla. She may date guys in public, but she prefers girls."

"How do you know?" It did kind of add up, if I thought about it.

"You can't possibly be that naive. Jules? Lucky?"

"LUCKY!" I stood up from my chair. "You don't know what you're talking about."

Liam stood up too, dragged me by the hand outside onto noisy Mass. Ave., away from the folks at the nearby tables who were leaning in to hear our conversation. "I'm sorry," he said. "I really thought you knew."

He tried to pull me into his chest—for comfort?—but I squirmed. What the fuck! I paced around, my mind whirling. When I went back to Mom's, I would get the story from Trina. She would know whether what Liam said was true; of course it wasn't. Liam took my hand and led me to a bus stop bench. We sat in silence a good long while as I got my head back together, calmed down. That was one thing I liked about him—he never forced conversation; he could appreciate a good silence.

A church bell rang in nine o'clock. Liam groaned. "Ah! I really am so sorry, I just assumed you knew. God, I feel stupid. Dad is all in this love-bliss stage with Mom again. Him and his stupid inspiration. He called me today and gave me this talk about me being some ignorant jerk, how if I had any brains left after what Dartmouth had sucked out of me I would show up to see you tonight, to see what . . ." His voice trailed off, his sentence, with whatever intentions it may have held, unfinished.

I waited, thinking he had more to say, and when he didn't continue, I spoke up. "Thing one," I said. "I'd have a hard time wanting to be with you right now after you just listed the reasons why you found Kayla so attractive. Gross. Thing two, you say all this to me, and yet you don't even have the guts to just ask me out for a proper date, to say out loud that you could want more from me than just random fooling around." His face looked downcast. He had the courage to come all the way to Boston to see me, yet he still didn't have the courage to state his case that maybe, just maybe, he wanted to be my boyfriend.

"Are we at least gonna be friends?" he said. His hand reached for mine, and this time I let him take it. His hand was sweaty, shaking. That only seemed fair.

I didn't answer, because I couldn't. I could never be just friends with Liam. I could be friends—and possibly more—with Henry, because we had a lifetime of friendship to draw on; with Liam, I just had unbearable physical attraction and, until now, a painfully unrequited desire to know him better, to know that he shared the longing I felt for him. I wanted the whole deal from Liam, the real deal, *romance,* and until he was ready to all-out ask me for it, I wasn't going to wait around for him to step up to the plate.

A loud bus passed by before Liam stood up to leave. He smiled a little, and my heart worked extra hard not to just jump into his arms. "Man," Liam said. "My number one favorite song of all time is 'Welcome to Paradise' by Green Day, and you know I never hear that song anymore without thinking of you. Congratulations—you're gonna haunt me for a lifetime."

"Good," I said. I let go of his hand and walked up the street, toward home.

Forty-three

Will the real Wonder Blake please stand up, please stand up? Who was she gonna be—the girl at the DQ longing for escape, the pop princess, the aspiring real deal singer-songwriter?

I knew Tig was waiting for my answer about what I wanted to do next with my career, but I had other things on my mind. I hurried to Mom's apartment after leaving Liam. Charles, Mom, Henry, and Tig were sitting around the living room waiting to celebrate my birthday, with presents and a cake on the table. "Where's Trina?" I asked.

Charles said, "She's in your room looking for a CD to play. Tell her if she chooses Mariah Carey she's not invited here anymore."

I found Trina in my room, sitting on my bed, reading a tabloid with a headline that screamed: KAYLA AND DEAN: THE INSIDE STORY BEHIND THEIR SHOCKING VEGAS ELOPEMENT. Aretha Franklin was wailing from my stereo about how if loving him was so wrong then she was guilty of that crime because she was bewildered, lonely, and loveless without her man to hold her hand. Sigh. Sister Ree, can I come to Detroit and take singing and songwriting lessons from you?

I kicked the door closed behind me.

"What took you so long?" Trina asked. She slapped the tabloid magazine. "And did you know Kayla and Dean were married by an Elvis impersonator! Wacky kids, who cares about the sacred institution of marriage anyway?" Trina placed the tabloid on her lap. "Does this rag belong to you? I found it in your bathroom."

"It's Mom's. She's always stealing tabloids from doctors' offices to throw away. Of course, she waits until after she's read them at home, but she doesn't like to see them in public places. Mom and I were reading that magazine in the checkout aisle at the supermarket a while ago when we turned to this 'Caught in the Act' page of paparazzi pictures and there was an awful, overexposed picture of me coming out of dance class, with sweat stains and my stomach sticking out through my leotard, with a caption that read, 'Wonder Bloat!'"

Trina said, "The same magazine that over the summer had you pregnant with Freddy Porter's baby and marrying him in a secret fairy tale ceremony that made you two the hottest new power couple in the music industry?"

"The very one!" I sat down on the bed Indian style next to Trina, took the tabloid from Trina's hands, and tossed it to the floor. "Question," I said to her. Deep breaths. "Is Kayla gay?"

Trina adjusted her seat to Indian style also, facing

me, like she knew there were more questions on the way and she needed to settle in. "Honestly?" Trina said. She tucked her front head of braids behind one ear. "Who knows with that piece of work? I don't think it's a coincidence that she married Dean right as her new album was released to disappointing sales, and just a few weeks after some tabloid printed front-page grainy photos of her topless on some beach with her topless assistant lying next to her." Looking at my wide-eyed shocked face, Trina added, "Don't think I don't also choose the longest line at the checkout aisle, girl."

I said, "How come Kayla doesn't just come out?"

"Well, aside from being afraid that her fans and all the advertisers whose products she endorses won't approve, I don't think she's come out even to herself. I think she fools herself into believing it's all experimentation until the right guy comes along. The girl is driven by hard-core ambition. I guarantee you, Kayla and Dean's marriage is a career move for both of them. Dean is as confused as Kayla, and he wants to look like a stud. Kayla knows she's not that great an artist, knows she's a studio singer with no songwriting talent and a limited pop music shelf life and she'd better branch out into acting if she wants to sustain a longer career."

"That's pretty cynical."

"Well, you be in a relationship with Kayla's ex-manager and I dare you not to become a little jaded about that girl."

I whispered the word, not sure how I would feel about the answer: "Lucky?"

Trina spoke low also, but her tone changed, from cynical to tender. "I wondered when you'd ask me about that. Do you really want to know?" I nodded. Trina paused, searching my eyes, as if she was trying to determine if I could deal with the answer. "Gay," Trina proclaimed. "All the way gay—Indigo Girls, Melissa Etheridge, was-gonna-change-the-face-of-alternative-music-one-day gay."

If there were tears streaming down my face, it wasn't because Lucky had been a lesbian. "How come she didn't trust me enough to tell me?" was all I could stammer in response. I couldn't believe that the sister with whom I had shared every day and every detail of my life had withheld something so fundamental about herself from me. I hurt enough from missing her every waking moment of my life, but now I grieved too for this piece of her that she had never let me know.

Trina rubbed my knee. "Lucky was only seventeen when she died. She'd just figured it out for herself, and she was just about to get around to telling you. If you really want to see that side of her, look at her songs; read deeper. I'm sure it's all there. She hadn't even told your parents."

"Was that weird for you, being part of Trinity when . . . Lucky and . . . *Kayla*?" In the here and now, I could get the possibility that Jules was more than

Kayla's leech of an assistant, but it was hard to wrap my head around the idea of my sister and the Kayla monster.

Trina said, "Tig had told us that if he was gonna represent us to the record company, Lucky and Kayla either had to be 'in' or 'out.' He said if he was going to take us to the record company, Trinity had to come packaged with an image—either wholesome pop girl group—or alternative chick singers; there was no middle ground there. He said he didn't care which direction we chose, but we were a risk either way: If we choose 'in' as a wholesome pop girl group, we would always worry that Lucky would be outted, but if we chose 'out' and went the alternative chick singer route, we would never achieve the mainstream success that Kayla craved. We were talented as a group, we sounded great together, but Tig really just took us on because of the family connection. I know he was ambivalent the whole time."

"Which direction did Lucky want?"

"Lucky wanted to go with 'out.' Kayla wanted 'in.'"

"And you?"

"I was getting pretty tired of being a third wheel to Lucky and Kayla's relationship, if you really want to know. I mean, it devastated me at first. My two best friends from when we were kids chalking up the sidewalk in Cambridge for hopscotch games, and then skip over to a few grades later, I arrive early for rehearsal in the basement at your old house and find them on the sofa kissing. I got to be okay with it eventually, but I come from a family of Baptist ministers, and that was not the type of thing I was raised to be around. I wish I could tell you I was all 'Oh yippee, you're girlfriends' cool about it, but the truth is, I wasn't. I didn't speak to them for weeks—I was freaked out. But Lucky brought me around. She always did. She could have brought the Pope around."

"So you were okay with it, you were going to stay in the group?"

"Um, probably not. The thing to remember about Trinity was that we were on the *verge* of signing a record deal, but it never happened, and not just because Lucky was killed. I think I ultimately could have dealt with a Trinity in which Lucky was gay, but I couldn't deal with Kayla's attitude that it was all just some experiment—and neither could Lucky. We never would have signed that contract; it just was never going to work out. *We* were never going to work out as a team. The dynamics were just too weird."

"Do you think that's why Kayla got to be so mean? Cuz she feels all this pressure to deny who she is in order to have her career?"

"Kayla's not mean—she's complicated. For all the nasty things she's done, let's also remember she was the person who looked out for you when you went to New York, who gave you a place to stay, who you may not realize was behind the scenes getting on Tig's case to not work you so hard, to give you some room to grow up. And for all that she and I don't speak any-more, do you know she still sends me a handwritten birthday card every year? That she still sends flowers to my mom every Mother's Day? I mean, this is a girl who had a first-floor apartment custom-built for her grandmother because of her heart condition, who calls her grandma every day, no matter what part of the world she's in. Kayla's a tough one. You can't just put her into this box of Wicked Opportunist Shrew, much as I'd like to, for all the grief she brought to Tig. But she made him a rich man. He's not complaining."

Ech; enough about Kayla. Maybe Kayla was "com-plicated," but for all her generosity to me, which I truly did appreciate, I knew my lasting memory of her would always be her playing for me Liam's lovesick voice mail to her—when I know she knew I cared about him.

I really wanted to hear more about my sister; birth-days and holidays were the days I especially hurt over Lucky. I asked Trina, "If Lucky were here today, what do you think she would be doing?"

Trina's face brightened. "I think she would be doing something similar to what you're doing. She would be singing in coffeehouses, honing her craft, writing songs, going to school, being Phi Beta Kappa president of the Smith College Proud to Be a Lesbian Society or something like that."

We both laughed. I was shaking my head. "Trina," I said. "Is every former B-Kid gay or what?"

Trina stood up from my bed; we could hear "Happy Birthday" being sung. Trina said, "Well, I'm not, for starters. And I heard about you and some not-so-subtle crush on Karl's son, and I have seen you with that nice very white boy in the living room, so I'd wager you're not. And I read that stealth date piece in, what, *Teen Girl* magazine? So I know you know Freddy Porter is all hetero dawg."

Charles kicked open my door, carrying a birthday cake with candles nearly burned all the way down, wax dripping into the white frosting, with Mom, Henry, and Tig behind him. "Just cuz you're a pop princess doesn't mean you can keep us little people waiting," Charles said.

Trina closed out the birthday song with an Aretha-esque gospel '*Happy birthday, dear Wonder, Happy Birthday to you,*' holding each note out, her voice so powerful and beautiful and pure, a complete contrast to the thin manufactured voice of Kayla that I'd truly gotten sick of hearing lip-synched during every performance of her tour. It gave me genuine birthday girl goose bumps on my arms.

Forty-four

I blew out the candles on my birthday cake and followed everybody into the living room. I was cutting the first slice of cake when Tig said, "So I think you've thought long enough. I already talked to someone high up at one of the majors out in LA. They're interested in hearing your new sound—think you can fly out there next week?"

Trina kicked Tig's leg. There was this silence hanging in the room, like everyone was waiting for me to make some big press conference announcement.

The pop princess answered, "Tig, remember that time when you picked me up at Kayla's to take me for a recording session and I was a little . . ."—I looked at Mom, couldn't quite say 'hungover' in front of her— "under the weather, and you told me my irresponsible behavior was strike one? That I was a kid working in an adult world and I couldn't afford to mess up like that?" Trina kicked Tig's leg again. I continued, "Well, can we just skip right over to strike three? I think I need to be out! For now, at least. I'm seventeen, and I wouldn't mind just being my age for a while. I'm kinda liking life as it is now. I don't want to sell my soul for record sales. I want to earn whatever I get, make myself in my own image, not some record company's. I think I need time to, like, figure out how to be a musician and all, figure out who I am."

Tig said, "Don't be all wise like that! You can't just walk away from all the opportunities a performer in your position has. It just doesn't happen."

Trina latched on to Tig's elbow. "It just did," she said.

Trina and Mom were in a lockstep beaming and nodding moment, a could-we-be-any-prouder-of-our-little-girl look on their faces. It was too sickening to witness, so I excused myself to the kitchen to get a glass of water. Get over it, Trina and Mom!

Henry followed behind me and handed me a plate with a slice of birthday cake on it. I took a bite standing in front of the kitchen sink. "Oh, yummy!" I said. "This one's a teeth tingler."

"A teeth tingler?"

"You know, when the frosting is so ridiculously sugary that your teeth tingle."

Henry just *looked* at me: a little admiring, a little nervous. I realized it was the same look he used to give me back at Devonport High—how come I'd never noticed it then?

He said, "That guy you stayed behind to talk to at the cafe. That was him, right? The Liam guy you told me about?"

"Yeah." I didn't want to lie.

"He looked like he wouldn't mind the chance to become your boyfriend again."

"He didn't want to be my boyfriend. And he wasn't ever my boyfriend. I've never had a boyfriend, at least not a proper one."

"What does 'a proper one' mean?"

The sugar from the cake and frosting must have shot right through my veins, because I went into rant mode: "It means, one who takes time to get to know me, who likes me for me and doesn't care whether or not I am or have been a pop princess, a guy who doesn't think it's the end of the world if we're seen in public together, who looks me straight in the eyes, one who doesn't expect to skip right to fooling around before he asks me out on a proper date—"

"Wonder," Henry interrupted my rant.

"Yeah?"

He looked me straight in the eyes. "If you want a proper date with a great guy, maybe *you* ought to ask *him* out."

Oh, he was really going to make me suffer for all those years of taking him for granted. And as Henry stood over me at the kitchen sink, all lanky and smiling, our first kiss might have happened right then and there if Charles hadn't skateboarded into the kitchen.

I said, "Don't ride that in here, you'll scuff the floor tiles."

"Shut up, butthole," Charles said. He handed me a gift. "Here, this is from Dad."

I unwrapped the present. Dad had sent me an exquisite music composition book made of Japanese rice

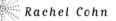

paper. "Wow," I said. "This is really nice. I'm surprised Dad sent anything at all for me." Since I'd been back in Boston, I'd been to Devonport to visit a few times, but mostly Dad and I worked very hard at being polite with each other while I was there, or ignored one another.

Charles opened the fridge to pull out a beer. I went over and took Mom's Sam Adams Light from Charles's hands and replaced it with a can of Coke. Charles rolled his eyes at me but popped open the Coke and took a chug. Then he said, "You and Dad are so similar it's scary. You'd better be the one to make up with Dad, because you're both the same way, stubborn, but he's like really old and settled in his ways, he's never gonna be big enough to do it."

"Why should it be me?" I said. "What am I gonna do, be all . . ."—and in a flash I was singing to the *Chew it, blow it, lick it, pop pop pop* "Bubble Gum Pop" melody, performing the old choreography, hands to knees to booty roll to twist, the signature move that girls at the mall were always asking me to show them—*"Forgive me, Dad, I was wrong wrong wrong?"*

Charles literally snarfed Coke out of his nose, he laughed so hard. When he finally caught his breath, he gave me this affectionate look that I don't think he'd used on a big sister since Lucky. He said, "I didn't know you could be so fun."

"I didn't either," I said. I danced the rest of the routine back into the living room to finish our birthday celebration.

Forty-five

My life as a pop princess officially ended at the Dairy Queen.

I seem cosmically unable to escape that place.

With my new driver's license (FINALLY), I had dipped into my modest "Bubble Gum Pop" earnings (modest by pop princess standards, at least) to buy a ten-year-old, mint-condition black VW Jetta with 80,000-plus miles on it and an awesome sound system. I was driving the Jettababy through Devonport when I recognized a familiar gray-haired figure sitting at an outdoor table at my old DQ.

I parked the car, kissed the steering wheel (I'll never get over loving that car), and walked over to where Dad was sitting. He was reading a Jane Austen novel and had a cup of hot chocolate in front of him. The ocean wind was whipping through what was left of his gray hair, but I don't think he even noticed that he was shivering in the December cold.

"Dad!"

He looked up. "Oh, hi." He didn't act surprised to me, just business as usual, like we hadn't been checked out of each other's lives ever since I checked into the pop princess lifestyle. He may possibly have been rude

enough to be about to turn his eyes back to his book, but I took the book from his hands and shut it. Men who think they're feminists because they've read *Sense and Sensibility* just make me wanna be crazy. I read that book, and not just the CliffsNotes. Lucky loved that book. But trust me, it's just another book about a corset-wearing English girl obsessed with marriage and money. Boring. Mostly.

"I have another book for you," I said. I took a book from my backpack, held it up for Dad, and ran my hands along the bottom and sides of it like I was one of Barker's Beauties caressing a brand-spanking-new La-Z-Boy chair on *The Price Is Right*. "*Ta-da*," I sang out.

"What's this? I don't understand."

"It's a G.E.D. test-prep study book. If you want me to take that test so badly, Dad, then you're gonna have to help me study for it. I'll be staying here two nights a week, beginning tonight." Charles said I had to be big in this situation, and this was as big as I got.

"Really?" he said casually. But I could see in Dad's eyes that he was pleased, that I was registering with him for the first time in a long time.

"Yeah, if I'm gonna go to Boston University one day and be a music major, then yeah, I gotta start here."

"Mom said you were thinking about giving up your career for a while, but I didn't realize it had progressed to this stage. Are you really serious about this?"

"I bought the book, didn't I?"

"And the career?"

"On permanent hiatus, to be continued, whatever."

Lecture face from Dad. "You know, it's very diffi-cult to come out from the stigma of having been an adolescent star as you were. I find it hard to believe you will be content with having just one hit song and then simply walking away. Are you really prepared for the implications of your decision?"

"What, have you been tuning into *Behind the Music* now that Mom's not around to hog the TV?" Dad blushed—he *was* watching TV! Shocker! The man who once unsuccessfully tried to ban Lucky and me from having a TV in our room because it was all "brain-rotting smut" was getting down with the cable hookup. I suppressed a laugh and said, "Yeah, I'm aware that this will be hard for me."

Dad must have been mad that I was on to his dirty secret, because he dug deeper into lecture mode. "If you're truly serious about going back to school, going to college, you know that you can't just have that life handed to you like the singing career was—there's no Cinderella angle for a proper education. Once you've taken the G.E.D., and assuming you pass, you'll have to go to junior college before any reputable university will consider you, and you'll have to excel at that jun-ior college. Your high school academic record was not exactly stellar. This will be a real challenge, Wonder—hard, very hard, work. Are you sure you're up for this?"

Oh, I wanted to strangle him. Give him an inch

and he takes a mile. "What are you saying, Dad, that you don't think I can do it? Because I don't appreciate that attitude! Show a little faith in me, will you? I mean I've earned enough money to pay for my college education myself. That took *work,* you know, and it took persistence and some smarts to get myself this far on my own, and maybe I won't have much money left over if I use what I've got for college and to keep that Jettababy running—"

Dad stood up from the table and snatched the Jane Austen book back into his hands. "That's not what I was implying at all."

I followed him as he stormed off toward our street. "Then what are you saying, Dad?"

He stopped, faced me. "If you really want to know, I was going to tell you I'm going back to work. I'll be teaching at the community college in Devonport starting in January, and I was thinking we could spend some time together going through the college's catalog, choosing some courses for you. It would be an excellent place for you to pick up with your education. But if you want to just assume the worst about my intentions like you always do . . ."

I actually jumped into his arms for a hug. "I'm sorry, Dad!" There was this tense moment from him. His body stiffened, like he didn't know what to do with my affection. Then he relaxed, gave me a nice pat on the back, and, like a typical uptight New Englander, pulled free of me and proceeded with his walk. I caught up with him and took his hand, whether he liked it or not. He clenched.

Dad said, "You're not going to leave that preposterous vehicle at the restaurant, are you?"

I said, "I'll go back for it. Nice to have a little Devonport-y walk. The cold Cape air feels nice, all clean and salty, like home."

"I thought you hated Devonport."

"Eh, love-hate. It's an evolving relationship." The sound of his small laugh was one I hadn't heard in forever.

We walked on toward our house. I let go of his hand just as we approached the lawn. I could hear Cash barking.

"Where are you going?" Dad asked.

I pointed to Henry's house.

This one-hit Wonder had renounced her nunnery prospects and had a proper date with the boy next door. *She* asked *him*.